FORGET-ME-NOT

BOOK 2 OF THE "WHAT HAPPENED TO MIA DAVIS?" SERIES

K.T. CARLISLE

Copyright © 2024 by K.T. Carlisle

All rights reserved.

No part of this publication may be reproduced, distributed, or transmitted in any form or by any means, including photocopying, recording, or other electronic or mechanical methods, without the prior written permission of the publisher, except as permitted by U.S. copyright law. For permission requests, contact K.T. Carlisle at ktcarlisle15@gmail.com.

The story, all names, characters, and incidents portrayed in this production are fictitious. No identification with actual persons (living or deceased), places, buildings, and products is intended or should be inferred.

Book Cover by Tamera Sims

CONTENTS

Prologue   1

Part 1
Elaine

    Chapter 1   9

    Chapter 2   17

    Chapter 3   37

    Chapter 4   53

    Chapter 5   77

    Chapter 6   101

    Chapter 7   123

    Chapter 8   145

    Chapter 9   167

    Chapter 10   177

Part 2
Catheryn

Chapter 11   197

Chapter 12   217

Part 3
Rachel

Chapter 13   233

Chapter 14   255

Chapter 15   279

Chapter 16   291

Chapter 17   307

Chapter 18   321

For AJ,

It's not easy being married to a writer, but boy are you amazing at it.

I love you.

PROLOGUE

May 18, 1996

Sweat glistened across Heather's forehead, thick streams of perspiration sliding down each of her temples as she squinted forward into the crowded playground teeming with screaming schoolchildren. The sizzling afternoon sun overhead was as intolerable as the blacktop radiating heat beneath her sneakers, threatening to melt straight through the rubber soles. She let out a sigh, the exhalation leaving her body thick and heavy as she gathered her tawny tresses into a loose ponytail, swiping away the moisture on her neck with the back of her hand.

As a child, she ached for the moments when the sun kissed her skin as she burst through the doors to the schoolyard, the humidity snaking up her shirt, causing the cotton to stick to her tiny torso. But now? Heather would have much preferred to trade supervising recess for a quiet lunch in the air-conditioned teacher's lounge.

"Ms. Martin, Ms. Martin!" a little girl with soft, brown curls and a cap-sleeved pink dress trotted up to Heather, the urgency in her voice instantly ripping the teacher from her daydream. Heather recognized the student as one of her second-graders—a smart child with a sweet disposition, albeit one that gave her a propensity for being overly sensitive at times. Heather suspected that now may be another one of those occasions as she searched the girl's face and spotted fresh tears glimmering in the corners of her eyes. She sighed.

"Yes, Suzie? What is it?"

"Ms. Martin, Michael and Mia wouldn't let me play with them!" the girl whined. Heather fought the urge to roll her eyes in response. *She's only eight*, she reminded herself. *This is your job, after all.*

"What do you mean they wouldn't let you play with them? What happened?"

"They said they were gonna play a secret game and when I asked them if I could come, too, they said, 'No!' And then they ran away from me," Suzie sniffled as the salty droplets were finally released from her eyes, streaking her face as they cut through the sweat on her round, pink cheeks.

Secret game? Regardless of how petty she felt that Suzie's complaint had been, even Heather didn't like the sound of that.

"Where are they now?" she demanded. The girl pointed a trembling finger in the direction of the field that bordered the blacktop, little blue flowers poking their heads through the thicket of tall weeds to greet the sun.

"They went into the field together and now I can't find them!" Suzie rubbed at her eyes, which had grown puffy and red from her unrestrained crying.

Ice formed in the pit of Heather's stomach despite the sweltering heat. She searched the playground for her fellow supervisor in a hurry, half-dragging the sobbing student to the teacher's side. Mrs. Turner was the other second-grade teacher at Sudbury Elementary—a tawdry woman with teased hair the color of honeysuckle and tanned skin the texture of leather. The chandeliers dangling from her earlobes swayed like two pendulums as she turned to face the panicked pair, a look of vague concern embedded in her amber eyes.

"Some students went into the field. Can you watch after Suzie while I go look for them?" Heather asked her coworker. Mrs. Turner nodded in response, placing her acrylic fingernails gently on the child's shoulder as she pulled the girl closer to her side. Satisfied that her student was in safe hands (no matter how inappropriately manicured she felt they were for school), Heather made a beeline for the field in search of the missing children.

They couldn't have gone far, Heather tried to convince herself as she jogged to the blacktop's edge, scanning the overgrowth beyond with frenzied eyes, hoping to land her gaze on a pair of blonde heads bobbing through the field. Though it was still considered spring in North Carolina, the mid-May sun had all but scorched the blades of grass below, the ends of the dried weeds bleached with exposure until they more closely resembled a sea of straw.

Heather knew the field wasn't on school property and therefore wasn't the landscaping crew's responsibility. Still, she cursed them for allowing the tangled meadow to grow wild and unkempt, its desiccated stalks climbing up past her knees. Locating the fair-haired children in the towering maze of unruly pasture felt like searching through a haystack for two flax-colored needles.

Heather pressed into the grassland, her head swiveling from side to side as desperation mounted in her chest. What would she do if she failed to find them before the bell rang and recess was over? What if one of them had gotten injured and couldn't find their way back? Or worse—what if they had been snatched up by a stranger lurking in the field? Dark thoughts swirled inside Heather's mind, threatening to overtake her as the edge of her vision blackened. She peered as if through a tunnel, sweeping the horizon from one end to the next, fighting against the anxiety blooming in her chest with each failure to find her students. Maybe she should turn back and get help. Maybe this was a job for the authorities. Maybe—

There!

Relief rippled through Heather's body as she spied a curious depression in the center of the otherwise knee-high grassland. She stumbled through the gnarled, knotted weeds at her feet, nearly tumbling into the parched and blistered earth as she raced to reach the obvious cavity in the field, confident that the children would be there waiting.

Though the thought of finding them at last filled her with joy, Heather couldn't ignore the familiar feeling of righteous indignation that often came with the territory of shaping young minds. The closer she drew to the indentation in the grass, the more justified she felt in delivering what she was sure would be an unforgettable scolding. How dare they misbehave this way? Didn't they realize how much their absence had frightened her? Didn't they care that they had broken school rules? They needed to be punished, and Heather was eager to fill her role as disciplinarian.

As she approached the small clearing in the center of the field and saw that her suspicions had been correct, she drew in a breath, steeling herself for a lengthy reprimand. But before she could speak, the words melted in her throat, the sight of the children's play-acting softening her resolve in an instant as she realized what they were doing. Situated atop Mia's shoulder-length golden locks was a makeshift crown of woven weeds that fell lopsided across her head, resembling a crooked halo. In her right hand, she clutched a withered bouquet of pale-blue forget-me-nots, while Michael held her left hand in his own as he looped a ring of broken stems around her dainty finger.

"There!" he said triumphantly as he secured the ring in place. "Now we're married!"

"Married, married!" Mia squealed with glee, giggling as she clasped her hands together.

"And we'll always be together—right, Mia?" Michael asked.

"Yes, yes!" the little girl threw her arms around her make-believe husband, planting a wet kiss on his cheek. "I promise."

Heather's throat seemed to constrict with tenderness, and for a moment, she briefly considered turning a blind eye to the entire situation. But the grass loomed tall over their tiny bodies, and she knew the chances were too high that the children would get lost on their way back to the schoolyard. She needed to escort them back, but maybe she could forego the formal punishment she had planned—just this once.

"Alright, you two," Heather announced her presence, parting through the weeds. Michael and Mia gave a start, realizing they had been caught breaking the rules by their teacher. Heather chuckled softly, placing a warm hand on each of their shoulders as she began to guide them back to the blacktop. "Recess is almost over. Time to get you back to class."

PART I
ELAINE

CHAPTER 1

May 13, 2023

The knife slid between my ribs and into my lung before I could draw a breath to scream. My eyes widened as pain stitched itself into the space where my attacker's blade had entered, freezing me in place on the kitchen tile. He knew what he was doing. He had done it before. I knew it with the same certainty that I knew I was going to die. I could see it in the fixed determination on his face as he continued to plunge the knife deeper and deeper into my body. He was hungry. Frantic. He needed this. And there was nothing I could do to stop it. Not anymore.

He withdrew the knife and I slumped forward, half expecting the nightmare to be over. But he was only getting started. Instinctively, my hands flew to the open wound in my chest, desperate to slow the deluge of blood that was leaking down my torso. The earth shifted beneath my feet and I stumbled straight into the arms of the man who was determined to kill me.

His left hand was like a vice around my arm as he gripped me, my lips parting in silent objection as I tried to produce the scream that never came. A strange satisfaction tugged at the corner of his lips as he drew his arm back before driving the dagger into my body once more, this time slipping into my intestines. I clutched his forearm, digging my nails into his skin with every ounce of strength I could muster, but it was no use. I could already feel myself fading.

The blows came slow and deliberate at first, each puncture through my flesh plotted with careful precision. But with every swipe of his blade, the fire behind my killer's eyes burned brighter, more violent. At one point, his gaze seemed to disappear into the flames entirely, a look of pure intoxication engulfing him, swallowing him whole. He became almost mechanic in his movements, an invisible veil falling over his features as his pace quickened faster and faster, the knife entering me over and over and over again until I became numb with agony, my nerves too overwhelmed with sensation to feel pain any longer.

With his muscular body pressed against mine, his breathing hot and labored against my skin, the rhythmic rocking as he pumped into me with eager, ravenous persistence, I was oddly reminded of the first night we slept together. I couldn't tell whether it was death's embrace or the thought of our naked bodies tangled in bedsheets that made my blood turn cold.

As though she could hear my dying thoughts about her husband, Cat let out a low groan from her place on the kitchen floor, still passed out from when he had subdued her mere moments before shoving his blade into my chest. I wondered how long it would be before he was finished with me and proceeded to kill her next.

The thought barely had time to plant itself in my brain before it was replaced with a sudden surge of inexplicable euphoria. All at once, warmth rushed through my veins as though I had been submerged in a sea of bathwater. My skin seemed alive with pleasure, little goosebumps of elation blossoming all over my body, consuming every inch of me. The muscles melted around my bones, all worldly tension erased as I surrendered to total ecstasy. As quickly as the sensation had overpowered me, it was over, substituted with a profound absence of feeling, a nothingness so complete, I didn't have to question what it meant.

It was over. I was dead.

I hovered in place, suspended above my bloodied, broken body, watching the soft glow of the streetlights that filtered in through the windows above the kitchen sink as they cast eerie shadows across Tim's face. He continued to stab me, seemingly unaware that he had already succeeded in taking my life. I tore my gaze from the sight, unable to stomach the gruesome nature of my own murder even in death, but the rest of my surroundings offered little comfort.

The room was in chaos. Blood oozed out of my wounds, soaking deep between the grout of the marbled tile floor as it collected in a pool around Cat's motionless body beside the kitchen island. More crushing to me than watching her thick, black curls become drenched with my body fluids were the remnants of our altercation that lay scattered around the room.

My tote bag sat in a crumpled pile beneath the refrigerator by the back door where Cat had thrown it after ripping it from my shoulder shortly following my unexpected arrival. I could see the claw marks from my fingernails gauged into her forearm from when I had tried to stop her from forcing me out of her home.

"Just stay away from Tim!" I had screamed, desperate to warn her about what I knew. I should have known before I got to her house that she'd be too drunk, too full of rage to want anything to do with me. After all that I had put her through with the affair, I deserved as much. But there was so much that she didn't understand, so many things I needed to say before it was too late. If only she had listened to me, if only she had let me explain, maybe things could have been different.

A wild, animalistic noise erupted from the place where Tim was still hunched over my lifeless body, effectively ripping my attention away from his wife. If I still had skin, I'm sure the sound would have caused my flesh to prickle with sheer terror. It was a haunting disturbance like the distinct wail of cattle being brought to slaughter, their screams full of panic, piercing and guttural. At first, I thought that perhaps the sound had escaped from my own lips—*was I coming back to life? Had he failed in killing me after all?* But I quickly realized that this was not the case. No, these howls had been produced by none other than my attacker.

I watched with sickening curiosity as his steady shriek slowly morphed into silent, sustained sobbing, uncontrolled tremors quaking through broad shoulders as his body racked with... grief? But how could that be? He had chosen to do this, after all. Willingly offered to take my life. Why would he—

"Mia!" he wailed into the shadows, his palms spread wide against the tile floor as he steadied himself, sticky with my blood. "I'm so sorry, Mia. I had to do it. I *had* to. You promised me. You *promised!* And now look what you've made me do..."

Kneeling over me, he swept blonde locks away from my face with his free hand, his right hand still clutched around the butcher's blade that he used to murder me. He cupped my face, his thumb lightly grazing my cheek as he leaned down and sealed his lips over my cold, immobilized mouth, still hanging slightly open around the scream that remained trapped inside my lungs. When he was finished, he slid his blood-stained fingertips over my eyelids, blocking the crystal pools beneath from view, placing me to rest.

"I love you, Mia," I heard him whisper. "We'll be together soon."

Stop calling me that you sick fuck!

Somehow watching this man defile my corpse with unwanted affection, listening to him call me by a name that was not my own—it made me feel more helpless than I had in the moments preceding my death. I wanted to push him away, kick him in the groin, scream in his face, *My name is Elaine!* But all I could do was float in the darkness, utterly undetectable. Invisible. Forgotten.

As though a switch had been flipped, his back straightened at once, the tears that stained his face evaporating like summer rain burned from a scorched blacktop. He appeared focused, controlled—completely abandoning the infantile wailing that I had just witnessed. With robotic rigidity, he snapped in the opposite direction to face his wife, the knife still clenched in his right hand as he loomed over her.

NO!

I lunged at him, determined to bring his murderous rampage to an end, but my spectral form would not comply. Each time I leaped into his path, I simply glided straight through his body, unable to stop him from moving forward.

As I continued to pass through him again and again with feverish desperation, I began to feel a strange darkness consume me. It was as though with each failed attempt to touch him, I had absorbed something hidden from deep within. Pieces of him seemed to take root inside of me, a horrible wickedness threatening to envelop me the more I tried to save the woman whom he seemed intent on taking next. I couldn't let him get away with this. After all, I had come here to protect her from this very fate. But there was nothing I could do. I was too late. I had failed.

He stopped short of Cat's body, nudging her torso with the tip of his boot, rolling her onto her back as he did so. She moaned in response but made no other indication of possessing consciousness—or life for that matter. If I could have held my breath, I would have. Instead, I watched in horror as he lowered himself to the floor, inching closer to her unsuspecting body with his blade.

Make it quick, I begged him. *Don't drag it out like you did with me.*

Just as I was certain that he would plunge the knife into her heart, he paused. He seemed lost in contemplation, temples pulsing as he ground his teeth back and forth, debating whether he should proceed with what he was about to do. The seconds passed with agonizing reluctance, each grain of sand through the hourglass stretching out like a millennium as I anticipated his next move. Finally, his shoulders sagged, and with them, the rest of his body as he melted down on top of her.

For a moment, I thought he had wedged the knife between her ribs, but the gentle rise and fall of her chest told me that Cat was still breathing, still unscathed. I floated closer to the couple, careful not to touch Tim as I tried to understand what was happening. Upon closer inspection, I could see that he hadn't stabbed her at all. On the contrary, he held her with all the tenderness and compassion that I had seen him embody on the day of their wedding. He planted his lips on her cheek, caressing the place where his mouth had been with the back of his hand as he raised himself into a seated position on the floor.

"Thank you," he whispered.

With that, he grabbed a fistful of Cat's tee-shirt and used the fabric to wipe the blade handle clean of his fingerprints before placing the knife carefully into her right hand. He stood up and made his way to the back door, stopping beside the doorframe as he plucked the landline from its cradle on the wall and proceeded to dial 911.

"There's been a murder at 29 Fieldstone Avenue," his voice was muted, hollow as he spoke the words. "Hurry."

He let the phone dangle by its cord, the sound of the 911 operator's panicked demands for answers coming muffled and tinny through the receiver. Before I could understand what had just happened, he slipped hastily through the back door, slamming it shut behind him. The force of the door closing sent a small gust of wind swirling through the kitchen, lifting a few of the discarded receipts that had fallen from my tote bag during my earlier struggle with Cat. One of them landed beneath me, the name "Michael Davies" printed across the top, mocking me with its unknown significance.

Stupid girl, it seemed to say. *You thought you could unmask a monster?*

I cursed myself for being so reckless, so confident that I could have stopped the inevitable. I should have been satisfied with calling Detective McGowen, letting her handle it. Now no one would know what I knew. What I had known for years—I just didn't understand what I was seeing.

CHAPTER 2

April 25, 2008

Looking back, the surprise party probably wasn't my best idea. But I just couldn't help myself. It's not like I enjoyed always having to be the one to help others realize their true potential. Nudge them in the right direction. Make them see what was best for them. Oh, who the hell am I kidding? I adored it. And while I was determined to give my boyfriend a full transformation from miserable, moody caterpillar to social butterfly, that was only part of the reason why I knew I needed to throw Evan a party that he would never forget.

***

May 18, 2007

The year before my brilliant plan began to take shape, Evan had brought me to his father's house to celebrate his twentieth birthday. Though we had been seeing one another for six months by that point, I had never met his family. I was beginning to think that he might never introduce me to them, so I was relieved when he finally asked me to accompany him home for a quiet birthday dinner.

I expected it to be a little awkward, maybe even a bit tense, with uncomfortable silences stretching between each icebreaker question, hanging in the air like a thick fog of humidity ready to burst into a torrential downpour. Nothing could have prepared me for the nightmare that actually unfolded after we arrived at his house that night.

I insisted on being the one to drive us there despite my boyfriend's many objections.

"We can just take the bus or something," he protested when I told him that I'd happily play chauffeur. But I wasn't having any of that. Why would I settle for being driven around town in a scummy bus like some license-less teenager when I had a perfectly good Mustang GT to take us where we needed to go?

"Don't be ridiculous," I had told him, perhaps with more aggravation in my voice than I intended. "We're taking *my* car, and I don't want to hear another word about it."

"You're the most stubborn fucking—"

"Look, I don't want to fight on your birthday, okay? So why don't you just say 'thank you' and drop it?"

Evan set his bony jaw in a rigid line, seemingly chomping down on the wicked words he still wanted to hurl in my direction. His pale green eyes flickered with poorly suppressed anger, strands of unruly, black hair casting shadows over his gaunt face, making him look too severe, too serious. And sexy, if I'm being honest. There was just something about that scowl of his, the way it made the corners of his mouth turn downward, his bottom lip pouting out like a piece of pink chewing gum that I desperately wanted to bite down on. Sometimes I'd push his buttons for the hell of it, just to see him make that face.

I laid my hand on his scrawny chest and pressed into his body before collecting my reward, savoring the taste of his melancholy as I gently sucked his lip into my mouth, giving it a soft nibble before finally releasing him.

"Now, what do you say?" I teased.

"Thank you," he grumbled before adding, "but if your car gets stolen, it's not my fucking fault. I warned you."

"Oh, c'mon," I nudged his arm. "It can't be that bad."

But it was.

Evan's childhood home was nothing like what I imagined it would be. It's not like I thought that he would direct me to a luxury mansion tucked away in a quiet corner of Green Valley's aristocratic suburbia. Being forced to attend public school in Williamsburg despite my parents' fortune had instilled in me early on that others were not as privileged as I was. Still, I wasn't expecting the house to be so bleak. So lacking in warmth or comfort, absent of all the hallmarks that made a house feel like a home. So much like where I had grown up after all—except slightly dilapidated and much, much smaller.

"It's just up here on the right," Evan instructed me to pull over in the seedy neighborhood where his father lived, not a sidewalk in sight, as though even the city planners wanted to deter others from walking through it. I killed the ignition, peering past my boyfriend through the passenger window to get a glimpse at the place.

It was more of a shack or a shed than a house, really, with cracked vinyl siding the color of coffee-stained teeth and front steps that led to a moss-covered entryway, the screen door hanging uneven, partially unhinged. The entire thing probably could have fit inside my parents' living room. I couldn't fathom how it could have housed just me and Evan, let alone an entire family.

"Let's get this over with," he mumbled, unclipping his seatbelt and flinging it over his shoulder before pushing out into the late spring evening. I rolled my eyes and sighed.

This was the way it always was with him—his sullen demeanor like a wet, heavy blanket thrown on top of a drowning victim anytime we did anything that might be considered remotely close to "social." It was annoying to me that he never wanted to just go out and have fun, be a normal college kid for once in his miserable life. We could be at the biggest frat party of the school year and he'd just stand there with his hands in his pockets looking ready to bite someone's head off. I hated it.

As I watched him storm off to the front steps, fists tightly clenched and jammed into his jeans as he skulked across the unkempt lawn, I chalked it up to his typical antisocial behavior. It didn't take me long to realize that there was a good reason for his downcast disposition.

I unfastened my seatbelt and followed Evan across the yard, up the crumbling concrete stairs, and through the front door. A menacing Pitbull signaled our arrival with a terrorizing howl from behind the next-door neighbor's chain-link fence as we filed into the house, neither of us daring to glance in its direction.

I heard the sound of heavy footsteps pound against the creaky floorboards that lay beneath our feet as we stood together in the foyer—if you could even call it that. The space was barely wide enough for me and Evan to stand shoulder-to-shoulder, with a tattered welcome mat that looked as though it had been stapled to the ground. There wasn't so much as a credenza to speak of, not even a small bench to sit down on and remove your shoes. Judging by the amount of visible dirt on the hardwood, that didn't seem like much of a concern to the people who lived there.

The footsteps thudded through an open archway to the left, revealing Evan's father to me for the first time. He was much larger than I anticipated—not overweight by any means, but rather thick and sinewy with muscles that threatened to burst through the fabric of his stained, gray tee-shirt. He towered over Evan, who I had once believed to be quite tall. But in the presence of his father, he seemed to shrink away, feeble and meek.

"Oh, it's *you*," he sneered. "Thought it was one of my real sons. The hell you here for anyway?"

My mouth fell open in shock. *What the fuck did he just say?* I turned to Evan, hoping he'd start laughing along with his father's insults. This had to be some sick family joke that I just wasn't in on—right?

"Thanks for the birthday wishes, Dad," Evan said sarcastically. "And many more where that came from, I hope."

His father blinked slow and blank, unfazed by his son's revelation, unembarrassed by the callous remarks that he had made. He simply grunted in reply, shrugging his powerful shoulders with an air of indifference that made me want to scream.

"Forgot today was the eighteenth," he muttered, the same green eyes that he passed on to his son locking on me as the words left his lips. "Who're you?"

Who am I? Who the fuck am I? I'm the bitch you're going to wish you never let inside your house, you miserable piece of human—

"This is Elaine," Evan spoke up before I had the chance to verbalize my silent tirade. "She's my girlfriend."

I watched as my boyfriend's father combed my body with cold, uncaring eyes, suddenly feeling the need to wrap my arms around myself, hyperaware of my pink crop top as his stare lingered a little too long on my exposed midriff. He sucked on his teeth, the smack of wet suction coming from his mouth making my flesh crawl with discomfort.

"Shame," he commented, his assessment complete. "She seems nice. Too nice for you."

He disappeared after that, back through the archway from where he had materialized, leaving me speechless and shaken and dreaming of wrapping my hands around his neck, squeezing until the life drained from his massive body. *Fucking asshole.*

I turned my attention back to Evan, my heart threatening to crack open at the sight of his deflated torso caving in around a broken heart of his own. I'll never forget the way he looked in that moment—like a little boy stranded in a sea of strangers, lost and frightened. Empty. I wanted to take his hand and run back to the car, speed away from his father's house back to the safety of the dorm room I shared with Cat. But instead, I let Evan show me to his childhood bedroom where we waited until his brothers inevitably arrived.

The room was located down a narrow hallway that stretched from the front door to the back of the house. Like the rest of the place, Evan's room was impossibly small, the only piece of furniture a twin-sized bed crammed against the right wall where it collided with the bedroom door whenever it swung open. Were it not for the collection of pencil drawings and doodles that littered the wall like a private art show, I wouldn't have guessed that the room belonged to Evan at all. He flopped down on the tiny bed, the mattress groaning beneath his weight as he sank into the covers.

"Well, that's my dad," he said, as though he had explained everything.

"I don't understand," I started. "Why is he so...? Why is he such a—"

"Such a miserable prick?" Evan offered.

"Well, *you* said it," I agreed, taking my seat on the bed beside him. "Why is he so awful to you?"

"It's... complicated," he sighed, running a hand through his thick, shaggy hair. "He's hated me ever since my mom died. Probably even before that."

A cold feeling settled stubbornly in my chest at the mention of Evan's deceased mother. I knew that she had died a long time ago—breast cancer, he had told me. She went in for a routine checkup and came out with a stage four diagnosis. Terminal. Five months later, she was gone. He was only eight years old when she passed.

I didn't press him on the subject, didn't ask prying questions that weren't my business to ask. Mama had taught me better than that. *Men prefer a quiet woman, Elaine. It's best you keep your questions to yourself.* Sometimes I wondered if she only said those types of things because she knew as well as I did that her husband was fucking his secretary.

Normally, I would have bit down on my tongue, forced the urge to ask for more information from my mind. But this felt different. As Evan sat dejected and forlorn on the edge of his mattress, his confession dangling in the air like an invitation, I got the sense that he wanted me to pry. He needed someone to talk to about this.

I reached out for his hand on the comforter and interlaced my fingers between his.

"You and your mom were pretty close, huh?" I said. He nodded, swallowing hard as he scanned the walls of his bedroom.

"She taught me everything," he said quietly, his gaze transfixed by a collage of charcoal drawings hanging on the wall across from us. It took me a moment to understand what he meant, but once it finally hit me, I felt like I was seeing Evan for the first time.

"She was an artist, too?" I asked.

"Yeah," he confirmed. "Fucking good one, too."

"Just like you," I told him, hoping to lighten his mood. But I didn't just say it to be nice. It was the truth. Even the amateur artwork that swallowed the room like poorly applied wallpaper was of far better quality than most of the abstract paintings that hung in my father's study back in Williamsburg, the haphazard squiggles and meaningless shapes like a kindergartner's work compared to my boyfriend's intricate drawings.

He drew mostly buildings—little beach bungalows dotted along sandy shorelines or elaborate cityscapes with high-rises that kissed the sun. As I looked around the room at each one, I wondered if he had chosen this subject matter for a reason. A sad image began to form in my mind of a sorrowful child mourning the loss of his mother, plotting his escape from the miserable home life she had left him in using the only tools she had shown him how. It made my throat thick with emotion.

Evan shook his head at my compliment with a mixture of modesty and melancholy.

"No, not like me," he insisted. "I'll never be that good. I'm not good enough for anything. Especially not for *him*."

"Oh, honey," I said, heartache swelling around my vocal cords, making me sound far more southern than I intended. Sympathy had a way of coaxing my mother's candied drawl from my lips, though I liked to pretend that when it came from me, it wasn't accompanied by the same insincerity. "You *are* good enough, baby. Why on earth would you ever say you weren't?"

As if on cue, the sound of the front door slamming shut echoed down the hallway, signaling the arrival of Evan's two brothers. I could hear booming voices exchanging enthusiastic greetings—the total opposite of the welcome that we had received moments before. Evan's back stiffened, his face ashen as he swiped away at tears that he thought I didn't see.

"C'mon," he got up from the bed and held his hand out to me. "Let's go."

I reluctantly placed my hand into his and allowed him to lead me away from the room, not yet ready to face what was waiting for me down the hall. The taller of the two brothers was locked in a one-armed hug with his father when he spied me and Evan walking toward the front entrance.

He looked a lot like Evan, with the same green eyes, the same striking bone structure, the same dark hair sweeping wildly across his face. But that was where the similarities ended. Compared to Evan's slight frame, his older brother's athletic form mirrored that of his father's, biceps bulging like an over-filled balloon on full display in his black tank top. A devilish grin spread across his pouty lips when his gaze landed on us. I gulped.

"Well, well, well," he purred with a sinister tone in his voice that I didn't like one bit. "Look what the fuckin' cat dragged in. The hell are you doin' here lil' bro?"

He released his father at once and pounced on his prey before Evan could return his greeting. In the blink of an eye, he had wrapped his thick arms around Evan's neck, squeezing him in a headlock and digging his knuckles into his younger brother's scalp in a way that looked more painful than playful. My insides twisted with rage.

"Let him go!" I yelled before I could stop myself. "You're hurting him! *Stop!*"

The meathead looked absently in my direction as though he were seeing for the first time that another person existed in the room. He dropped Evan promptly from his grasp, leaving him to rub at the tender spots on his skull. I was grateful that he had released Evan so quickly, but my relief was short-lived. He inched closer to me, licking his lips with a hungry expression on his face that made me feel queasy and self-conscious.

"And who is this knockout?" he whistled, looking me over from head to foot like I was a prized pig at a county fair. My cheeks flushed red.

"Shut the fuck up, Tyler," Evan growled, still rubbing the top of his head. "Leave her alone."

"No, I don't think I will," Tyler answered casually, still raking over my body with eager eyes. "Fine piece like that is worth gettin' to know. Tell me who you are, beautiful."

"She's my fucking girlfriend, you dickhead, and I told you to *leave her alone!*"

Anger radiated in the space between the two brothers as Evan stepped in front of me, shielding my body from Tyler's probing gaze. I thought that the two might start throwing punches, but the sound of a new voice interrupted their standoff.

"*Girlfriend?*" Evan's second brother stepped into view from behind Tyler's hulking body. He was less chiseled than Tyler or his father, but still more strapping than Evan could ever hope to be, with blue eyes instead of green and a full beard to match the thick, black tresses that covered his head.

"Yeah, Rob, my girlfriend," Evan squared his shoulders, obviously trying to make himself appear bigger than he was in his brothers' overwhelming shadow. Rob snickered in response.

"That's funny," he said. "I always thought you were gay."

My jaw fell to the floor for a second time. What the hell was wrong with these people? How could they be so cruel to their own brother? And on his birthday, no less. Although, it was beginning to dawn on me that none of them seemed aware that there was a birthday celebration to be had. Weren't we supposed to be having dinner, cake, *something?* As though reading my mind, Rob spoke up once more.

"What're you doing here anyway? Thought we wouldn't have to see you again until the summer. Just wanted to show us you don't like dick after all?"

"Fuck you, Rob," Evan spat. "It's my birthday. My *twentieth* birthday. I wouldn't be here if I didn't need to be."

Tyler and Rob exchanged a sideways glance, a palpable tension building between the three brothers. I got the feeling that they all knew something that I didn't. Before I could open my mouth to ask what the hell was going on, Evan's father interjected with a dark, biting laugh.

"Ohhhh, so *that's* what you think, huh?" he jeered. "Well, I hate to be the bearer of bad news, but you're not getting shit from this family."

I felt lost, like a stranger in a foreign country only understanding bits of conversation. But Evan didn't seem to share my confusion. He looked just as lost as I did, and yet his face was full of understanding. His shoulders sank.

"You can't do that," he whispered. "You can't—"

"I can, and I did," his father snapped. "You honestly think you deserve it after everything you've done? Over my dead body."

"You can't do that!" Evan protested, louder this time, his voice cracking around a flood of tears. "Mom left me that money for when I got old enough. It wasn't yours to—"

A thick, heavy hand clapped down hard across Evan's face, slapping him speechless. I clasped my hands to my mouth as I watched my boyfriend's father grab a fistful of his hair and yank him back, forcing his son to look him in the face.

"You don't get to talk about her, boy. Not in this house. Not to me," his voice rumbled like thunder through a black sky. "Your mother didn't know you'd turn out to be a disappointment. A *criminal*. I saved her from making a mistake."

My veins felt as though they had frosted over, an icy tundra creeping under my skin. *What did he mean by criminal?* As though I had spoken the question aloud, Evan's father looked at me with a curious expression in his eyes that almost seemed like concern. I felt paralyzed.

"Does she know what you've done?" he was speaking to Evan, but his gaze was fixed on me as he posed the question. "Does she know who you *really* are?"

Evan tore away from his father, leaving a few strands of black hair in between his fingers as he did so. His eyes were red with unsuppressed turmoil as he turned to look at me. I wanted to reach out for him, wanted to hold him and soothe him the way I knew that he needed. But I was still trapped inside his father's stare, still wondering what he had meant, frozen by the possibilities.

"C'mon," Evan muttered. "Let's get out of here."

He took my trembling hand into his own and began to shove past his brothers towards the front door. As we passed, his father seized me by the wrist of my free arm, holding me in place with a firm grip.

"Be careful with him, girl," he warned. "He's not what you think."

With that, he released me, and I continued to follow Evan out into the front yard on shaky legs, my gut spiraling in a cyclone of cryptic messages that I still didn't understand. I reached into my pocket, fumbling for the car keys to unlock the door. Neither of us bothered to buckle our seatbelts as we sped away from the place, not caring what might happen to us should an unexpected collision keep us from reaching safety. We were three blocks from the university parking lot when Evan broke the weighty silence with an ear-shattering scream.

"FUCK!" he yelled, smashing his fist into the dashboard. "FUCK! FUCK! FUCK!"

He punched the space above the glove compartment over and over again until his knuckles turned red and swollen, blood blisters forming under milky skin, threatening to burst. I felt sorry for him, but seeing him that way frightened me—especially with his father's warning still ringing in my ears.

Does she know who you really *are?*

I cringed.

"Evan, stop it," I begged. "You're scaring me. Please!"

"Goddamn it, Elaine, don't tell me what the fuck to do!" he yelled, throwing his fist into the dashboard in defiance. It was horrifying, the way the nighttime shadows played off his sharp features, accentuating his anger, making him look deranged. I selected a parking spot in a hurry and killed the ignition.

"Get out!" I screamed at him. "Get out of my fucking car! You're acting like an animal!"

"Fuck you!" he shot back.

"Fuck *me?*" I demanded. "Fuck *you*, Evan! What the hell is wrong with you? You're a psycho! Look at yourself!"

"You don't know what you're talking about!" he yelled. "You don't know a fucking thing about me! You're just like everybody else!"

"You're right," I said, tears flowing freely down my cheeks. "I don't know you at all, and after tonight, I don't think I want to."

My words seemed to sting more than the imprint of his father's palm still hot and pink across his face. All at once, his features melted into a pool of instantaneous regret. He reached for my hand, but I flinched away, exiting the car in a hurry.

"Elaine—*wait!*" he stumbled out of the passenger seat, pursuing me as I stomped across the pavement toward the brick building that housed my dorm room. The air was humming with humidity. It smelled like rain.

"Get away from me!" I hollered over my shoulder.

"Elaine, *please!* I can explain."

I whipped around to face him, heart hammering in my chest with angry adrenaline.

"Explain then," I demanded. "What the fuck was that about tonight? Why does your father think you're a criminal? What aren't you telling me?"

Evan stepped back as though I had assaulted him. He looked wounded, drained. Again, I felt compelled to comfort him, but not until he told me what was going on.

"I should have told you this sooner," he started. "I just didn't know how. Elaine, I'm... what you saw tonight doesn't hold a candle to the kind of shit that man has put me through. Every day of my life since my mom died has been a living hell, and it's only because of him. He hates me. Always has, always will."

I softened a bit, recalling the way his father had greeted him. The way he had left his mark across his son's face without a second thought. But then I remembered his warning.

He's not what you think.

"That still doesn't explain why he thinks you're a criminal, Evan," I pointed out. "Out with it. Now. Or I'll never trust you again."

He took a deep breath, expelling the air from his lungs with a long, heavy sigh.

"I did something really stupid when I was about twelve years old," he started. "I was being bullied at school, bullied at home. I just didn't know how to handle it. One day I got so mad, I just knocked this kid out on the school bus for talking too much shit. They ended up in the hospital for weeks in a coma. I was sent to juvie for three years, had to go to anger management and everything. But Elaine, I swear to you, I'm not that person anymore. I would never, ever hurt you like that. You have to believe me."

I thought about the fresh bruises forming on his knuckles from where they had made impact with my dashboard. I turned away.

"You really scared me tonight, Evan," I complained. "I don't like that side of you."

"I know," he whispered. "I'm so sorry. Really, I am. But that fucker just makes me so goddamn angry, I don't know what to do with myself. And he took something from me. He took the only thing I had left of her and I just…"

He trailed off, staring up at the inky sky overhead.

"You just what?" I prompted.

"I… I miss my mom," his voice was strangled. "I miss her so fucking much, Elaine. You have no idea. You have no idea what this is like. I feel like I'm sinking and the only one who wants to keep me from drowning is already dead. Do you have any idea what the fuck that feels like? Do you have any idea how much this hurts?"

I didn't. My parents and I didn't have the best relationship in the world—their jobs too important, too busy to do such trivial things as spending time with their only daughter—but I didn't hate them. I couldn't imagine either of them being dead. The thought alone was enough to make me feel as though I were stranded in the waves beside Evan, swallowing mouthfuls of salty water as I succumbed to the riptide that wanted to take me under. Take us both under.

I took a step towards him, feeling guilty that I had added to his grief. Feeling even guiltier that I had nothing to offer him to make it any better, wishing that I had ignored his insistence to forego an extravagant birthday gift—or any birthday gift for that matter. I cupped his face in my hands, used my thumbs to smear away the tears from his bony cheeks.

"I'm sorry, baby," I told him, sealing my lips over his own. Though I didn't know how yet, I promised myself in that moment that I would make it up to him.

***

June 3, 2007

A few weeks after Evan's birthday, the semester was coming to an end, which meant that he'd be forced to return to his awful father's house for the summer while I had to head back up to Williamsburg. I was still feeling guilty about the way everything turned out—especially the part about me not getting him a present on what I'm sure was the worst birthday of his life. Although, judging from the way his father treated him, I was sure there were more horror stories than I could stomach in that department. I couldn't leave him stranded in that house without making some sort of grand gesture, and I thought that I had chosen the perfect thing.

"Hey, handsome," I chirped in his direction as he exited the lecture hall where I knew his art final was being held. "Been waitin' for ya."

I skipped into his arms and dove in for a deep kiss, excited to wipe the sour look off his face with the surprise I had in store.

"I got you a present," I smiled, unable to contain myself any longer. His lips quirked up in a confused half-smile.

"Oh?" he asked. "What for?"

"For you to have a little fun this summer," I said, slipping an old library book into his hands. He held it up for closer inspection, a quizzical look on his face as he read the title out loud.

"Green Valley University Class of 1956? What the fuck is this?"

"Just open it, stupid," I chided. "I think you'll like what's inside."

He raised a doubtful eyebrow in my direction before flipping the cover open. As he bent the binding back, a plastic card tumbled to the floor. I snatched it up quickly before anyone could see, not wanting any prying eyes to ruin what I had planned.

"Don't let anyone see," I said, placing the smooth, plastic piece into his hand. He turned it over and his eyes lit up at once.

"A fake ID? Are you serious?" he said in a low, excited whisper. "Where the hell did you get this? Did you make this yourself?"

I giggled, pleased to see my man looking as delighted as I wanted him to be.

"No, I didn't make it myself, silly," I nudged him in the chest, "but I have my ways."

I gave him a wink as I thought about my trip to the restricted section of the university library where rumor had it that someone was selling fake IDs to students looking to score drinks on the sly. It was almost impossible for me to get through undetected—especially since Cat always seemed to be manning the front desk. But I had memorized her work schedule to seize the perfect opportunity, and when I asked the red-headed receptionist named Stephanie to give me the key to the eighth floor, she was all too happy to comply.

It only took two trips: One to submit the order in the back of the old yearbook that Evan now held in his hands, and one to collect the ID. The perfect plan.

Evan's smile faded a bit from his lips as he turned the plastic over in his hands.

"I don't know if I can take this," he said. "I could get in a lot of trouble if I'm caught. I've got a record, you know?"

I smiled wide. I was hoping he'd say that.

"I know," I said. "That's why I had the guy just put a random name in. Check it out."

I grabbed the plastic out of his hands and pointed to the name beside his photograph—a picture I had stolen from his dorm room when he wasn't looking one afternoon. He squinted at the words, an involuntary grin pulling up into his cheeks.

"Michael Davies, huh?" he laughed. "Has a nice ring to it."

CHAPTER 3

April 27, 2008

I loved Cat. As the only other rich kid in our Podunk public school system, she and I were destined to be the best of friends. I didn't have to explain to her things that were commonplace to me—like why there were four forks set at the dinner table or what a cruise ship looked like or how to tell if a diamond was fake. We understood these things, which meant we understood each other. But even though I considered her to be more of a sister than a friend, there were certain things I knew that I couldn't trust her with, and keeping secrets was one of them.

One summer during high school, our families decided to go on a joint vacation to a lavish retreat in Jamaica. Our parents had given us each a wad of spending money with a warning to stay within the resort's boundaries, but I was feeling a bit rebellious. I had seen the street vendors that paved the way to the tourist center through the window of our limousine, the unmistakable skunky odor of marijuana wafting into the stretch cabin, telling me there was more fun to be had than tanning on the beach.

I had never smoked weed before—had only ever caught whiffs of it coming off the clothes of stoner kids spilling out of smoke-filled vehicles in the school parking lot—but I was curious. More than curious, I was eager to make the most of our trip with a taste of something naughty. And who better to share in my virgin voyage to the land of psychedelics than my best friend?

"Come *on*, it'll be fun," I had said to her, applying precisely the right amount of peer pressure to get what I wanted. I was good at that.

She hesitated at first but ultimately gave in. Before our parents even had time to register that their daughters had flagrantly disobeyed them, we had made our way back to the resort with a sixty-dollar dime bag (how was I supposed to know they had charged too much?), a lighter, and a pack of brittle rolling papers in hand. We selected a private alcove along the shore, tucked away behind a set of tall boulders as we folded the sticky nuggets into an unevenly packed joint and began to puff away.

With two hits each, we were stoned. I felt like a warm honey glaze slowly melting over a homemade biscuit fresh out of Mama's oven, fits of giggles washing over me as silky smooth as the waves that seemed to meld with my skin as I dipped my toes into the sea. The same could not be said for Cat.

Mounting paranoia had left her shellshocked and speechless in the sand, her eyes bloodshot and fidgety as she scanned the cerulean horizon. She kept smacking her mouth like a dying fish desperate for water, the sound of her dry tongue clicking against her teeth instantly deflating my high.

"Something's wrong," she said. "I don't feel right. I think there was something stronger in that stuff..."

"You're just being paranoid," I assured her. "Just relax. It'll pass."

But it was too late. Cat was already bounding back towards the hotel, crying out to Mommy and Daddy that Laney had forced her to do drugs. I got in huge trouble after that and didn't speak to Cat for the rest of the vacation. We eventually made up and were best friends again by the time we had made it back to North Carolina, but the experience made me think twice about letting her in on anything that needed to be kept secret. Maybe that's why I didn't go to her for help when I wanted to plan Evan's surprise party.

Still, I knew I couldn't pull it off all by myself, even though I would have much preferred to do exactly that. As my father used to say, *If you want something done right, refrain from delegation.* But with coursework and final exam prep taking priority, I needed the extra help. Besides, the only suitable venue I had access to was the two-bedroom apartment that I had moved into four months earlier with Evan, Cat, and her boyfriend, Tim. Trying to plan an entire party there without raising my boyfriend's or my best friend's suspicions would have been damn near impossible.

It didn't take me long to figure out where to move the party. The Sigma Nu house was a ten-minute walk from the brick duplex that contained our apartment across the Greene Street Bridge. It was a narrow, colonial-style house with white, straight-lap siding and a small porch out front that was littered with cigarette butts. Not the most breathtaking place to have a celebration, but the frat house held a special significance for our tight-knit group. After all, this was where Cat and I had attended our first real college party—the same party, as it turned out, where we ended up meeting both of our boyfriends.

I'll never forget that night. How Cat and I had locked our eyes on Tim as his pinstriped button-down called to us beneath the blacklights like a phosphorescent traffic cone. Daring one of us to make a move.

I had wanted to make him mine the moment I set my sights on his herculean body, thick biceps stretching out the fabric of his shirt, begging me to tear away at the long sleeves to find the prize beneath. He was exactly my type with bronzed skin and sandy blonde hair, haunting eyes that looked to be pale blue or gray, or maybe a mixture of both. But when I saw the way Cat looked at him, her string of recent breakups prompting our wild night out to begin with, I knew I had to back down. But not without making her sweat for it a little first. I wasn't about to let her walk away with the hottest guy at the party *that* easily.

We played rock, paper, scissors to see who would win his affection, but I made sure to throw the game at the last minute. Like I said, Cat was terrible at keeping secrets. From the time that we were kids fighting over who got to wear my mother's Jimmy Choos while we played dress-up in her walk-in closet, I had been able to pick up on her projections. When she intended to throw scissors, her left eye would squint ever so slightly. Rock, her eyebrows would raise up to kiss her scalp, almost disappearing into the wild, black curls on top of her head. If it was paper, she would do this stupid thing with her mouth, scrunching it up in a puckered, wrinkled ball below her dainty nose right before she made her move. That's how I knew to let my fist come down in the last round, allowing her flat palm to cover me in misplaced triumph. It was almost too easy.

When the battle was over, I took a look around the crowded room and spotted Evan leaning against the wall. He wasn't the kind of guy that I normally would have gone after—too artsy-looking with brooding eyes that screamed for me to just leave him alone. It was that scowl that did it for me, though. One look at those pouty lips of his and my heart was off to the races. The rest, as they say, is history.

The four of us spent a lot of time at that frat house together, albeit almost always against Evan's wishes. I knew that he probably wouldn't have agreed to hosting his birthday there what with the fact that he spent most parties with his back firmly planted against the wall, radiating hatred at any brother who dared look in his direction. But to me, the house was symbolic. That was the place where we had first met, where we had shared our first kiss. Besides, could having the party there have been worse than the shit show that unfolded at his father's house the year before? I didn't think so.

It had to be the Sig Nu house. That was final. The real trouble would be convincing a group of frat brothers that my boyfriend openly despised to allow us to use the place for his birthday. To be honest, I didn't necessarily trust any of them to be up to the task, either. At least, not without an ulterior motive.

Most of them had made it pretty clear that they wanted to do much more with me than dance whenever we attended one of their parties. It was innocent for the most part, but Pete was the worst offender, his sweaty body always grinding up against my backside much too close for my comfort when the music played. I hated the way he'd sneak up from behind, grabbing at my hips, gyrating into me with what I prayed was just a roll of quarters for the Third Street Laundromat. Although, I have to admit that I did like the way his unwanted advances always got a rise out of Evan. It was almost worth enduring the borderline assault just to watch him turn green with jealousy, those little pink pillows on his face looking puffier and more kissable with every thrust on the dance floor. I was terrible back then.

With a house full of horndogs hell-bent on hitting on me, I couldn't risk turning to any of them for the help that I needed lest they seize the opportunity to pull some sort of sick prank at Evan's expense. Still, I did need someone on the inside who could coordinate with me without also trying to get into my pants. It seemed like an impossible catch twenty-two until I realized that I already had the perfect person to ask for help.

Tim was a brother at Sigma Nu—a fact that was easy for me to forget given that he lived with us in an off-campus apartment rather than the frat house that his fellow brothers called home. Even if he hadn't been my best friend's boyfriend, I still would have turned to him for help. Compared to the rest of the animals that lived at the fraternity, Tim was a perfect gentleman. He was quiet and reserved, always preferring to dress in long-sleeved button-downs despite the fact that he had much more of a body to show off than any of the other brothers by far. And yet his bizarre fashion choices and conservative demeanor didn't seem to diminish his authority among the other frat members. On the contrary, he seemed to hold a special place in each of their hearts, some unspoken admiration that placed him a step above the rest in their strange little hierarchy.

Whatever it was that placed Tim on a pedestal, I didn't dare question it. He had the precise qualities that I needed from a co-conspirator: tight-lipped, connected, and zero underlying sexual desire towards me whatsoever. Even though we lived together, there weren't many opportunities for me to get Tim alone to discuss my plans—especially not without tipping off Cat or Evan in the process. Thankfully, being in college meant we all led pretty predictable lives, so it wasn't difficult for me to find my opening.

One Wednesday while Cat was busy working her shift at the library and Evan was in class, I texted Tim to meet me at the Sig Nu house alone. I couldn't tell if it was the unseasonable chill in the late April air or the possibility that Tim might reject my request that made me feel strangely nervous as I approached the frat house on Fifth Street that day. It was as though even Mother Nature was trying to warn me that the party was destined to fail. But I didn't care. All I cared about was making Evan happy—especially since my last attempt to lift his spirits hadn't turned out the way I hoped it would.

It seemed that instead of using the fake ID to have some good, old-fashioned college fun with the guys, Evan was more determined to find the bottom of any whiskey bottle that he could wrap his thirsty hands around. I pretended not to mind as much as I did. After all, I was the one who had enabled him in the first place. Besides, didn't acute alcoholism just come with the territory of being in college? We were all drinking much more than we should have been in those days. Who was I to cast judgment?

Still, part of me knew there was something darker about Evan's newly formed habit. Something permanent. I especially didn't like the way it seemed to take his anger to new heights. All that hard work he had put in at anger management following his stint in juvenile detention seemed to dissipate as soon as the liquor reached his lips. On more than one occasion, he had found himself on the receiving end of a serious ass-kicking thanks to his drunken behavior. And of course, I had to forgive him. If it weren't for me, he wouldn't have touched the stuff nearly as much as he did. At least, that's what I told myself.

I put the thoughts about his most recent beating at the Sig Nu's annual Valentine's Day party out of my mind as I made a sharp right turn off the sidewalk and up the worn, cement pathway to the frat house's front porch.

It won't be like that this time, I had told myself. *You just need to show him how to have fun. You just need to show him he's loved.*

Tim was already standing on the veranda as I approached, a small stack of what appeared to be textbooks squeezed under his arm. The long sleeves of his shirt gave me genuine pangs of envy as a crisp breeze bit my cheeks.

"Hey, is everything okay?" Tim asked, concern pinching his eyebrows together in a wrinkled line across his forehead. The two of us weren't that close at the time and all my text had said was to meet me at the frat house alone. He had every right to be confused, maybe even worried that something was wrong.

"Yeah, sorry," I laughed away the apprehension in his features. "Didn't mean to scare you. Just had something I wanted to talk to you about—in private."

"Um... okay? What's it about?"

As I opened my mouth to answer, a gust of arctic air blasted across the yard and up the porch, sliding its icy fingers beneath my cashmere sweater with bitter persistence. I sucked in a sharp breath and squeezed my eyes shut.

"*Sheeeeeoot!*" I yelled out, vaguely wondering what Mama might say if she had heard me. *You sound like a hick, darling. Wherever are your manners?* Probably at the private school you didn't send me to, Mom. Why don't you put your debutante sash back on and have another glass of chardonnay while your husband works another "late night" at the office?

Thankfully, I wasn't alone in my discomfort. Even with his long-sleeved shirt protecting him from the worst of it, Tim clapped his hands together and gave a surprising holler of his own.

"Son of a *bitch!*" he yelled. "Can't believe how cold it is today."

"I *know!*" I agreed emphatically. "Do you think we can talk about this inside instead?"

"You bet," he said, turning around to face the front door. No sooner had he spun around than a body materialized in his path, sending his textbooks crashing to the floor in the collision. I watched them tumble from his hands as if in slow motion, a familiar-looking yearbook splaying open as it landed spine-first on the ground. Plastic cards and photographs of fellow students scattered across the deck like marbles spilling from a drawstring bag.

"Oh my goodness, I am so sorry!" a twangy voice called out. My heart hardened at once. I'd recognize that sickeningly sweet, sing-songy bullshit anywhere, even if it hadn't also been accompanied by Mia Davis's blonde-haired, blue-eyed, infuriatingly perfect-looking figure. Flashes of the Valentine's Day party burned into my retinas until my vision turned red. *This bitch.*

"Here, let me help you with those," she offered, bending down to reach the floor and scoop up the mess that her clumsiness had made. I beat her to the punch, falling to my knees and gathering all the evidence that Tim seemed too preoccupied to care was lying at his feet for the entire world to see.

"I've got it," I snapped, "you've done enough."

It probably wasn't fair for me to be as mean to Mia as I was. After all, we were neighbors, and what happened two months earlier wasn't her fault. Evan had been drinking all day before we made our way to the Valentine's Day party, his moodiness causing all sorts of needless argumentation leading up to our arrival. When Pete came up behind me with his typical grabby behavior, I expected Evan to get jealous, but not enough to do the unthinkable. Before I knew what had hit me, he was wrapping his arms around Mia, forcing himself on her, trying to stick his tongue down her throat with the same hungry enthusiasm that Pete kept poking me with his poorly restrained manhood. It wasn't long before Mia's boyfriend stormed into the room, ripping Evan's scrawny body off of her and punching him out cold in front of the entire party.

Evan and I made up afterward, of course. I knew it had only happened because he had been blackout drunk. But that didn't make it hurt any less, and it certainly didn't help quell any feelings of anger or jealousy that I held toward Mia. I had long suspected that Evan had once been enamored with her, though he would never admit as much to me. There was something he was hiding from me when it came to her, and when I saw them together that night, I couldn't shake the feeling that his inebriation had inspired his true feelings to surface. I hated it. And even though I knew it was wrong and she didn't deserve it, I hated Mia for it.

I was still hunched over Tim's library books, sliding the fallen IDs discretely between the pages so Mia couldn't see, when I saw a pair of white tennis shoes occupying the doorframe next to my nemesis.

"Geez, Mia, what the hell happened here?" Tennis Shoes asked with a teasing tone.

I raised my gaze to get a better view of the girl who had entered the picture and saw that it was Lisa—one of the frat brother's girlfriends whom I had met before at a few parties. She wore a big, goofy grin framed by a pair of plump, pink lips that were shiny with too much lip gloss, her long, dark hair collected in a fishtail braid, cascading down into a gentle curl just above her belly button. Behind her, I could see her boyfriend, Sean, standing in the frat house foyer, tufts of ginger hair poking out beneath his Tar Heels baseball cap. He had a pack of Marlboros in hand, ready to add to the pile of cigarette butts that I was certain were sticking to my knees as I raced to gather Tim's questionable collection of plastic cards and photographs.

"I was just coming through the door when I knocked straight into Mike here and—"

"It's Tim," I interjected fiercely, not even bothering to disguise my annoyance. "But don't worry, you've only met him what? Fifty times since we moved in above you?"

That was an exaggeration, but I didn't care. I wanted to make Mia feel small and stupid. Inferior. The same way I had felt when Evan had his hands all over her.

She clapped her hand over her mouth, cheeks flushed red with embarrassment. *Nailed it.*

"Shoot, I'm so sorry, sugar," Mia said to Tim, touching his shoulder apologetically. I noticed him give an involuntary flinch at her touch, which put a smile on my face. "I don't know why I thought your name was Mike. Sometimes I can be so forgetful."

Lisa snaked her arms around Mia's waist from behind, rubbing her hands across her friend's belly with a look of mischief on her face.

"Don't mind Mia and her baby brain, you guys," Lisa giggled. "Somebody's thinking for two these days."

"*Lisa!*" Mia hissed. She wriggled out from beneath her friend's grip with a mortified expression stitched into her features. I couldn't hide my delight, a villainous sneer pulling my mouth wide with understanding.

So, Little Miss Perfect went and got herself pregnant? Thoughts of Mia's thin frame tacking on pounds of baby weight made me feel lighter, less insecure.

Lisa tossed her braid over her shoulder, tilting her head back as echoes of her laughter carried on the cool spring breeze.

"Oh c'mon," she nudged Mia's shoulder gently. "I'm just messing with you, girl. Everyone's gonna find out soon enough anyway."

Mia crossed her arms over her torso, her cheeks still burning scarlet at her friend's unwanted revelation. She pressed her lips together in a thin line, casting a worried look at the apartment complex across the street.

"Well, not everyone knows just yet," she said vaguely.

I clutched Tim's books to my chest and got up from the floor, brushing away the ash and stray butts that had stuck to my jeans. An uncomfortable silence passed as we stood there awkwardly, Mia's unplanned pregnancy pressing its wrinkled flesh against our skin like an invisible elephant consuming the space between us.

"And on *that* note," Sean chimed in for the first time, attempting to ease the tension. "We'll see you guys around. Tim, you and I have to talk later, man. Lost my ticket the other day to that bitchy bartender at Lucky's, so I'm gonna need a replacement you feel me?"

Fresh darkness blackened the storm clouds still swirling behind Mia's eyes as she snapped her head in Sean's direction.

"Ex-*cuse* me, but that 'bitchy bartender' just so happens to be my *best friend!*" she said, effectively lodging Sean's foot into the back of his throat. She proceeded to stomp down from the porch and out to the sidewalk as Lisa gave chase behind her.

"Ah, shit," Sean sighed, slowly making his way across the porch. "Looks like I'm headed for the doghouse. All the more reason why I'll be needing that replacement. I'll catch up with you later, man, alright?"

He clapped Tim on the shoulder and jogged off to catch up with Lisa and Mia, who were already hugging it out on the sidewalk, their display of forgiveness as palpable as it was nauseating. The spiteful part of me had wanted their fight to last just a bit longer. Although, I was more than happy to relish in Mia's misery, images of her fattening belly making my own stomach do somersaults of joy. Soon enough, she would be the size of a potbelly pig and not even all the liquor in the world would make her attractive in Evan's eyes. The thought made me all the more excited to start planning his surprise party.

"C'mon," I nudged Tim in the arm and motioned towards the still-open front door. My touch seemed to jolt him into consciousness, his vacant stare coming into focus for the first time since bumping into Mia. "You good?"

"Yeah, yeah," he shook his head as though clearing away the cobwebs tangled around his mind. "Just thinking..."

He let the statement hang in the air unfinished as we crossed the threshold into the frat house. I wondered if his preoccupation had anything to do with the library book filled with fake licenses that I still had wrapped inside my arms. I took a look around the living area to make sure we were alone before confirming whether my suspicions were correct. Although, from the sound of Sean's cryptic requests, Tim's secret dealings didn't seem to be all that secret—at least not to the Sig Nu brothers. Was that why they all held Tim in such high regard?

"Thinking, huh?" I smirked, holding the yearbook out for him to take. "Thinking about what's inside that library book? I'm surprised at you, Tim. I didn't peg you for much of a rule breaker, let alone a criminal."

Red splotch marks crept along Tim's neck as he snatched the yearbook from my hands.

"You're not supposed to know about that," he stammered. "Not even the guys are supposed to know about that. Goddamn Sean and his loud ass—"

"*Relax*," I stopped him mid-sentence. "I knew before Sean said anything. All your shit spilled out on the floor, but don't worry. I'm not going to tell anybody. I'm a customer, after all."

I gave him a knowing wink. His muscles relaxed a bit as he allowed the breath that he had been holding to escape his body. The relief didn't stay for too long as a fresh source of terror caused his shoulders to stiffen once more.

"Please don't say anything to Cat," he said. "She doesn't know about this. She thinks I'm selling homework, which is already bad enough. I don't want her to think... she can't know that I'm... what I really am."

"Like I said, your secret's safe with me," I assured him, inserting an imaginary key into my sealed lips and tossing it over my shoulder. "But since we're on the topic of secrets, I need you to help me with one of my own."

"Oh?" Tim asked. "What did you need help with?"

I told him all about my idea for Evan's surprise party. Just a small get-together, I assured him—nothing too crazy. Yet despite my reassurances, he didn't seem convinced enough to help. So, I did the only thing I knew how and applied a bit of pressure.

"Of course, if you don't help me," I began, "I might accidentally tell Cat what you've been up to in the restricted section. Your call."

His knuckles whitened as he tightened his grip around the yearbook in his hands.

"Fine," he relented, though his tone suggested that he felt otherwise. But as he allowed the idea to simmer, I could see his aggravation slowly morph into genuine excitement. He smiled at me, his great, white teeth pristine and plentiful—how I imagine sharks might look shortly before consuming their prey. "Actually, this is a great idea."

"Really?" I asked, slightly stunned by his about-face.

"Yeah," he assured me. "I really do."

CHAPTER 4

May 14, 2023

Religion never factored much into my upbringing. I guess my father never could get behind the whole, *thou shalt not covet thy neighbor's wife*, thing. Mama probably would have enjoyed attending the occasional service, if only to partake in the Eucharist—she wasn't one to miss an opportunity to place a wine glass to her lips. But even without all the built-up anticipation of pearly gates and heavenly angels (or, you know, the other place), being dead was not what I expected it to be.

I have to admit that part of me was disappointed. It's not as though I were expecting to be fitted with a custom set of wings and matching halo, but I did think that it would be a bit more glamorous than simply floating through the ether like some neglected pet goldfish. Shouldn't there have been a guide? Some wise, mysterious entity to show me the ways of the afterlife? It didn't seem right that after enduring such a brutal attack, I had been cursed to a state of purgatory, not a single explanation provided for how I might navigate my non-existence. I felt abandoned, angry, helpless—emotions that were only compounded by the fact that I could do nothing but watch as the officers swarmed Cat's kitchen.

"She didn't do anything!" I had screamed at the uniformed women who dragged Cat to the back of their squad card. "You have the wrong person! She's innocent! STOP!"

But no one cared what I had to say about the matter. No one could hear me.

"Hey!" a familiar voice called from across the street. I could almost feel the thrum of a skipped heartbeat echo through the place where my ribcage used to be as I turned to face Evan. For one glorious moment, I thought that he could see me, but no sooner had hope burgeoned than it was vanquished by the painful realization that he was speaking to an officer standing just behind me.

Evan jogged to the edge of Cat's driveway, his sneakers barely kissing the stamped concrete surface as the officer stepped forward into my plasma. She walked straight through me in less time than it took to suck in a breath, but I didn't need her to linger more than that to hear the thoughts inside her head.

Stay where you are, her warning planted itself inside me with the same lucidity as though the thought had been my own. It was so clear, the sound of her voice so loud that I almost didn't understand why she felt the need to repeat herself as she approached the end of the driveway. Only after hearing her deliver the message aloud did I realize that she hadn't spoken a word. It was as though in the moment it took her to pass through my body, I had absorbed a piece of her.

My thoughts drifted back to my desperate attempts to stop Tim from reaching his unconscious wife on the floor, the darkness that swallowed me with each sweeping movement through his body still lurking somewhere inside like a parasite waiting to overtake its host. Had I taken something from him, too?

"No, that's bullshit!" Evan protested, unhappy with the officer's demand that he keep his distance. "I have a right to know what's going on here."

"Do you live here, sir?" the policewoman asked.

"Well, no, but—"

"Then I have to ask you to take a step back," she said firmly. "This is a crime scene."

"A crime scene? What the hell are you talking about?"

"This is an active investigation, sir. I can't speak to the details surrounding—"

"Oh my God!" Evan's anger was replaced with genuine shock as his gaze fell past the officer's shoulder and landed on a stretcher, the body bag containing my corpse lying on top zipped shut and ready to be hauled away to the morgue. He watched the coroner load my body into the back of a transport van, his eyes glistening through the darkness, saturated with terror.

"Please," he begged the officer, the aggravation in his voice taking on a more desperate tone. "You have to tell me what's going on. I know the woman who lives here, okay? She's my... she's a very close friend. Please, I just need to know she's alright."

The officer softened a bit, empathy erasing the severity of her features as she cast a furtive glance over her shoulder and lowered her voice.

"Look, I shouldn't be telling you this, but there's been a homicide here," she admitted, the confession drawing an audible gasp from my former husband's lips. His milky skin seemed to pale beneath the moonlight, taking on a sickly complexion that reminded me of the way my lifeless body had looked sprawled across the kitchen floor.

"Oh God, was it Cat?" his voice was barely above a whisper. "Is she—is she—was that... her?"

The woman winced at Evan's words, her lips screwing up in an involuntary grimace as she dared to ask a question of her own.

"Blonde hair, blue eyes—is that the woman you're talking about?"

Evan shook his head.

"What? No. Black, curly hair, brown eyes—*that's* Cat," he clarified. The officer's expression changed again, her frown peeling back into a rigid line, blue eyes blackening to two lumps of coal within her sockets. She squared her shoulders and spoke in a flat, authoritative tone.

"Well, I'm sorry to say but that woman's been taken into custody," she said without sounding one bit remorseful. "We have reason to believe that she was responsible for what happened here tonight."

Evan's dark brows furrowed together, confusion threatening to tear straight through the skin of his forehead.

"I don't understand," he said. "If Cat's been arrested, then who...?"

He didn't have to complete the thought, a cruel and unrelenting understanding draining whatever color was left from his cheeks as his knees sank to the pavement. His body quivered like dead leaves rustling through a violent wind. I thought he might have been having a seizure, the tremors quaking along his extremities, erupting like seismic energy ripping through tectonic plates. He placed his hands on the concrete, sucked in a staggered breath, and vomited on the ground.

"Oh no," he moaned, tears dripping down his nose, mingling with the snot and sputum that dangled in a stringy mess from his face. "No, no, no, no, no..."

His strangled refrain dissolved into the air, hollow and empty, as though he, too, were just a ghost in the night. Though I had no body left to speak of, my heart had never felt as broken as it did in that moment. We hadn't waited until death to part. Our divorce was finalized months before my murder could hold us to our wedding vows. Still, I ached to wrap my arms around him, to hold him close, to absorb his hurt. He didn't deserve this. And neither did Cat.

Cat!

A fresh wave of powerlessness swept through me as flashes of my best friend rotting away in a prison cell danced before my eyes. It wasn't just the fact of her innocence that plagued me, the knowledge that I alone held all the answers that might have kept her from a concrete tomb if only I had gotten the chance to share them. It was everything that had happened between us leading up to my death. Every crossed wire, every bitter insult, every screaming match and swung fist—all of it had coalesced to bring our thirty-year friendship, our sisterhood to a screeching halt.

Cat wasn't just doomed to serve what would likely be a life sentence for a crime she did not commit. She would do so while still believing that I had died hating her. That she had been nothing more to me than a liability at best, a rival at worst. And there was no way for me to change that.

Unless...

A new thought began to blossom within me. I had passed through Tim, the imprint of his malevolence leaving an indelible mark behind that I still struggled to comprehend. And that policewoman's thoughts had been etched into my eardrum as clearly as if she had spoken them aloud when she had stepped through my phantom figure. I might not have had the spirit guide that I wanted, but I was learning. If I could capture fragments of the living souls that surrounded me simply by slipping through them, then there had to be a way for me to pass on a message of my own. There had to be a way for me to still tell Cat what I knew.

It was four o' clock in the morning before the crime scene investigators packed it up, the evidence of their assessment left behind in the form of little yellow markers placed with care along the kitchen tile. Caution tape was strung along the wraparound porch of the Halls' Victorian farmhouse, transforming the appearance of the three-story home from one of grandeur to something altogether grim. Ominous.

I thought about Cat's mother—a skilled interior designer who had left her legacy in her daughter's hands following her untimely death—and what she might say about the ghastly additions to her estate. Though I had spent many Halloween nights at the Hall family manor, Cat and I traipsing through our upper-class neighborhoods as we collected our bounty of sweets in silk pillowcases, I had never seen the house look more haunted than it did as I watched it fade into the distance from the back of the police car that I had slipped inside, undetected.

"Hasn't been a homicide like this in I don't know how long," the officer driving commented. I recognized her as the same policewoman from earlier, black hair undulating down her neck from beneath her peaked cap in a sea of soft waves.

"And in the *nice* neighborhood, too," the male officer in the passenger seat agreed. He lifted the hat from his head and rubbed the smooth scalp that was hidden beneath as though he were trying to sweep the images of my bloodied body from his mind. "God, I need a drink after that."

"At least we caught the killer," the policewoman offered.

"Yeah, well... all the more reason to raise a glass," her partner replied, nudging her in the shoulder with a half-smile on his face.

"Another victory for the WPD," she nodded.

Bullshit, I thought in stony silence. *If you only knew what I know.*

The remainder of the drive to the Monroe County Sheriff's Office passed in silence, though not for lack of my trying to break through the invisible sound barrier that seemed to keep the officers from hearing my screams. It was like being submerged in water, the sound of my voice garbled and unintelligible. No matter how loud I tried to yell, no matter how many times I pled with them that they had placed an innocent woman in jail, no matter how much I insisted that they had let a killer escape, it didn't matter. I had even tried to telepathically communicate, reaching my spectral fingers inside each of their brains, hoping to implant a seed of doubt inside. But all that my efforts had earned me were a fresh set of stolen thoughts, most of which were self-congratulatory in nature. An internal pat on the back for a job well done. *Way to go, guys! Great fucking work.*

As the squad car pulled into the darkened parking lot outside the sprawling brick building that comprised the county jail, I drifted out from the backseat and left the police officers in their state of undeserved celebration. It was less important for me to break through to either of them than it was for me to find Cat.

I entered through the front door (literally) and surveyed my surroundings. It reminded me a bit of the administrative office in high school. The floors were a dull, slate-colored linoleum that I imagined might stick to the soles of my shoes if I still had feet that touched the ground. Strips of navy-blue carpet runners were situated along the most highly trafficked areas, including the front of the trapezoidal reception desk which sat below a set of loudly buzzing fluorescent lights. The smell of sweat and burnt coffee beans permeated the air in a nauseating cloud. Aside from the overweight officer who sat sleepy-eyed behind the front desk, not a soul occupied a single of the black plastic chairs that lined the left-hand wall.

I searched the walls for a map, a directory, a placard—anything that might tell me where I was in relation to Cat. Unfortunately for me, no such convenience existed. With nothing but instinct to guide me, I glided through the locked wooden door beside the reception desk and into the maze beyond.

The hallway on the opposite side of the door was long and narrow, entombed in stark, white cinderblocks that were so blinding, for a moment I thought that I had entered a tunnel of light, my spirit finally being welcomed into Heaven. I wandered into the empty space, twisting and turning down the labyrinthine passages that snaked through the county jail like a vast and unpredictable serpent.

Though there were metal signs strategically placed in regular intervals indicating where each corridor led, they did little to help guide me in the right direction. I had only ever been to the police station one other time in my life—a drunken screaming match between my parents about my father's infidelity had ended with him being carried off in cuffs after shoving Mama into a glass China cabinet, the explosion of shards that followed wedging deep into her bronzed skin.

While the entire ordeal was traumatic for everyone involved, I was too young when it had happened to remember any pertinent details about Daddy's processing experience. All I remembered for certain was that he was placed inside a holding cell to sleep off his stupor (Mama had dropped the charges before he was transferred to a more permanent setting). But Cat was accused of murder—a serious crime that warranted a lengthy stay. If I was going to find her, then I would need to find the place where the long-term prisoners were held.

I floated aimlessly into the jail, my phantom figure passing through concrete walls and locked doors as though moving through water. It was strange to have such freedom, to be uninhibited by physical obstacles. So much of my life had been dominated by the material, the tangible, things that were seen and felt and admired. Part of me felt liberated by the absence of touch, my body melting into each moment as easily as a snowflake dissolving into the earth. But there was another part of me—the part that still felt human, still felt *alive*—that craved the structure that came with physicality. Especially when I found myself slipping unaware into the male restroom only to come face-to-face with an unsuspecting officer whose stream of urine shot straight through me before I stumbled out of his path, desperate to erase the image of his flaccid member from my mind. *Disgusting*.

After spending what felt like hours passing through every corner of the county jail, I finally discovered the sign to the female detention center in front of yet another locked metal door in the basement. I passed through unobstructed, expecting to find a long stretch of hallway lined with iron bars and noisy occupants begging to be released on the other side. Instead, I was met with an eerie quiet, the white cinderblock walls broken up by a single metal door in six-foot intervals. Each door contained a small glass window in the center that more closely resembled an oversized bookmark than a means to peer into what lay beyond. I looked through the tiny pane on the first door and saw nothing but shadows inside. Frustrated, lost, and eager to find my friend, I drifted through the doorway and into the darkness beyond.

On the other side of the door was a collection of four cells, each designed to house two inmates with a set of matching twin-sized cots and a single toilet bolted in the center. Only three of the units remained at full capacity—none of the prisoners inside looking anything like Cat. The last of the cells was home to just one soundly sleeping Spanish woman. Even in her state of slumber, the sight of her unruly tresses laying in a tangled mess across her mattress, scowl stitched across her thick, menacing lips told me she was not a woman to be trifled with.

I moved back through the door and into the hallway, continuing to the next pod of prisoners. And the next. And the next. I checked each unit at least three times, just to be certain that Cat was nowhere to be found. By the time my inspection was complete, the lights had come on in each cell block, prisoners stirring from their cots, ready to greet the day's planned monotony. Seeing no point in searching each cell for a fourth time, I decided to retrace my path back to the main hallway on the ground level of the county jail. Maybe I had missed something. Maybe Cat was in a holding cell after all, and I needed to find her there.

I propelled my ghostly figure through the ceiling, resurfacing in the main stretch of hallway behind the front lobby just in time to hear the sound of unfamiliar voices approaching.

"—smiled for her mugshot, I shit you not," I heard one person say.

"You're kidding!" another replied in a squeaky tenor. A pair of officers rounded the corner down the hallway towards the booking station, making their way towards my place at the junction between detention and holding. The woman on the left looked like an ogre with large, hulking shoulders and thick, bushy eyebrows that bunched together in a hairy line across her forehead. I judged her to be at least six feet tall, her body more massive and muscular than the puny rodent of a man who walked beside her.

"I swear on my mother's grave," the woman asserted, raising a meaty hand as though making a promise before God himself. "Never seen anything like it."

"Where's she at now?" the other officer asked, his short, skeletal legs jogging five steps for every stride that his lumbering counterpart took.

"Got her in CID 10 with Slater and Horne," she answered. "They're in for a real treat with that one, that's all I can say. I mean, who smiles at the fucking camera after stabbing a woman to death? Like nothing even happened! The bitch is crazy."

"Sounds like it," the man agreed.

Stabbing?

They had to be talking about Cat. How many women in Monroe County could be arrested for such a brutal crime in one night? But what the hell was CID 10, and where could I find it? Maybe the answer to both questions was hidden down the same hall where the officers had just been.

I glided down the corridor marked "BOOKING" until I reached another metal door on the left-hand side of the hallway. Inside, the booking station was abuzz with the sound of shuffling paper and idle chatter exchanged between the officers working there. Beyond the camera operator and fingerprinting station was a cramped cubicle where a set of payphones were bolted to the wall on the right. To the left was another small, unmarked hallway. I decided to take my chances and see what was held beyond.

The corridor was lined with wooden doors on either side. To the right of each doorway was a black, metal placard bolted to the cinderblock walls, the letters "CID ROOM" printed in white with a corresponding number displayed beneath.

CID 10!

The place where my heart once lived seemed to swell with excitement as I located the last door on the right and slipped inside. It was a gray, dismal box of a room with nothing but a flimsy metal table and matching chairs decorating the space. The smell of vomit hung thick in the air, seemingly able to trigger my gag reflex even in death. It didn't take me long to realize that Cat was the source of the foul odor, her head buried in a trashcan, stomach contents spilling loudly against the plastic container with a sickening splash. A pair of chubby detectives looked onward in horror from their seats on the left-hand side of the room. The male detective curled his lip in disgust as he waited with obvious impatience for Cat to finish her retching.

"What did she want?" he growled as she straightened in her seat. A stony expression washed over Cat's face, her nostrils flaring out as her lungs pumped hot, angry air through her dainty nose.

"She had these papers with her," she said darkly.

"Papers…?"

"Receipts," she clarified. "Yeah, her little fuckin' trophies. Like she owned him or something."

"Receipts for what? Who did she own?" the detective stoked the fire raging behind Cat's eyes with his questions.

"She was fucking my husband," she seethed through gritted teeth. "They were hotel receipts."

I let out a frustrated scream that fell on deaf ears. That wasn't exactly the truth. Yes, I had started an affair with Tim, and yes, I had come to Cat's house with a bag full of receipts, but the two things weren't related to one another. Not in the way Cat thought, at least. Tim and I had only started sleeping together within the last two months of my life. Out of all the receipts that I had in my bag, not one of them had come from a hotel room that we had shared. I wasn't there to claim ownership. I was there to protect her. But she was too full of hatred to hear me. I needed her to understand, but how?

Cat began to sob, her face streaked with tears and eyeliner, chest heaving around painful gasps as she tried to collect herself but couldn't. The female detective in the room placed a tissue box in her lap, much to the disapproval of her partner. She paid no mind to his irate scowl as she patted Cat's knee, leaned back in her chair, and proceeded to change the subject.

"Let's take a break from Elaine for a minute," she said, running a hand through her frizzy, graying hair. "Walk me through what you did up until the time she arrived at your place."

Cat dabbed at her eyes and pinched the tip of her nose with a tissue, wiping away the mucus that bubbled out from her nostrils.

"It was our wedding anniversary," she choked, sucking in a staggered breath to suppress a whimper. I cringed. "We would have been together ten years. I took the day off. We were gonna..."

She trailed off, gazing out into the distance as though peering into a memory that could have been. A memory she might have had if it hadn't been for me.

"It doesn't matter," she decided with a shudder, shaking the what-ifs from her mind. "I didn't do much before she got there. I was feeling horrible. Spent all day drinking, looking at old pictures, eating junk food... the whole day was kind of a blur, to be honest. I was wasted by noon. Maybe even before then."

That wasn't surprising to me. Cat's drinking had gotten so out of control in the past few years that the reputation of the interior design firm we co-owned with Tim and Evan was dangling by a thread. It had become such a problem that I was forced to take matters into my own hands (as usual), consulting with a business attorney to explore options for her forced removal, sending her away to rehab just to keep her away from our clients. At least, that was the lie I had chosen to tell myself to justify my actions.

"Did you go anywhere? See anybody?" the detective prompted, using a thick finger to slide her wire-framed glasses up the bridge of her nose as she peered up from her notetaking.

"No," Cat shook her head vehemently. "My parents were killed by a drunk driver. I would never be that careless."

Visions of Cat's sedan parked on my front lawn in her most recent display of disorderly drunkenness the week before flashed inside my mind. As though he shared my memory, the other detective scoffed at the remark, earning him a sharp look from his female counterpart. He smirked and put up his hands in defense, choosing to remain quiet rather than voice the source of his amusement. The woman turned her attention back to Cat, still leering at her partner from the corner of her eye.

"What's the last thing you remember doing before Elaine arrived?" she probed. Cat closed her eyes, deep in thought. It was a long time before she finally spoke.

"I was in the kitchen, I think," she offered, the vague response sending the male detective over the edge. Before his partner could keep her momentum going, he seized control of the conversation, unable to mask his irritation any longer.

"Okay, so Elaine knocks at the door—what does she say to you?" he demanded.

"I can't remember, man," Cat groaned.

"You have to try, Cat," he asserted, his face growing purple with frustration. "C'mon, you can't be that drunk anymore. You had time to sleep it off. I know you can remember. What did she say to you?"

He looked as though he wanted to pounce on her, the flaps of his cheeks quaking with rage as he leaned in closer, urging her to comply. This wasn't going to end well for her. Not when I was the only person in the room who knew what really happened. I moved to Cat's side, my hand hovering above her head as I debated whether or not I should attempt to communicate. If I made contact and I scared her witless in front of the detectives, she'd be deemed psychotic. If I let her answer their questions, she'd incriminate herself. Either way, it seemed she was doomed to be locked away. What more harm could I possibly cause by trying to intervene?

Without a second thought, I sank my hands inside Cat's head, a strange vibration buzzing through my fingertips as I focused all of my energy on implanting my memories inside her brain. It wasn't the same sensation as I had while diving into the minds of the officers who drove me to the county jail. This was different. Visceral. Like sticking a wet finger inside an electrical outlet.

We need to talk, I willed the words to come to her, etched the image of me standing at her doorstep into her mind with all the power I could muster. The pulsing feeling between us seemed to snap like a rubber band as Cat straightened in her seat with a start.

"She wanted to talk about something," she said in a shaky voice, tilting her head as though draining pool water from her ears. *Holy shit—it worked!*

"About the affair?" the female officer prompted before her partner could speak.

No, no, not the affair! I raced to place my hands back inside Cat's head, injecting the memory of what I had said mere moments before my life had been taken.

"Just stay away from Tim!" I had begged her, my hand planted firmly around her wrist as she tried to force me from her home. "I need you to listen to me, *please!* He's a monster, Cat. He's done horrible, horrible things, and he's going to do it again. I'm sure of it. Listen to me!"

I was frantic, the vibrations pulsing through my fingertips in sporadic, panicked bursts as I desperately tried to convey the message that she failed to heed the first time.

"She told me to stay away from Tim," she said tearfully, grabbing for another tissue.

"And what did you say to that?" the male detective pressed. Cat's eyes fell to her forearm where the evidence of our struggle was still carved deep into her pale skin.

"She grabbed me and I pulled away," she said. "Her nails scratched my arm and I was bleeding pretty bad."

Yes, yes! Now remember the rest, I begged her.

"Then what happened?" the detective continued.

"I pushed her and told her to get out," Cat answered.

"And did she leave?"

"No," she whimpered. "She kept turning around and yelling, and I just kept screaming at her to leave."

What was I yelling, Cat? Come on, I just told you. You can say it.

"So, what did you do?" the detective redirected the conversation, pulling Cat away from the memory I needed her to explore.

"So, I went into the kitchen," she said.

"Okay," the detective copied the answer down in his notepad.

"And I grabbed the knife," she continued.

"Okay." *No, no! It's not okay! This isn't what happened. This is all wrong!*

"And I just started slashing at her."

Before I could attempt to communicate once more, the door to the interview room swung open in a rush as two men entered. On the right was the small mouse of a man that I had overheard in the hallway, his pointed nose twitching like a rat on the hunt for a hunk of cheese, sweat streaking down his temples, beady eyes shifting with nervous apprehension. I recognized the man on the left as well, his slicked-back hair full of salt and pepper, warm, brown eyes shrink-wrapped with age. It was Owen Strong—the attorney that I had hired months ago.

What is he doing here? I wondered. Cat wouldn't have known to call him; I was fairly certain that she didn't even know who he was. Tim was the only other person who knew that I had hired legal counsel following the mess his wife had made. But why would he send a lawyer to help the woman whom he had willingly framed mere hours ago?

"Okay, detectives, I think that's quite enough," Owen's declaration tore me from thought as he strode into the room with the air of assumed authority that only a lawyer could possess.

"Sorry, Hurley, he just bust in here like a bat outta hell," the squirrelly officer quickly explained to the pudgy male detective still seated at the table. Hurley fixed him with an intimidating glare, his lips clamped together in a tight line.

"Any other questions you'd like to ask my client will be under my supervision from here on out," Owen continued as though the officer hadn't spoken a word, placing a glossy business card on the table in front of Cat. The look of befuddlement on her face as she read the name on the card told me that she definitely wasn't the one who called him.

"It doesn't matter anyway," Hurley snatched the recorder off the table in front of him and began shoving papers back into the manilla folder that contained Cat's case details. "Your client's already confessed. We're done here."

The pair of detectives waddled out of the room like twin penguins marching across a frozen tundra, their icy stares at the mousy officer in the doorway frosting the path forward as they moved past him without a word. No sooner had the door slammed shut behind them than Owen was opening up his black, leather briefcase on the table, settling into the seat that Hurley had just abandoned. He retrieved a single manilla folder from within and laid it neatly on the table between him and Cat, giving her a tight smile as he did so.

"It's not usually so empty," he joked, nodding at the briefcase. "I would've been in here sooner, but the damn photocopier jammed—so *they* say. In any case, I'm here now and I'm going to help you, Mrs. Clark, don't you worry."

"It's Cat," Cat snapped, her obvious aversion to hearing her married name twisting my spectral stomach in knots. I had been so wrong about so many things over the past few months. It didn't matter what my reasons had been. None of them could justify hurting her in this way, even if the assumptions I made had been proven correct. I wished I could take it all back. At the very least, I wished I could explain.

My focus shifted back to the conversation in time for me to hear Owen's explanation for his arrival.

"Your husband called me about the message you left him this morning," he informed Cat. "Ms. Reid and Mr. Clark hired me on retainer a few months back out of liability concerns over your recent behavior at work."

So Tim *had* called Owen—but why? Was he simply playing the role of concerned husband so as not to attract suspicion? I had to admit, it wasn't the worst idea in the world. Part of me was even a little grateful that he had thought to send help for his wife, no matter how self-serving the gesture had been.

Gratitude, however, was the furthest thing from Cat's features as she absorbed the truth of Owen's identity. Confusion melted into pure disdain as she sank into bitter silence, animosity radiating off her skin like a sun-soaked blacktop. It was as though the darkness swirling inside her mind was boiling over, leaking into the space between us, permeating the air like a thick fog too oppressive to ignore. I didn't need to touch her; the tendrils of her hatred rooted themselves inside me without warning.

You fucking bitch, she spat without speaking. *It wasn't enough that you shipped me off to rehab? You had to get a lawyer involved to keep an eye on me? You always blew things way out of proportion. I didn't have a problem. I was doing fine. I was fucking handling it!*

"*Are you sure about that?!*" I yelled back, unable to bear the lies she was telling herself. Yes, I had been wrong about some things and yes, my decision to send Cat to rehab was partially caused by those false assumptions, but that didn't matter. She needed help, and I was the only one with enough balls to do anything about it. Why did that make me the bad guy?

In an instant, the anger that suffocated me was sucked from the room as Cat jerked her head in my direction. Her eyes seemed to lock with my own, tears of terror threatening to spill down her cheeks. It wasn't as easy for her to rationalize the sound of my voice in the room as it was for her to shrug off the thoughts I had implanted inside her brain as her own. She knew that she wasn't alone now. The realization was written all over her face.

She shifted back in her seat to face Owen once more, shaking her head as though trying to convince herself that she hadn't just heard what we both knew she had. Though I didn't fully understand how or why it was happening, it seemed that I was right after all. I *could* communicate with the living—or at least, I could communicate with Cat. There was something between us, some unseen connection that anchored us to one another. But I didn't seem able to control it. The rules eluded me in the same way Daddy's chessboard remained an unsolvable enigma despite his many attempts to teach me the art of the game. Still, I needed to keep trying. I needed to figure this out.

I barely registered the conversation that transpired between Cat and Owen over the next hour, too consumed by the concept of mastering the ability to make myself heard, maybe even seen. But when the attorney posed his final question, not even the hope of materializing as an apparition could distract me from the words that were spoken.

"So, did you do it?" he sized her up, daring her to answer honestly. It seemed like an eternity passed before Cat finally obliged.

"I don't know," she sighed. "I must've. But I really don't remember."

No, no, no!

Why was she still remembering this wrong? Why was she so willing to accept the blame? I could almost understand feeling pressured into a confession by the police, driven to admission due to some misguided belief that doing so might result in a more favorable sentence. But this was her attorney she was speaking to. Surely, she could summon the courage to deny fault in his presence—couldn't she? It didn't appear so.

With her statement seemingly sealing her fate, Owen wrapped up the conversation in a hurry, informing Cat that they would meet again at her arraignment the following morning. Almost as quickly as he had left the room, the burly female officer who I had seen thundering through the hallway hours before came to collect her prisoner. I followed them through the booking station, into the maze of corridors, and down a separate staircase at the end of the hallway that was home to the holding cells. *Guess I was wrong about that.*

Cat was shoved into a concrete hole much smaller than the cells I had inspected in the detention center on the opposite side of the county jail. The four-by-four unit contained a single twin-sized cot bolted to the wall, beside which was a toilet that seemed to overflow with the putrid remnants of her vomit. She flopped down onto the bare mattress with an audible thud, tossing and turning in obvious discomfort. Despite our minor disagreement in the interrogation room regarding her alcoholism, I couldn't help but feel sorry for her. I craved nothing more than to comfort her, to give her peace, to apologize—for everything.

I curled up on the bed beside her, allowing my arms to melt inside her body as I tried to hold her close. In a strange way, it almost reminded me of the sleepovers we'd have as children, our bodies snuggled up inside the same bed, whispering to one another until the darkness swallowed our secrets. Unlike those nights spent worrying about which boys had a crush on us, however, Cat's mind was tangled with a new kind of self-pity that made me feel more hollow than my lifelessness ever could. I watched the movie of our struggle in her kitchen replaying over and over again inside her mind, the sequence disjointed and jumbled—a mosaic of missing pieces scrambled beyond repair. No matter how hard I tried to grab each piece, secure it in its rightful place, I couldn't fix the fracture in her thoughts. She was broken. Had I broken her?

Please! Just show me how it happened, she cried without a sound. I wanted to weep but no tears came.

"I can't," I whispered, desperate to make her understand. I was trying, I really was. But I didn't know how this worked. None of it made sense.

She bolted upright in the bed, darting nervous eyes around the cell.

"Wh-who said that?" she demanded with all the strength of a terrified child facing the bogeyman. She had heard me again, but how? Why couldn't I figure this out?

Hearing nothing in return, she fell back onto the bed, shielding her face from view with her hands as she allowed herself a moment of weakness. I stroked her hair as she lay there beside me, berating herself in silence.

That's right, just cover your face with your hands, you stupid girl, she said to herself. *The same hands that killed Elaine.*

"No!" I shouted, unwilling to let her live with this guilt. "You're wrong, Cat! You didn't do this!"

At the sound of my voice, Cat sprang from the mattress with a start, spinning around to face me. This time her eyes didn't just appear to gaze in my direction. They absorbed my body, consumed me with the same certainty that she knew she was locked inside of a cage. Her mouth fell open in horror, a noiseless shriek failing to escape from her lips.

She sees me—but how?

CHAPTER 5

May 15, 2023

I couldn't communicate with Cat for the rest of the night. It was as if by showing myself to her, I had severed the connection that existed between us, depleted whatever powers I thought that I possessed. Not even placing my hands inside her body would allow me the luxury of hearing her thoughts as I had done so freely before. She was closed off, separate, the silence of her mind more oppressive to me than it had been to feel her anger overpower my senses without disturbing a single hair on her head. I hoped that it was only temporary, but there was no way for me to know for certain how long the isolation would last.

Between the utter lack of control and the complete absence of explanation as to just how the fuck any of this worked, I was becoming more disillusioned by the second that I might be able to offer Cat the answers she needed to prove her innocence—something Owen didn't seem at all willing to assist with. When he arrived at the arraignment that morning with mere minutes to spare before court was called into session, the best advice he could offer was to submit a plea of "no contest." As though acknowledging that the prosecution had enough to convict was somehow different from admitting guilt in the eyes of the public.

Don't do it, Cat, I had pled with her, hoping she could hear me, knowing deep down that she could not. I could barely watch as she rose from the stiff, wooden bench in the front row of the courtroom, the imposing judge looming down from his perch behind a mahogany podium, waiting without patience for her response to his question.

"Mrs. Clark—your plea?" he demanded, the sweet molasses of his southern drawl rolling around his tongue seemingly at odds with the irritation on his wrinkled face. Cat bit down on her lip, glancing over her shoulder at Owen for a fraction of a second before turning back to face the judge once more.

This is it, I thought miserably, no longer able to pierce the veil that separated us. *She's getting locked up for God knows how long and it's all your fucking—*

"Not guilty," she announced. For a moment, I thought I might have heard her incorrectly. She had been so convinced of her involvement the night before. Was it possible that my attempts to communicate had been more helpful than I thought? Whatever the reason for her open defiance of her legal counsel, I was grateful for the change of heart, which was more than I could say for Owen.

He burst into the attorney meeting area promptly following the arraignment, a stormy expression clouding his features, melting away the warm chocolate of his irises until they appeared black with rage. I recognized that glare, the palpable disappointment glowing from his retinas like an iron poker burning inside a roaring fireplace. Two months ago to the day, he had fixed Cat with a similar expression as she stumbled into the office stinking of whiskey, pupils dilated and dizzy as though it were a Saturday evening and not ten o' clock in the morning on a Wednesday. That was the day that everything changed. The day I had ensured my death sentence without even realizing what I was doing.

***

March 15, 2023

It was an accident, finding those receipts. Okay, so maybe *accident* is the wrong word to use. I fully intended on snooping through Cat's office, searching through her desk drawers to find what I already knew would be there. The fact that she was drinking at work wasn't exactly a secret, yet she still flat-out denied the accusation when I confronted her about it back in January.

"I'm *fine*," she insisted, the offensive odor clinging to her breath completely contradicting her assurance. "It's just a minor setback, okay? You're overreacting."

"Minor setback, my ass!" I hissed. "You fucked up—*big time!*"

Despite what she believed, I wasn't overreacting. Whether she wanted to admit it or not, her drinking had cost our firm nearly half a million dollars, and that was being generous. She had failed to file for the proper permits so we could break ground on a new student center in Chapel Hill, setting the entire project back by two months and placing us in breach of contract. It wasn't just a "minor setback," an inconvenience that could be easily explained away to the client. It was a catastrophic display of negligence that had the potential to get us sued by one of the most prominent property developers in the region. A developer I had worked my ass off trying to secure for months. And yet there she was, denying fault, shrugging it off as if it were nothing.

"Do you even care what you're doing to this company? What you're doing to *me?*" I stared her down, searching her hazy eyes for a single ounce of remorse, receiving nothing but a blank expression in return. Fourteen years of my life I had sunk into the firm—fourteen years that I could have spent pursuing a career in event planning like I had intended to do after graduation but didn't, Cat's pleas for help in starting Burg Interiors too desperate, too heartbreaking to ignore after losing both of her parents so suddenly. But my sacrifices didn't matter to her. I was nothing but a nag in her eyes, a bossy, overbearing witch trying to fix a problem that, in her opinion, didn't exist. It was more than infuriating—it was disrespectful.

"I don't have time for this." She shoved past me, slamming the door to her office and locking herself away for the rest of the day. I was livid, and I wasn't going to let her carelessness cost us everything we had all worked so hard to build. If I couldn't get through to her simply by talking, then I had no choice but to seize control of the situation another way.

I knew it wouldn't be easy. It wasn't as though I had the power to fire her. She, Tim, Evan, and I were all equal partners at the firm, and any decision to terminate that partnership needed to be unanimously agreed upon by the other three team members. By the time January came to a close, Evan and I had been divorced for nearly a year, his own battle with alcoholism (and denial thereof) too much for me to continue suffering through. The tension between us had become so taut with animosity, it was a miracle that either one of us could get through an entire day of work without screaming at the other. I suspected that any attempt to get his blessing for Cat's removal would be swiftly dismissed—especially with the reason being so similar to what had ended our marriage.

Tim, however, was a different story. True, he probably wouldn't have been on board with terminating his wife, and if I was being honest with myself, I didn't want that either, no matter how justified I would have been in doing so. Despite everything she had done, I still loved her, and I knew that Tim did, too. If he cared for her as much as I thought he did, as much as *I* did, then maybe I could convince him to get her the help she so obviously needed.

"You and I need to talk—*now*," I announced as I rushed into his office early one February morning. I locked the door behind me, drawing the Roman shades shut around his office window to block us out from the rest of the world.

"Um... okay," he said, shutting the laptop on his desk, his golden eyebrows arched with concern. "What's going on?"

I took a seat in the tufted armchair across from him, running my sweaty palms along the navy-blue suede material, crossing and uncrossing my legs, trying to summon the courage to stab my best friend in the back. Rather than face Tim's expectant gaze, I peered around the room at the teak bookcase in the corner, the white sheepskin rug on the floor, the abstract artwork hanging from pale-gray walls, almost identical in color to the man's irises that I could feel hot on my skin, urging me to speak.

"Elaine?" he pressed. "What is it?"

"It's your wife," I blurted out. "She's fucked everything up in Chapel Hill, and I can't take it anymore. We're probably going to get sued after this is all over, and it's all her fault. She has a serious problem. I... I'm scared for her. I'm scared for all of us."

"Oh..." he trailed off solemnly.

"Oh?!" I half-yelled, trying to reign in my anger so as not to attract the attention of Cat and Evan who were lurking somewhere within our small office building. "*Oh?!* I come to you talking about your wife's drinking problem and all you have to fucking say to me is 'Oh?' She's a mess, Tim! And Chapel Hill is only the half of it."

He cocked his head and scrunched his brows together.

"What do you mean? What else has she done?"

Shit. I hadn't meant to say that last part out loud. It just sort of slipped out.

"Nothing I..." I bit my lip, searching for the right words to say, trying to swallow the urge to confide in him what I had no real proof to believe. The truth was that there was a deeper reason why Cat's drinking had bothered me so much. One that had nothing to do with Chapel Hill and everything to do with the long nights spent at the bar with my ex-husband on their many business trips together. I could never prove that something was going on between them—both of them had fervently denied it—but that didn't quell my suspicions. Still, it wouldn't have been fair to saddle Tim with those poisonous thoughts. Not without the evidence to support it.

"I just mean that if she doesn't get help soon, then who knows what kind of damage she'll cause?" I backtracked, hoping he couldn't see the images of Cat and Evan swimming behind my eyes. "She's killing herself, Tim. And she's going to take us all down with her. You have to see that."

It was his turn to look away from me then, the shame and sadness transforming his eyes into anvils too heavy to lift in my direction.

"I don't know what to do about it," he whispered to the floor. My heart wedged itself in my throat at the sound of his voice, so empty. Vulnerable. I walked around the desk and knelt at his side, forcing him to look at me.

"I think we should talk to a lawyer," I told him. His body seemed to flinch at the suggestion, back pinned against the leather desk chair in which he sat.

"A lawyer?"

"Yes," I confirmed. "I've talked to her several times about her drinking and it's no use. She's convinced she doesn't have a problem. But maybe if we talk to a lawyer, they can help us figure out a way to send her for the help she needs. I mean, she's a liability at this point. There's got to be some sort of action we can take. Our livelihoods are on the line here."

"I don't know," Tim rubbed his face with his hand. "What if this makes everything worse? What if they want to get the cops involved or something? I don't... I can't do that to her."

"Hey, no one is saying anything about cops, okay?" I assured him. "I'm not trying to get her in trouble, but we can't just let her go on this way. It's affecting us all, and there's no way for us to just fire her. I'm sure if we talk to a lawyer, they'll be able to tell us what we can do, or at least be a mediator if we have to stage an intervention or something."

Tim let his hands collapse in his lap, hanging his head in defeat.

"Fine," he relented. "But this stays between us for now, okay?"

"Of course," I promised, taking his hand in mine and giving it a gentle squeeze. "We'll get through this, okay? All of us. I swear it will be worth it in the end."

His lips quirked upwards in a feeble attempt to smile, the heat of his hand in mine flushing my cheeks pink as the warmth of his touch radiated through my body. I released him at once and cleared my throat, standing up to exit the room.

"I'll make some calls, alright?" I told him. "I'll let you know what I find out. Just... just hang in there. It'll be okay, I promise."

Later that day, I found the number for Owen Strong, Esquire III, a business liability attorney based in Green Valley. The following week, we met for our first consultation. Owen was kind enough to make the forty-minute trip to Williamsburg so Tim and I wouldn't have to raise Cat's suspicion by sneaking off to the city—not that she was ever lucid enough to have noticed such things. The three of us met at Sally's Diner to discuss our options over mugs of lukewarm tar that the glorified truck stop passed off as coffee to its otherwise tasteless clientele.

"I'll be honest with you," Owen began, the red vinyl surface of his booth seat squealing beneath his weight as he leaned back, "lawyers don't typically get involved with staging an intervention."

He let the statement hover as he raised a stained mug to his lips, dragging out the suspense for what I assumed was dramatic effect. *Were all lawyers just wannabe actors?*

"But," he continued, choking back his coffee as though it were scotch, "here's what I *can* do: I can review your partnership agreement and see if there are any loopholes we can find that might allow you to take some sort of disciplinary action. I can also review the contract with your client in Chapel Hill to see what we can do to avoid a lawsuit down the road. Of course, you'll be responsible for my retainer fee, which, frankly, pales in comparison to the thousands, if not millions in legal damages you'd likely owe to your client should they decide to take action against you. Not to mention all the lost business such a case would cost you in the long run."

I glanced at Tim whose vacant eyes were busy drowning in the mud which sat untouched within his coffee cup. He had barely uttered a word for the entire meeting, not exactly the united front I was hoping to portray. *Guess this is up to me—like every fucking thing else.*

I stretched my hand across the table, eager to accept whatever help that Owen could provide.

"It's a deal," I said. "Just tell me what you need from us, and I'll make it happen."

Owen clasped my hand in his and shook. I swore I saw a flash of green twinkle somewhere in his umber eyes.

"Great," he smiled. "I'll have my staff draw up the paperwork today. But just to reiterate, Ms. Reid, my hands are tied in terms of getting your partner the help she needs. Unless she's a danger to herself or to others, we can't have her committed involuntarily. I can give you my advice on how to best approach voluntary commitment, but that's all I can give you."

Despite his parting warning, I left the diner feeling confident that Owen would be able to help us. As promised, his secretary emailed me and Tim a copy of the retainer agreement outlining the services we had agreed to before the day was through. Along with the signed agreement, I sent Owen a copy of the articles of incorporation for Burg Interiors as well as the contract for the Chapel Hill client, hopeful that he would find something to help us buried within the legalese that I could never wrap my mind around.

He didn't.

It was the first week of March when he finally completed his assessment, not a single word of good news detailed within his report. He had a way of speaking that was infuriatingly complex, navigating his emails no more digestible to me than combing through the contents of the very documents I had hired him to evaluate on my behalf. From what I gathered, however, my initial instincts had been correct: Outside of a unanimous agreement between me, Tim, and Evan, there was no way to oust Cat as part owner or even pursue formal disciplinary action. Since it was her first real mistake in fourteen years at the company, she didn't have the negative track record of disorderly or negligent conduct that would make either termination or probation a viable option.

Equally disappointing were Owen's findings with the Chapel Hill contract. Cat's behavior did give the client grounds for litigation—especially since the project delay resulted in lost profit as the school would no longer be able to market the student housing that we had promised in time for the upcoming fall semester. So, on the one hand, she wasn't negligent enough to get rid of; on the other, she was so negligent that the client would be well within their rights to financially ruin us. I could never understand how a legal system that was forged from black and white could have so many gray areas. It made me want to scream.

"I think your best bet would be to stage the intervention and get her to agree to voluntary commitment," Owen informed me over the phone. I breathed a heavy sigh, frustration twisting my insides in an angry knot.

"I've tried talking to her about it before," I attempted to sound calmer than I felt, but the aggravation was becoming overwhelming. "Nothing works. She doesn't fucking listen to me."

"Then you need to *make* her listen," Owen asserted.

"What, like, tie her down or something?" I thought about the likelihood that I might be able to overpower Cat, strap her to an armchair, force her into submission. Though she was a petite woman, I didn't have much on her in terms of physical size or strength. Tim could handle the job just fine, but he had become increasingly aloof about the entire situation, hardly participating to the degree that I had expected after our first conversation.

Owen broke through my thoughts with a genuine chuckle, the sound of which grated on my nerves more than his unfavorable findings. *Just what the fuck is so funny about my life falling apart?*

"No, I don't mean tie her down," he snickered. "But if you want her to listen, you need to present her with facts. Not feelings. Don't just throw accusations at her. Show her the proof. Make it undeniable. The stronger you make your case, the more likely she'll be to see that you're only trying to help."

There he was, talking like a lawyer again. Still, what he said made sense to me. I thought back to the first time that I had tried to broach the subject of Cat's alcoholism after one of the most mortifying meetings that we had ever had with a client in Sudbury back in 2018.

I had caught her the night before the presentation, cozied up next to my husband at the bar despite the fact that they had told me they were "caught in traffic." Evan and I got into such a heated argument that night that I refused to let him stay in our hotel room, forcing him to seek shelter elsewhere (perhaps with his newfound mistress). Instead, he took the opportunity to hole up for the night in some seedy bar, his face sporting bruises the following morning from an ass-kicking he had endured at the hands of some stranger he had pissed off. He never did get a good enough grip on his anger issues.

If I hadn't been so infuriated by his behavior, I probably would have felt sorry for placing him in harm's way. Instead of sympathy, I was filled with embarrassment and rage as he stumbled into the client meeting the next morning nearly fifteen minutes late, appearing as though he had been hit by a car, smelling even worse than he looked. Served him right, in my opinion. Then again, that was before I had the opportunity to get Cat's side of the story.

I demanded her presence at the City Tavern, choosing a public setting on purpose so she couldn't cause a scene or evade my questions as easily. According to her, I had everything all wrong. The secrecy that I had initially interpreted to be an act of infidelity had in fact been an effort to cover up another of Cat's mistakes—a minor one by comparison to Chapel Hill, but a mistake nonetheless. She had left the original design presentation behind at our office in Williamsburg, three hours away from the place where our meeting was held.

I had to admit that the explanation made sense to me. What she presented to the client that morning was a far cry from the caliber of work I had expected to see from her. It was astonishing to me that the developers were impressed enough to give us their business at all. Though she blamed the whole thing on being overworked, I suspected her forgetfulness had more to do with the thermos she carried around in her purse than juggling too many projects.

It was ironic to me that the person who ratted me out to our parents for smoking a joint was the same woman whose life had become dominated by the desire to drink. I guess that's what grief does to some people—changes them until they become something unrecognizable. Ever since her parents died, it was as though a switch had been flipped. She carried that damned thermos around with her everywhere, sneaking sips of whiskey as though it were the elixir of life itself. I had kept my mouth shut about it for years, choosing to turn a blind eye to her pain rather than have a difficult conversation. But that trip changed everything. Already emboldened by the thought of her stealing my husband out from under my nose, I didn't shy away from seizing the opportunity to tell her how I felt.

To say that she was unhappy with my accusations would have been an understatement. She was fierce, defensive, unwilling to entertain the possibility that her oversight could have been caused by the liquor swimming in her bloodstream at all hours of the day. But I had the evidence in that thermos, and she couldn't ignore it.

"I'm just trying to help you," I pled with her, the container in question sitting between us on the high-top table in the center of the restaurant, the dark wooden fixtures mirroring the nature of our conversation. Maybe it was the desperation in my voice or maybe it was the irrefutable proof of her addiction resting in plain sight. Whatever the reason, she closed the discussion with a promise to me that she would stop drinking in the office altogether.

That's it!

I thanked Owen for his advice and hung up the phone as quickly as I could, assuring him that I would reach back out if I had any further questions. His legal guidance might not have given me the answers I had hoped for, but his suggestions on how to break through to Cat had spawned an idea that I couldn't believe hadn't entered my mind before. It didn't matter that I could smell Cat's deceit billowing from her lips like a pungent cloud of paint thinner; I needed to prove to her that I was not only right but that she had broken her promise to me. I needed to find her stash.

The morning after my conversation with Owen, I came into the office early, the sun still too weak to marble the sky with its usual display of pinks and purples as I unlocked the unassuming building that held our surprisingly stylish workspace. It would be at least two hours before any of the other partners joined me there—plenty of time for me to poke around Cat's office without her knowledge.

Despite her substance abuse, I had to admit that she kept an organized space. Her desk was free of clutter, concept boards for our upcoming presentation in Charlotte tacked to the walls behind the wooden bureau in neat little displays, each phase of the design color-coordinated and labeled with care. A collection of potted plants sat in the corner, healthy and watered. Not the typical state of disarray that one might expect of an addict at all.

There weren't many places where I thought she could have hidden her liquid treasure. I didn't think she'd be stupid enough to simply store it in her desk drawer. But with no filing cabinet to speak of and a bookcase that held mostly trinkets and framed photographs of past projects, I couldn't find another hiding place that made sense. Just as I was contemplating where best to begin my search, the sound of the furnace groaned to life and hot air crept down my neck, sending welcome goosebumps down my spine as my cool flesh embraced the warmth. I looked up at the source of the disturbance, an air vent with a suspiciously loose screw grabbing my attention. *Maybe that's where she hides it.*

    I dragged the navy-colored armchair over from the front of Cat's desk—an exact match for the one in her husband's office—and placed it beneath the register, hoisting myself up so I was eye-level with the slatted opening. My fingers pinched at the loose screw, trying and failing to twist until it popped out. It was no use. I needed a screwdriver or something to open the damned thing—perhaps there was one hiding in the desk drawers that I still had yet to explore.

    I stepped down from the armchair and made my way towards the desk. There was a set of three drawers with deep cubbies on the left-hand side, a long, thin drawer that spanned the width of the desk at the top where one might store their pens and stationery—or a screwdriver. I pulled it open only to find a few spare pencils and a pack of spearmint chewing gum. *Damnit.* I continued to the top drawer on the left, nothing but a stack of past issues of *Architectural Digest* and *The World of Interiors* waiting for me within. The drawer beneath it was equally unhelpful, the closest thing resembling a tool being a measuring tape wedged between the side of the drawer and sheets of unused graph paper.

    Angry and frustrated, I yanked the final drawer open with enough force to shake the entire desk, the vibration causing a manilla folder within to spill open, obscuring the rest of the drawer's contents from view. I reached inside to grab the folder, stuffing the loose papers that had fallen out back where they belonged. As I extracted the file from the drawer, my gaze fell to what lay beneath, the shock of my discovery enough to send the papers crashing to the floor.

I don't know why I was surprised to see the Jameson sitting there. Maybe I was hoping that I would end up being wrong about the whole thing. But one look at the quarter-full bottle was all the confirmation I needed. There was no way that Cat could deny the truth of her problem with this evidence in hand.

"Shit," I sighed, bending down to pluck the bottle from its not-so-secret hiding place, setting it on top of the desk before kneeling back down to the floor to scoop up the mess of papers I had made. Why did she even have these tucked away in the same drawer? It seemed silly to keep what looked like important files stashed alongside a bottle of whiskey. Then again, nothing Cat did these days seemed to make much sense to me.

I picked one of the papers up and skimmed its contents, nosiness getting the better of me. It was a hotel receipt for a Holiday Inn in Sudbury dated May 17, 2018. I recognized the date immediately. This was from the same trip that we had taken back when I originally approached Cat about her problem. But it didn't make sense. We had stayed at the Marriott—not some dingy Holiday Inn. What sort of impression would that have made on our clients? As the person responsible for coordinating our hotel stays, I would never allow such a thing.

I continued reading below the invoice date until I came across a brief note above the summary of costs. My hands began to shake, cold sweat collecting on the nape of my neck, eyes burning with tears that came involuntarily, blurring the vision I wished that I didn't have.

Those fucking liars!

I let out a scream, the anguish erupting through my throat like hot lava frothing from an active volcano. The alcohol I expected to find. The alcohol I could one day even learn to forgive, but this? There was no forgiving this. Right above the cost breakdown were the only words I needed to see to confirm what I had always suspected but never wanted to believe:

> *Dear Mr. Michael Davies,*
> *We hope you enjoyed your stay at the Holiday Inn.*
> *Please find a summary of your expenses outlined below*
> *for your convenience.*

I knew of only one person who sometimes went by the name Michael Davies. A name that I had given him purely to help him see the light at the end of the dark tunnel that was his home life. Now I was the one who was trapped in the shadows, vision blackening at the corners until I felt as though I had gone blind. It didn't matter that we were divorced. The truth of his affair, of my so-called best friend's betrayal, was as painful as though I had learned of it while Evan and I were still married. I hated him. I hated both of them.

By the time I had the strength to pick myself off the floor along with the rest of the receipts, the clock above the door to Cat's office read eight-thirty. That rat bastard who was lucky enough to call himself my ex-husband would be getting to the office at any moment, with Cat and Tim not too far behind. Though I wanted to shove the evidence in Cat and Evan's faces, rub their deceitful noses in my sickening discovery, I knew that I couldn't make a scene. It wasn't just the fact that doing so would ruin my chances of getting Cat the fuck out of our lives and into rehab where she belonged. I didn't want to be the one responsible for hurting Tim in that way. Not yet, at least. I needed time to think, to breathe.

I grabbed the bottle of Jameson and the folder full of receipts and stormed into my office, locking the door behind me. Evil thoughts pulsed through my racing brain, stomach quaking uneasily, threatening vomit. All the years of paranoia and jealousy that I had convinced myself were unfounded flashed before my eyes, mocking my naivety. I wanted to run away. Hide in a corner. Cease to exist. But I knew that I couldn't. I had obtained the evidence that I needed to send the bitch away. It was time to take action. Still, I couldn't trust myself to make the request peaceably—not on my own, at least.

I placed the Jameson and the manilla folder on my desk and reached for the phone. The law firm wasn't open yet, but I had Owen's personal cell. He would have to understand. This was an emergency.

"Hello?" relief and adrenaline coursed through my veins at the sound of his voice.

"I need you to come to the office," I told him in a rush.

"Now?" he balked at the request.

"Yes, *now*," I snapped. "It's urgent, and I really need your help. How soon can you get here?"

He let out an aggravated sigh.

"I guess I'll make my way up there now," he griped. "But you're getting charged extra for this. This is completely unprofessional."

"Do whatever you have to," I told him. "Just get here fast."

"Whatever you say, boss," he chided. "I'll see you in forty minutes."

In the time it took him to get to Williamsburg, Evan had made his way into the office, but there was still no sign of Tim or Cat.

Good, I thought to myself. I wasn't ready to face her just yet. The sight of Evan skulking past the small pane of glass that peered from my office into the reception area was abhorrent enough as it was, but at least I was practiced in the art of hating him. It was easier to swallow down the familiar feeling of disgust that came from his mere presence. I didn't think I could say the same for Cat—at least not without someone there to stop me from going over the edge.

I saw Owen's bright-red Corvette pull into the parking lot before he strolled into the front lobby of our small office building, his face full of bitterness, not bothering to disguise the feelings of irritation that my last-minute request had inspired within. I welcomed him at the reception desk, not even the amber glow from the golden candelabra that dangled from the ceiling enough to soften his features.

"You've got some nerve," he muttered. "What the hell is so important that you've got me driving all over North Carolina so early in the goddamn day? I *do* have other clients, you know."

"Just quit your cryin' and get into my office. We can't talk here," I cast a nervous glance over my shoulder, hoping that Evan hadn't overheard Owen's booming voice from his open office down the hall. Owen followed me into my own office and I closed the door behind us, taking another peek out the window to the parking lot to ensure that Cat was still nowhere to be found.

"You sure *you're* not the one with the drinking problem?" Owen remarked, eyeing the bottle of Jameson on my desk with an air of judgment I didn't appreciate.

"That's Cat's, smartass," I informed him. "I found her stash this morning. Along with... some other things."

"Oh?" he said, his expression quickly morphing from one of accusation to one of piqued interest. "What other things?"

I could feel the color drain from my cheeks, the tears filling in my eyes faster than I could control. *Shit.* I didn't want to cry in front of him, but I couldn't help it. I clamped a hand around my mouth to stifle the sound of my sobbing, placing my free hand on my desk to steady myself, keep from crumbling to the ground. *Get a hold of yourself, you blubbering idiot!*

"Hey," Owen's voice was gentle, soothing. "What's going on? Was it worse than you thought? Is she abusing drugs or something, too? Take a deep breath, okay? In through your nose, out through your mouth. Atta girl. One more time. Good, good. Here, take a seat."

He guided me into my desk chair, moving the folder out of the way to move a box of tissues closer, completely oblivious to the contents within and what they signified. I grabbed for a tissue and blew hard into the absorbent paper, the lavender-scented moisturizer calming my senses. Owen waited for me to regain my composure as I dabbed at my eyes and smoothed my skirt.

"They've been sleeping together all this time," I finally choked out.

"Who has?" Owen prodded, perplexed by the admission.

"Cat and my dipshit ex-husband," I clarified, my tone much sharper than I intended. It wasn't Owen's fault, after all. "Sorry," I whimpered, "I'm just so fucking angry. I found all these receipts in her desk next to the whiskey. They've been having an affair for years from the looks of it. All on company time, too. Wouldn't even be surprised if they used the firm to pay for their hotel rooms. Fucking assholes!"

"Jesus," Owen offered, just as blindsided by my discovery as I had been. "I'm sorry, Elaine. This is… I'm so sorry. But, why exactly did you call me here?"

I shot him a look that I'm sure could have stopped his heart cold if attorneys possessed such organs in the first place.

"Because I have the proof now!" I barked. "It's a pattern of behavior, isn't that what you called it? Can't we do something now? Fire her? *Light* her on fire? Anything?"

"Okay, well, for the record, we're not setting anyone on fire, let's make that clear," Owen smirked. "And I'm sorry to say this, but it doesn't change much of anything in terms of your legal recourse. You and your husband are divorced now, and even if they did charge the company account for a hotel room here and there, it wouldn't hold up well in court. Not when y'all are traveling around the state so often as it is."

"So what? I'm fucked, then? There's no way to get rid of her. Is that what you're telling me?"

"No, I wouldn't say that," he countered. "You know what you have to do. Voluntary commitment is still your best option if you really want her out of your hair."

Movement in the parking lot caught my eye from beyond the window. I could see Tim's silver sedan coming to a halt, Cat tumbling out of the passenger seat, staggering towards the office. *Fuck.*

"She's here," I gasped, still not ready to face her. Owen placed a firm hand on each of my shoulders and looked into my tear-stained face.

"Listen to me," he commanded. "You have to do this. It's what the business needs. It's what *you* need. You have to face her. And, if I can make a suggestion, I'd leave the affair out of it. She'll get too defensive and angry. It'll only make it more difficult for you to convince her to leave."

Cat and Tim had entered the building, each of them making their way to their individual offices. Any moment, she would discover the missing bottle from her drawer. How soon after would she come storming into my office as a result? The thought made my stomach flip.

"I'm too angry about it," I said miserably. "I can't just let it go."

"If you want this to work, then you *have* to," Owen told me. "You know that I'm right."

I sighed. He *was* right, but that didn't make it any easier to accept what I needed to do. Before I could speak any further, Cat had flung the door to my office open, swaying slightly in the doorframe as she fixed me with an accusatory glare. *The fucking nerve.*

"I'll be right outside if you need me," Owen promised. "You can do this. It's time."

He excused himself from my office to leave me alone with the woman whom I now loathed with every fiber of my being. As I watched him depart the room, I couldn't help but take comfort in the way his eyes became two daggers, piercing through Cat's flesh with a look of repulsion that mirrored my own. It filled me with a sense of strength and righteousness that I didn't think I'd be able to locate in time to do what needed to be done. But that look was all I needed to know that I wasn't alone in this. He was on my side. I could do this—even if it killed me.

CHAPTER 6

March 16, 2023

The day that Cat checked into rehab was the same day Burg Interiors was due to arrive in Charlotte for an upcoming presentation. It was seven-thirty by the time we checked into the Hilton. Tim had delayed our arrival by several hours as Evan and I waited for him to finish dropping his wife off at the Green Valley Recovery Center before making the long drive to the Queen City. He looked muted, expressionless, the usual brightness behind his icy eyes dulled to a sullen charcoal as they absorbed the veins of granite tile swirling beneath his shuffling feet in the hotel lobby.

I felt sorry that we had to make the trip on the same day he was forced to place his wife in rehab—not exactly the excuse for postponement that a client would happily oblige while still planning to trust our team with their student housing design. I felt even sorrier that it meant having to spend the next three days in Evan's company, although Tim was still in the dark when it came to Cat's infidelity. This was obvious from the way he endured Evan's cordial conversation in the hotel lobby while I busied myself checking us in at the reception desk. I cast a malicious glare in my ex-husband's direction, unable to disguise my disgust.

Piece of shit, I wanted to scream. *How dare you speak to him after what you've done?*

Part of me wanted to make a scene, break the news to Tim right then and there, watch him sink his powerful fists into my former husband's face, leaving him bruised and bloodied on the floor like he deserved. Instead, I bit my tongue, collected our room keys from the concierge, and passed one each to the two men in my company.

Evan snatched the key to room 506 from my outstretched fingers without a word, turning on his heel and darting for the elevator to escape my presence. *Good riddance.* Tim, on the other hand, took his time claiming his hotel key, his hand clasped around an unmarked prescription bottle which he pocketed discreetly before accepting the card to room 510.

"What're those?" I nodded to the breast pocket of his blazer where he had stored the bottle. I could hear Mama's disapproving voice lecturing me from miles away. *Mind your business, Elaine, wherever are your manners?* Gee, I don't know, Mom. You probably swallowed them down while you were busy chasing your own pills with a glass of wine.

"Just something I take when... when I can't take it anymore," Tim replied vaguely. My heart gave an involuntary lurch at the statement. He gave me a sad smile and began to walk away, but I grabbed him by the hand before he could leave.

"Hey, you know you can talk to me, right?" I told him, dark thoughts clawing their way out of my brain, digging their nails into my throat.

Cat had told me all about Tim's troubled mind, how he had tried to end his life by jumping from the Greene Street Bridge. The same bridge where Mia Davis's body had been found following her unexpected suicide at the end of our junior year at Green Valley University, her actions apparently inspiring Tim to take a leap of his own. I knew he had gone to therapy after that, but I didn't know he was still on medication. The thought that I could have possibly reawakened his demons by forcing his wife away into recovery terrified me.

He squeezed the hand that had tethered him in place, my fingers trembling in his grasp. A shameless tingle of desire erupted somewhere in the pit of my stomach, reminding me of that first night I saw him at the Sig Nu party all those years ago. It had been almost twenty years since then, but the man who stood before me remained unscathed by the passage of time, as handsome as if I had just discovered him sipping in silence from his red plastic cup. How Cat could ever cheat on him, I would never understand.

"Thanks, Elaine," he said, the smoothness of his voice melting my insides. "I'll be okay."

"Okay, well, if you need somebody to talk to, I'm just a room away," I flashed my hotel key, a reminder that I wouldn't be far if he needed a shoulder to cry on (or something more). *What the fuck is wrong with me?*

I tore my hand away abruptly, embarrassed by the unexpected thoughts vying for my attention. It didn't matter what I knew about Cat, what I knew about Evan. As far as Tim knew, he was (somewhat) happily married. I wasn't going to act on some long-held schoolgirl crush just because I was feeling broken and angry and, yes, okay? I was lonely. It's not like Williamsburg was overrun with bachelors—at least not any that weren't missing a significant number of brain cells, and teeth. If Evan and I had been divorced for a year, then it had been at least that long since the last time I had sex. Probably longer. A girl had her needs, but this wasn't the way to fill them. I wasn't that person. I wasn't *Cat*.

"You coming up?" Tim gestured towards the same elevator that Evan had just taken. His question was innocent, not at all the invitation that my vile mind wanted it to be. That didn't stop the heat from rising in my cheeks, heartbeat echoing in my chest, each thud against my ribcage seemingly screaming, *kiss him, kiss him, kiss him.*

"I, um... I think I left my phone in the car," I lied, feeling the vibration of an incoming email buzzing around in my purse. "I'll catch you later, okay?"

"Okay," he shrugged, unfazed by my deceit.

"And Tim?" I stopped him yet again before he could turn away. "I really am sorry. About Cat, I mean. You don't deserve all this mess."

"It's not your fault," he said, placing a warm hand on my shoulder. "It had to be done. And now thanks to you, she'll be all better when she gets out."

"Yeah, *right*," the sarcasm left my lips faster than I had time to reel it back in. Tim picked up on the insincerity in my voice, his brows raised slightly in response. "Sorry I—" *know that your wife is a lying, cheating whore who doesn't deserve you*, is what I wanted to say but didn't, "my mom had a problem, too. Still does. I know how tough it can be to get ahold of."

Tim's face softened at the confession. It wasn't a lie, but it wasn't the truth that I wanted to share, either.

"I'm sorry," he said with genuine empathy in his voice. "I didn't know that."

"It's fine," I told him. "I'm sure you're right. Cat will be okay."

The words tasted like bile as they left my mouth, but what else could I say? I was still conflicted about whether or not I should tell him what I knew. And if I *was* going to tell him, it sure as hell wasn't going to be in the center of the Hilton lobby.

He gave my shoulder a final pat before heading towards the elevator, the smell of spiced pine and worn leather lingering behind in the place where he had touched me. In all the years that we had spent traveling together across North Carolina meeting with clients and vetting new business, how had I never noticed such an intoxicating aroma? I wanted to bathe in it.

Instead, I rushed out of the hotel, letting my duffel bag collapse to the concrete as I closed my eyes and leaned against the cool, brick exterior, the late winter air like a cold shower, shocking the stupid out of my system. I felt ridiculous, dirty, ashamed—of what I wasn't entirely certain. Maybe it was because I couldn't seem to get the thought of Tim's naked body out of my mind. Or maybe it was the overwhelming desire for a drink swelling within, the irony of which wasn't lost on me. But I wasn't the one with the problem. Sure, I had my fun in college, but I had abandoned my partying ways the moment I exited the graduation stage. I could have a drink if I wanted one. Hell, I could have three of them if I felt so inclined. After the bullshit I had endured, the disgusting lies that I had uncovered, wasn't I entitled to blow off a little steam?

My eyes flicked open, landing on a Holiday Inn hotel that shared a parking lot with the Hilton where I was staying. The sight of it reignited the fire that threatened to burn me from the inside out as

Cat had sat across from me in my office the day before. I somehow managed to get through the conversation without making a single mention of the Holiday Inn receipts that I had found in her desk, *Michael Davies'* name written all over every single one. That didn't mean that I had kept my composure. I was crying and sputtering the whole way through, choking on the words that I wanted to scream into Cat's face.

"You promised me," I kept repeating to her. "You promised, and you did it anyway!"

She thought I was referring to her promise to quit the office day drinking, the nearly empty bottle of Jameson on full display on top of my desk. She either didn't see the manilla folder sitting next to it or didn't realize that it belonged to her.

"I'm sorry," she hung her head, unable to face me. "I promise I'll do better."

"Your promises don't mean shit to me, Cat!" I shrieked. "Either you go to rehab, or you're getting terminated from this company. It's as simple as that."

"You can't do that." She faltered, uncertainty staining her features.

"Try me," I challenged. "You think Tim and Evan want to put up with this shit? When you're destroying everything we've worked for years to help *you* build? You need help."

She remained quiet for a long time, eyes locked on the whiskey bottle like a caged animal longing for food. All at once, a heaviness fell over her as she sank into herself. If I hadn't wanted to rip her head from her body, I probably would have held her. She looked so defeated.

"Okay," she whispered. "I'll go. Just give me until after the Charlotte presentation, and I'll check myself in next week."

"No," I argued. "You go today. Tomorrow at the very latest if you need to make some arrangements. I'm not fucking around here, Cat."

"Okay, just... just let me talk to Tim," she relented. "I need a day to make a plan, get my shit in order before I go. But I swear I'll check myself in tomorrow."

"You'd better," I warned her.

"I will," she promised, rising from the armchair in my office to approach my desk, her drunken stagger no longer present, sobered by the severity of our conversation. "Elaine, I'm... I'm really sorry. I'll do better. I really will."

She placed a hand over mine, her unwelcome touch causing me to recoil in response. The wounded expression that consumed her features gave me a tiny surge of joy.

"Just go," I commanded.

And that was that.

Though I was happy that she didn't make the whole thing harder than it needed to be, that didn't make it easier for me to contend with the betrayal I felt. And seeing that Holiday Inn looming against the backdrop of a dusky Charlotte skyline—visions of Cat and Evan's would-be escapades taunting me from across the parking lot—certainly didn't help.

Fuck it.

I bent down, scooped up my duffel bag, slinging it over my shoulder as I marched back inside the hotel, past the reception desk, ignoring the elevators altogether and making a beeline for the bar.

The Hilton's interior was swanky and impressive—even by my silver-spooned standards—with cathedral ceilings illuminated by a soft, peach hue that glowed from the curved overhang above the bar's quartz countertops. Lengths of matching high-top tables dotted the dining area, all lined with leather upholstered stools, their cream-colored cushions identical to those situated at the bar. Breathtaking chandeliers dangled from above, and on the far wall, strands of their delicate beads appeared to drip down from the ceiling, draping a copper backsplash in a curtain of crystalline pebbles like a waterfall of glass. If I hadn't been in such a terrible mood, I might have basked more in my surroundings. Instead, I sank into one of the barstools and flagged down the bartender.

"Welcome to the Hilton," he smiled, flashing a set of white teeth that made me feel strangely self-conscious about my own. "What can I get for you?"

"Jack and diet," I answered. "And make it a double."

"Coming right up," he flung a red terrycloth over his shoulder and turned away, grabbing one of the glass tumblers from off the back counter along with a bottle of Jack Daniels. All at once, the sight of the brown liquid made my stomach turn, the very knowledge that it was Evan's drink of choice enough to make me gag.

"Actually," I piped up before he could pour the bottle, "I think I changed my mind."

"No problem at all," a dimple deepened in his cheeks as his lips curled upward. "What can I get you instead?"

I paused. Did I even know of another alternative? I had consumed plenty of drinks at frat parties during my college days, but none of them had been particularly memorable—probably a result of the blackouts that followed.

"Dealer's choice," I decided, trusting my soon-to-be inebriation to the hands of the professional. He sized me up with a pair of cool blue eyes that I tried to pretend didn't remind me of Tim's, his hand stroking a carefully trimmed black beard that matched his slicked-back hair. With a snap of his fingers, he spun around, selecting a tall glass bottle that looked as though it were filled with sapphires. I watched him pour a sizable amount into the tumbler he was still holding, adding a splash of tonic to the mix before setting the cocktail down on the counter in front of me.

"A classic choice for a classy lady." He gave me a wink. I felt myself blush and murmured a quiet thank-you in response. He lingered a moment, waiting for me to take a sip with expectant eyes. I brought the liquid to my lips and sipped it slow at first, quickening my pace as floral notes lit up my tastebuds, demanding to be saturated in whatever flavorsome concoction he had just presented to me. It went down smooth despite the fizzy tonic tickling my throat, a warm sensation burgeoning in my belly as the alcohol worked its magic. The bartender struggled to suppress a hearty laugh.

"Guess you liked it," he commented, picking up my now-empty glass. "Can I get you another?"

"Abso-freaking-lutely, you can!" I said emphatically. "What the hell *was* that?"

"Just a gin and tonic," he beamed with pride at having satisfied his customer.

"Yeah, you can keep those coming if you don't mind," I told him, my mouth suddenly feeling too dry in the absence of my newfound favorite drink. *If I didn't have a problem before, I was certainly on my way.*

I slid my room key across the counter so he could start my tab before he turned away to fix my second beverage of the night.

"Would you like to see a menu?" he suggested, placing the drink down in front of me. I fought the urge to down it in one gulp as I had the first time.

"That's okay," I told him, a low rumble building in my stomach to spite me. "This will do for now."

"Well, if you change your mind, you know where to find me," he knocked twice on the countertop and turned his attention to another customer seated at the opposite end of the bar. I sipped in happy silence over the next half hour, plucking my phone from my purse to thumb through the litany of client emails that had gone ignored for the better half of the day, too busy driving to give them the attention they demanded. Among the sea of mind-numbing workplace minutia was a message from Owen. I rolled my eyes, assuming it would be related to the extra fees he charged for my insistence that he make the forty-minute trek to our office the previous day. It was a pleasant surprise when I opened it up to read what was inside:

> **Subject:** *About Yesterday*
> **Sent:** *Thursday, March 16, 12:32 p.m.*
> *Elaine,*
> *I just wanted to say how proud I am of you for doing the difficult thing yesterday. I know that couldn't have been easy for you, and I'm glad you gave me a call. All*

things considered, I think you've suffered enough, and I'm not going to add to that by charging you for the trip up there. I had a clear schedule anyway so no harm, no foul. I hope today's a better day for you.
All best, Owen

I hadn't expected such a demonstration of kindness from someone I believed to be nothing but greedy. Perhaps I had misjudged him. I raised my glass to my lips and took a final swig in celebration. *Thanks for the savings, Owen. Next round's on you.*

I signaled the bartender for a third drink, those white teeth of his glimmering against the rosy bar lights, making my head feel dizzy. Or maybe that was just the gin. Within a few moments, he had sat another glass down in front of me, placing a menu on the counter beside it.

"At the pace you're setting, I think you ought to eat something," he commented. "My managers are kind of sticklers about over-serving customers. You don't want to get me into trouble now, do you?"

"I'm *fine*," I hiccuped, hating the way Cat's words sounded coming out of my mouth. "I promise not to tell on you."

I hoped the overt flirtation would be enough to send him away without forcing food into my system. I was enjoying the way the alcohol had numbed my senses, made me forget about... *what exactly? Damn, gin and tonics are good. Why had I never had one of these before?*

My charm seemed to do the trick, and the bartender chose not to push the subject any further, leaving me alone with my drink.

Time seemed to melt away and I was halfway through the glass when I thought I heard a familiar voice sneaking up behind me.

"You have *got* to be fucking kidding me right now," Evan sneered. The hairs on the back of my neck prickled in response, involuntary goosebumps of sheer hatred trailing down my spine. "Guess you're the only one around here who's allowed to have any fun, that right? Fucking hypocrite."

Though I hadn't noticed him at the bar, his words were slurred. Judging from his past expense reports from the hotels that I did know about, he had probably consumed whatever Jack was stocked in his room's mini-fridge.

"Fuck off, Evan," I spat, my tongue struggling to form the sentence. "Or is it Michael now?"

"What're you—"

"Welcome to the Hilton, sir," the bartender interrupted. "What can I get for you?"

"He'll take your whole bottle of Jack if you let 'em," I chimed in before Evan could speak. "Your wife, too, if you've got one."

The bartender raised his brows in response, nervous laughter escaping from his lips in an effort to break the tension.

"Jack it is," he said, quickly turning around to make his escape.

"What the fuck are you saying?" Evan hissed at me.

"I think you know exactly what I'm saying, *Michael*," I shot, tossing back the rest of my drink. He clamped his lips together, silencing whatever hurtful insults he wanted to hurl my way. "What's the matter? *Cat* got your tongue? Thought you'd be used to that by now you piece of fucking—"

"One Jack, neat," the bartender interjected once again, leaving a tumbler full of brown liquid in front of Evan's stunned face. He cleared his throat and nodded to my empty glass, "Can I get you another, miss?"

"No thanks," I said. "This bar just got a bit too crowded for my liking. You can close out my tab if you don't mind."

"Not a problem," he assured me, clearing the countertop of my mess. I slid off the barstool and collected my duffel bag, the action making the room spin in circles around me. Evan scoffed as I clutched the edge of the counter, muttering something under his breath while I attempted to regain my composure. I ignored him and staggered out of the bar towards the elevators to make the ascent to my room. Maybe there would be more gin in the mini-bar.

As the elevator climbed higher up into the building, I could feel myself growing more incensed, Evan's unwanted presence diminishing the buzz that I had worked so hard to build. *Asshole*. Pretending as if he didn't know exactly what I was talking about. Like he was innocent. *I'll show you innocent. Just watch me "innocently" tell the man whose wife you're fucking exactly what it is you've been up to.*

The elevator came to a halt at the fifth floor, doors parting around the furious inferno my body had become. I navigated down the hallway, past Evan's room, tossing my luggage in front of the door to my room, abandoning it there before continuing to room 510. My knuckles rapped against the surface in a rush of adrenaline, the alcohol coursing through my veins making me feel bolder, wilder than I anticipated. I waited for a long time before knocking on the door again. Maybe Tim was in the bathroom and hadn't noticed my intrusion the first time? I pressed my ear against the door, hoping to hear him stirring within.

Nothing.

I knelt down by the purse I had carelessly thrown to the ground and extracted my phone. *Jesus*. How was it already ten o' clock? How long had I been at the bar?

Why wasn't Tim in his room?

Maybe it was a good thing he had stepped out. The more I gave myself a chance to calm down, the more I started to second-guess my irrational urge to spill all the secrets I had been keeping. I sighed, moving back to the abandoned luggage in front of my hotel room as I shoved my room key into the slot above the handle and made my way inside, kicking my duffel bag in along with me.

It was a nice room with a king-sized bed situated in the center against the right-hand wall. A floor-to-ceiling window overlooked the city, twinkling lights from towering skyscrapers creeping in between taupe drapes, spilling onto an indigo chaise lounge that was tucked away in the corner. But I didn't care about the fine furnishings or the impressive view of the skyline. My heart was set on the mini-fridge, and what I might find inside to help regain the buzz that Evan had single-handedly squashed.

Maybe I do have a problem.

To my delight, the fridge was stocked with a selection of airplane-sized liquor bottles, among them a now-familiar blue glass that seemed to call out to me by name. *Jackpot!* I grabbed the gin and a small bottle of tonic that was conveniently placed on the refrigerator door, as though the hotel staff had somehow anticipated my drunken downfall. On top of the fridge was a plastic cup, which I quickly filled with equal parts gin and tonic—okay, maybe there was a *little* more gin than tonic.

I brought the mixture to my lips and felt a temporary calm wash over me as I popped on the television to distract my wayward mind. But my relaxation didn't last for very long. The universe seemed hell-bent on forcing the image of Cat and Evan down my throat along with whatever alcohol I could get my hands on. A commercial for the Holiday Inn & Suites taunted me on the flatscreen, its pleas to book my stay grating on my already frayed and fragile nerves. I punched the remote with my thumb, clicking to the next channel. It was The CW, some investigation-style reality show that I had never seen. Mama and Daddy never approved of what they considered to be such low-brow entertainment. Maybe that's why I decided to keep it on.

I let the show play in the background, not paying it much attention as I continued to sip from my cup, unpacking my belongings from my duffel bag and folding them as neatly as my intoxicated hands would permit before stuffing them into the bureau beneath the TV. After I downed the last drops of gin, my brain feeling fuzzy and light, I decided to hop into the shower. The developers would be meeting us in the conference room the following morning by ten o' clock, but from what I remembered about hangovers, I'd likely need to sleep in longer than I originally planned if I was going to appear presentable—or functional.

There. I don't have a problem, I thought. Alcoholics didn't think about things like that—did they?

I shook the thought away from my addled mind and stepped into the bathroom, running the tap in the walk-in shower as I undressed, letting the steam from the water fog the glass enclosure before making my way inside. It felt nice, the way the droplets burned against my flesh, turning my skin pink beneath the shower head. I closed my eyes and enjoyed the moment for a while, holding onto the grab bar that was fixed to the tile wall to steady myself, sobriety still too far away to keep my body from swaying.

It was a large shower, surprisingly so. Easily big enough to hold two people. I wondered if all hotels had showers this big. If the Holiday Inn across the parking lot had them. If Cat and Evan had spent hours inside them together, lathering each other up with cheap soap, enjoying the acoustics that the tile walls afforded as they filled the bathroom with moans of pleasure.

Great, now I'm pissed again.

I slammed the faucet handle down to shut off the water, my fingers pruned and wrinkled. *How long had I been in here?* It seemed that gin had a way of making me oblivious to time. I toweled off and headed back out to the room, selecting a set of silk pajamas that I had packed from the drawer where I stored them away. The alarm clock on the nightstand blared ten fifty-five—how I had stayed in the shower that long without drowning or scalding the skin right off my bones was beyond my comprehension. I ducked back inside the bathroom to dry my hair, pondering all the while whether it was too late to enjoy one last drink before bed.

By the time I made my way back to the mini-bar, it was a quarter past eleven. It seemed whatever reality show had been playing earlier was on some sort of marathon. What the hell was this trash anyway? Drunken curiosity caused me to click the volume up a few notches as I brought a fresh glass full of gin (no tonic this time) to my lips, just in time to catch a few closing words before the show faded to commercial break.

"When we come back to *Cheaters*," the announcer's dramatic voice broke through my clouded head. The video cut to a woman shrieking profanities at some ashen-faced man as he sat clammed up on an armchair in his house, photographs flung at his feet from the hands of his enraged spouse. *You've got to be kidding me.*

Of all the shows I could have selected, I had unwittingly chosen one in which married couples accused each other of the very things I was trying to force from my mind. My gut twisted in gnarled knots like centuries-old tree roots breaking through cracked soil.

That's it!

I tossed back the rest of the gin, grabbed my room key off the nightstand, and headed out the door. Tim had to be back from wherever he had gone off to by this time of night. I didn't care if I was waking him from a dead slumber. I no longer wanted to be the only person tortured by this ugly secret that was eating away at my insides. It was time to tell him what I knew.

I knocked on the door like a mad woman, my knuckles turning a bright scarlet from the sheer force of my fist swinging against the wooden surface. From beneath the door, I could see the light was on inside—proof that someone was alive within. In the middle of my persistent knocking, the door cracked open an inch, the security chain preventing it from opening any further.

"Elaine? What're you do—"

"I need to talk to you," I cut Tim off mid-sentence, unable to disguise the disgust in my voice.

"Okay just... give me a second," he closed the door, leaving me standing in the hallway. Several moments passed in silence and I thought perhaps he had forgotten me there until the sound of the chain sliding back assured me that he had not. The door opened slowly, Tim obscuring his body behind its surface as he permitted me into a room that was identical to my own. I headed for the chaise lounge in the corner and took a seat, watching as Tim emerged from the shadows of the small foyer.

He was wearing nothing but a white bathrobe emblazoned with the Hilton logo over the left breast, his damp, blonde hair evidence that he had just gotten out of the shower himself. My lips parted slightly, envisioning what he was wearing beneath. *Hopefully nothing.*

"Elaine, is everything okay?" Tim pulled me away from my perverted imagination, concern mounting in his voice as he took me in. "You seem tense. Did something happen?"

"I need to tell you something," I said, my jugular pulsing around an angry heartbeat. "It's about Cat. And..."

I bit my lip, confidence slipping away from me the longer I stayed in his room. Maybe I had been wrong to go to him. Maybe I was just drunk. Maybe—

"And what?" he prodded.

Too late now.

"And Evan," I blurted. Tim's eyebrows pulled together in a knot across his forehead, perplexed by the statement.

"What about Evan?" he ventured.

"They've been sleeping together behind our backs," the confession left my body in a rush. Tim didn't seem to have understood the words, his features stuck in a state of confusion rather than the anger and hurt I had expected to see. I continued, "I only just confirmed it. But it's the truth. I always thought they were too buddy-buddy on their trips. All those hours at the bar together, that time in Sudbury I caught them lying about being in traffic. I didn't want to believe it, but... yeah. She's been cheating on you. For a long time now."

Realization slowly settled across Tim's body. First, his head as it hung heavy towards the floor, then his shoulders, sagging beneath the weight of my revelation, and finally the rest of him, slumping down onto the bed at his side. He covered his face with his hands, the silence that bloomed between us more unnerving than it would have been to see him break down and cry.

"How long?" It was a question, but the words were flat, absent of inquiry.

"I'm not sure exactly," I told him, "but I think it's been going on for years."

His hands slipped from his face and into his lap with a soft thud, eyes fixed on the wall across from him, devoid of feeling. A slight tremble quaked through his body as he wrestled internally with the information. I wanted to comfort him, soothe him in the way I wished I had been soothed when I first made my discovery in Cat's office, surrounded by receipts of a love affair that I didn't want to admit was real. Before I could overthink it, I walked over to the bed and sat down beside him, taking his hand in my own.

"I'm sorry I have to be the one to tell you this," I whispered. "You're such a good man, Tim. You deserve so much better."

He turned to face me then, a curious expression lingering in his eyes that I couldn't quite place.

"No, I don't," he finally said, the words ripping a hole through my heart. He was blaming himself. I couldn't allow it.

"Hey, that's not true," I told him. "This isn't your fault. It's *hers*. It's *both* of theirs."

"No, it isn't." Though he was sitting right beside me, I could barely hear the words. "I'm not good enough. I'll never be good enough."

"Don't say that," I urged him, cupping his head in my hands to force him to look at me. Somewhere in the recesses of my mind, I could see the image of Evan sitting on the edge of his childhood bed, waiting for a nonexistent birthday celebration. Those same words escaping his lips. That same sadness. I could feel that familiar response bubbling to the surface before I could stop it, "You *are* good enough, baby."

Why did I say that? Goddamned alcohol. I was never drinking gin again, no matter how good it made me feel. I dropped my hands into my lap and stood abruptly from the bed.

"I'm sorry," I said, mortified by my behavior. "I'm sorry. I should go. I should—"

"Stay," Tim reached for my hand and pulled me back down to his side. "Please stay."

"Okay," I whispered. "I can do that."

"Thank you," he murmured, his hand still wrapped around my own. I could feel his thumb caressing my skin, his fingers lacing themselves in between mine. My heart was hammering in my chest. Was this really about to happen?

We stayed like that on the bed for what felt like hours, just holding hands, my head eventually finding its way to his shoulder, his head nestling on top of mine. Despite the awful circumstances that had made it possible, I found the moment deeply romantic, the gentle slip of our fingers as they glided across each other's skin. The only imperfection was his wedding band stubbornly fixed around his finger, reminding us both that what we were doing was wrong, no matter how right it felt.

"I should have thrown scissors," I lamented, thinking back to that night at the frat house when I had thrown the game on purpose, willingly handed Tim over to Cat on a silver platter. *What a fool.*

"What do you mean?" the movement of Tim's lips against my scalp as he spoke made my heart skip a beat.

"Cat never told you?" I breathed, eyes still fixed on our intertwined fingers, not yet bold enough to face him. "We both saw you at the Sig Nu house one night, so we played rock, paper, scissors to see which one of us would be lucky enough to take a shot with you. I felt sorry for her, so I threw the game on purpose. I wish I hadn't. I..."

I trailed off, my head dizzy with desire that I didn't dare verbalize.

"You what?" Tim purred, urging me to continue.

"I wanted you," I confessed. "I still want you."

Maybe it was the warmth of his hand melting away my better judgment, or maybe the gin had done a good enough job of that already. Whatever it was that forced me to lift my head and close the distance between us, place my hungry lips over his, slide my eager tongue into his mouth, I wasn't angry at it. And neither was he.

He returned the favor with so much enthusiasm that I thought at first it might have been a dream, my fantasy finally coming to fruition after years of bottling it inside, keeping my distance to protect a woman who didn't deserve my protection. His lips moved from my mouth to my neck, pulling me deeper into his embrace as he did so. I closed my eyes, hands grabbing for his robe to remove it from his body, the shock of bumpy skin that greeted my fingertips forcing my lids open at once. I pulled away and looked down at what was hiding beneath my palms, an audible gasp leaving my lips.

"Tim, what happened to you?" I demanded, the skin of his back a scarred and puckered mess of mottled flesh. His forearms weren't in much better shape, deep, purple lines decorating his skin in a manner that looked to be self-inflicted.

He pulled away, embarrassed by my discovery, pulling the robe back up to cover his body.

"Shit," he muttered. "I'm sorry. I... I'm so fucking ugly."

"No, no, no," I backtracked, worried that I had ruined the moment. "You're not ugly, I promise. I just was... surprised is all."

I pulled his face back to mine, kissing him again, bringing the robe back down.

"Don't stop," I begged him. "Please don't make me stop."

"I won't," he whispered. And he kept his promise.

CHAPTER 7

May 19, 2023

It was awful not being able to figure out the nuances of being dead—especially as I was forced to watch Cat wrestle with the ugly symptoms of her withdrawal, unable to offer any comfort. Monday had been the worst of it, terrible tremors rattling through her body like a set of skeleton keys dangling from the pocket of some ancient caretaker. By nightfall, she had started to hallucinate, bellowing into the darkness of her jail cell at some terrifying specter that only she could see. From the things she was saying, I could only guess that she thought it was my ghost that had come to haunt her once more.

"I WISH I HAD KILLED YOU, YOU FUCKING WHORE!" her words echoed off her cement enclosure with a horrible ring. *Real nice, Cat.* Guess I deserved that after everything that had happened between us. That didn't make the profanities any easier to endure.

It turned out I was right about that feral-looking Spanish woman whom I had found sleeping in her half-empty cell on my first night at the county jail. She was as mean as she had appeared, even in the clutches of a deep slumber. At the sound of Cat's screaming, the woman rose from her cot, crossed the room in an angry rush, and punched her delirious cellmate right in the jaw, knocking her out cold. Even then, all I could do was watch.

I was beginning to think I had broken some holy rule by making myself heard, making myself *seen*. The involuntary isolation made me feel as though I were being punished—as if being stabbed to death hadn't been punishment enough. How was I supposed to know it was frowned upon to speak to the living? I didn't even know how I had made it happen in the first place. It wasn't fair that I had been seemingly disallowed from making contact, forced into a private prison of my own, not even an hour of recreation to break the monotony. But I knew my agony paled in comparison to Cat's.

She was so alone, so confused, spending hours each day scribbling notes to herself, trying desperately to access the recesses of her mind that held the answers to proving her innocence, if only she knew how to reach them or what questions even to ask. Though I couldn't speak to her or hear her thoughts, I refused to leave her side. I couldn't abandon her. I owed her that much, at least.

It was a relief when Thursday came and Owen arrived, alleviating her of the loneliness she undoubtedly felt, perhaps even bearing good news related to her case. That hope didn't last for very long. Why was it that this man seemed incapable of relaying anything positive to his clients?

They met in the same room where they had argued following Cat's arraignment—a cramped, gray square of a space almost identical in nature to the place where she had first been interrogated. He sank into the metal chair across from her, nothing but a flimsy, matching table separating them. His forehead was a wrinkled mess of worry where smooth skin normally rested, the apprehension making him appear more his age than usual.

"This is a fucking nightmare, Cat," he snapped, as though it were her fault. "Really. I don't know what you expect me to do here."

I wanted to rip out his throat at the remark. How could he be so cruel? So heartless? This was his job, after all. Maybe I had been right about him all along, the kindness he had shown me in his email months ago a rare display of decency from an otherwise indecent man. *Lawyers.*

Still, I had to admit that as he disclosed the details of Cat's case, it really didn't look good. If I were an outsider looking in, I wouldn't have believed anyone else could have killed me. No signs of forced entry, no evidence of anyone aside from Cat being in the home, thirty-eight stab wounds (*Had it really been that many?*) inflicted by the same knife she had been holding when the police arrived. It all added up to just one person. Tim had made sure of it.

But there were some things that Tim couldn't ensure, no matter how careful he had been. It seemed that Cat's scribblings in the days leading up to her meeting with Owen did help shake some memories loose.

"Elaine's ex-husband, Evan—you must have seen him at the firm—I saw him parked across the street after the cops put me in the back of the car," she professed. Though I was happy to see she was no longer willing to take the blame for my murder, I wasn't thrilled about the fact that she was shifting the load onto Evan's shoulders.

No, Cat, I willed her to hear me. *Don't do this to him. Think about what you're saying, please.*

It was no use. At least Owen didn't seem as convinced of Evan's involvement as Cat did. He chalked her memories up to nothing more than drunken hallucinations, desperate attempts to refuse responsibility for her own actions. But Cat wouldn't let her accusation be swept under the rug so easily.

"Ask Evan where he was that night," she commanded. "And while you're at it, ask him if he fucking drugged me."

If my heart could stop any more than it already was, it would have. In the chaos of trying to locate my friend and communicate with her from beyond the grave, I had almost forgotten about how it was that she had been subdued on the floor, writhing unconscious on the kitchen tile while her husband sank his blade between my ribs.

Owen was quick to point out that there were no drugs found in Cat's system according to her medical intake, but she was insistent on the matter. His curiosity piqued, he decided to give her the benefit of the doubt.

"How do you think you were drugged?" Owen invited her musings. Cat hesitated a moment before answering.

"I don't know," she confessed.

But I did.

***

May 4, 2023

All things considered—the absence of our lead designer at the meeting, the sickening knowledge of Cat and Evan's affair looming in the room—I hadn't expected the presentation back in March to go as well as it did. Maybe it was the memory of our unbridled lovemaking that made it easier for me and Tim to play nice with Evan in front of the clients, the giddiness of our secret tryst infectious enough to convince the developers to give us their business. Or maybe it was the concept board that Cat had put together before her impromptu stay at rehab that had made the right impression. Whether it was our positive attitude or the quality of work we presented that ultimately earned us their trust, I didn't care. I was just happy to have the excuse to spend more time alone with Tim in the city that had finally brought us together.

There were mountains of emails waiting for me on my phone as I sat in the familiar dining room at the Charlotte Hilton months later, sipping on coffee and wolfing down pancakes, fueling myself for the long day that stood before me. Trips like these were common for me and Tim during the earliest stages of project development, our commitment to meeting with local vendors and contractors one of the many reasons why clients trusted Burg Interiors in the first place. We offered a personal touch that most other firms didn't in that regard—something Tim had been passionate about from the very beginning.

I had admired that about him, the way he constantly sought out ways to make the company better, expand our horizons. If it had been left up to Cat, I doubted the firm would have ever done anything more than residential renovations, which, while fun, weren't nearly as lucrative as the commercial projects we had graduated to after those first few years. Tim's drive to do more was a big reason why we were able to make a name for ourselves in student housing design. His work ethic was commendable, and something I normally strove to imitate. But that was before our shared business trips began to take on a new meaning.

While I usually would have spent the first night in town combing through the emails that had gone unanswered from the comfort of my hotel room, I had spent the previous evening screaming out in ecstasy as Tim ravaged every inch of my body, much to the chagrin of our neighbors, I'm sure. Though he had moved into my house shortly after that first trip to Charlotte, there was a distance I detected from him in Williamsburg, a need to sneak around, a quiet reservation that sometimes made me wonder if he regretted sleeping with me. I suspected it had something to do with the fact that our hometown was saturated with painful memories of a life he no longer had, hurtful reminders of a marriage that had failed, a love he had lost.

But once we were in the hotel room, everything was different.

He'd pin me against the mattress, the wall, the floor, tearing away my clothes, thrusting himself into me with an eagerness that I welcomed over and over and over again. Evan was always fantastic in bed—a truth I couldn't deny even when all I wanted to do was punch him in the face. But Tim made me forget everything I thought I knew about what it meant to feel pleasure.

I forced the urge to straddle him from my mind as he took his seat across from me in the hotel dining room the morning following our arrival, his conservative button-down somehow inviting my imagination to run wild about what I knew was hidden beneath. I had often wondered why he always chose to adorn himself in long sleeves, the curiosity of his wardrobe a riddle that I never could solve. We did live in North Carolina, after all, the heat and humidity suffocating to even the toughest of Tar Heels. Yet Tim never wore so much as a tee-shirt, dressed in long sleeves no matter how high the temperature soared. I couldn't understand it—not until after that first night together.

He didn't tell me how he had gotten the scars. I didn't ask. Maybe it was Mama's voice in the back of my head urging me to keep quiet or maybe it was the fact that my initial reaction to learning his secret had almost cost me the feel of his touch altogether. Either way, I felt it best to let him talk to me about it on his own terms. In the meantime, I found the fact that he trusted me with his true form to be strangely arousing. As though it were confirmation that whatever was blossoming between us wasn't some meaningless affair as it sometimes felt while we were at home. I had to admit that I was falling for him fast. Perhaps the comfort he felt in displaying his deformities was a sign that he was falling for me, too.

Get a grip, Elaine, I chastised myself, shaking the thought from my mind as I focused my attention back on my phone and the emails I still had yet to open. *He's still fucking married, you idiot. Get back to work.*

I scrolled to the top of my inbox, ignoring the magnetic pull of Tim's gaze as he watched me pore over the illuminated screen in my hands, sipping his coffee in silence as he did so. Pangs of guilt and anxiety mounted in my chest as I realized the sheer volume of messages I had chosen to ignore, some of which were related to the very meetings I was meant to attend that day. *Damnit.* Maybe Evan was right about me. I was a fucking hypocrite, sleeping with someone else's husband when I should have been working. The thought made my stomach turn to ice, but not as much as the sight of the first unanswered email on my list.

Oh no. What does she want now?

My finger gave an involuntary tremble as it hovered over yet another message from a woman who had been hounding me for weeks, pestering me with questions that I didn't want to acknowledge. I swallowed my fear down with my coffee and clicked on the email:

> **Subject:** *MD*
> **Sent:** *Tuesday, May 3, 12:02 a.m.*
> *Elaine,*
> *Why did you lie about Michael Davies? I know you know that name. Please just talk to me.*
> *—Detective McGowen*

"You okay?" Tim's voice tore me away from my phone. "You look like you've seen a ghost."

"Yeah," I lied. "I'm fine. Just have more emails to get through than I thought."

"Sorry," he smirked. "Guess we were both a little distracted by *other things* last night."

I blushed, forced a smile, tried not to think about the contents of the email I had just read or the woman who had sent it. Her persistence had started to wear on my nerves, daring me to entertain possibilities that I didn't want to face. I couldn't. It was bad enough that I had to come to terms with the fact that Evan had been a cheater. A liar. I wasn't ready to think about what else he could have been. What else I had been too blind to see.

"I've got to get going. Got a meeting at the university starting soon," Tim got up from his seat, downing the rest of his coffee in one gulp. He planted a kiss on top of my head, tucked my hair behind my ear, and said in a low whisper, "We'll pick back up where we left off tonight."

I tried to cling to that promise for the rest of the day as I navigated meetings of my own. It was easier for us to split up the workload during our trips, Tim usually meeting with the stakeholders at whatever university happened to need a new student center, myself choosing to avoid such settings, the memory of those final semesters at Green Valley University flooding back to me in a painful rush any time I was forced to step foot on a college campus. I much preferred the company of general contractors and zoning regulators to the recollection of a time when my peers had believed me to be an accomplice to murder.

Like I said, Evan's surprise party wasn't my best idea, no matter how carefully I had planned out every detail, Tim helping me every step of the way. I had kept my promise that I wouldn't spill the beans about Tim's side hustle, and he had held his end of the bargain (or blackmail, whatever you wanted to call it), convincing the Sig Nu brothers to let us use the house, getting Evan drunk beforehand to help loosen him up a little. Boy, did that backfire on me.

I don't know if it was the pressure I had placed on him to get involved or just a slip of the tongue, but when Evan questioned where it was that we were going as we made our way to the frat house that night, Tim let the cat out of the bag without even thinking. It was infuriating to me, and I had half a mind to make him suffer the consequences by telling the whole world what I knew about his secret dealings in the university library, but I never got the chance. Not with Evan screaming at me in the street, his drunken obscenities so devastating that Tim's disloyalty seemed to dissolve from my mind entirely.

We never did end up making it to the party. Evan had stormed off in an angry whirlwind, promises of heading to the local liquor store fresh on his lips—as if he needed more whiskey to help him over the edge. Tim had chased after him, trying to calm him down while Cat and I walked the streets aimlessly, her comforting arm around my shoulder, willing the tears to stop falling down my cheeks.

By the time we made it home, it was eleven o' clock and Evan was passed out on the floor of our shared apartment, a fresh bottle of Jack still clutched in his hands. *Fucking idiot.* I had no idea that just a few hundred feet from where his unconscious body lay, Mia Davis was drowning in the riverbed beneath the Greene Street Bridge, visible from the windows of our living room.

The cops had come to our apartment the next day, asking us questions about what we knew, claiming that Mia's roommate had seen Evan lurking by her car the previous night, insinuating that he might have had something to do with her death. They had even called him in for additional questioning later that week, the rumor mill churning out all sorts of hateful speculations as a result. It didn't matter that the police had ultimately deemed it a suicide. Evan's name became equivalent to the bogeyman's after that. And I was the bitch who was stupid enough to stick by the monster's side.

Sure, I hated Mia. With her perfect body, her undeniable popularity, the way every boy in school—my boyfriend included—seemed to kiss the ground she walked on, who could blame me? But if I thought for one second that Evan had anything to do with murdering the poor girl, I would have come clean about it in an instant. After all, we hadn't exactly been on the best terms at the time what with the failed surprise party and the fierce argument that it had inspired between us. Even taking his anger into account, the dark past I knew he harbored, the violent tendencies he struggled to reign in—I didn't think he could resort to taking another person's life. Much less a girl who he seemed to have a crush on.

Others weren't as easily convinced.

Mia's roommate, Rachel, lived in the apartment below us. She was a bit of a loner and, if I'm being honest, I thought she was kind of a freak, her stringy, auburn hair always dangling haphazardly down the sides of her freckled, perpetually sweaty face. I never once saw her out at a party, a club meeting, *anywhere* where other students might be. But after Mia died, she became an unavoidable pest. Though she had only dared to corner Evan once, hurling accusations at him as though she were a seasoned police officer from the way he told the story, I could feel her eyes on us whenever we passed one another in the stairwell of the brick duplex that housed each of our apartments. Her watchful stare stamping itself onto our skin, daring us to make a wrong move.

That experience had changed Evan forever. What had started as a mild taste for alcohol became a full-fledged addiction as he tried to escape the pain of scrutiny at the bottom of any liquor bottle he could find. I felt sorry for him. It seemed he was destined to live a life of misery, and no matter what I tried to do, no matter how I tried to help, he just couldn't see the light. The thing that haunted him had ultimately been enough to end our marriage, his need to drown the memories too much for me to bear. Imagine my surprise when the ghost responsible for his hurt showed up fifteen years later, fresh accusations waiting on her lips.

Weeks earlier, she had stopped me in the parking lot one morning after our first trip to Charlotte, calling me out by name, asking questions about our stay at the Hilton as though she already knew everything about it. I didn't recognize her at first—truth be told, she had grown into herself, no longer the frumpy twenty-something-year-old that I remembered with her hair pulled back into a neat ponytail, posture straight and confident. But as soon as she flashed her badge in my face, the words "Detective Rachel McGowen" engraved beneath a golden shield, all the memories came rushing back.

"Leave me alone!" I screamed at her. "I don't want to talk to you."

But she wouldn't take no for an answer. She halted me in my tracks, a wild, desperate look in her eyes that frightened me as she spoke.

"Girls are dying, Elaine!" she yelled at me, as though I had any idea what the hell she was talking about. What girls? Where? She didn't wait long to get to the point, "You wanna know what Green Valley, Sudbury, and Charlotte all have in common? Three girls dead. One in every city where Burg Interiors just happened to be working nearby projects. Three girls dead in Holiday Inn hotel rooms that just happened to be right next to where *your* team was staying. Where *Evan* was staying."

I froze. *What did she just say?* No. I knew what Evan was doing at the Holiday Inn. Why else would those receipts have shown up in Cat's desk drawer? I wasn't going to let Rachel's wild theories make my already difficult life even more difficult. In so many words, I told her to fuck off, let me get back to work, leave me to my misery. But she was dogged.

"Just one more thing," she said to me as I was poised to enter the office. "Have you ever heard the name Michael Davies before?"

Once again, the blood in my body seemed to frost over. How in hell did she know that name? I felt as though the ground was falling out from beneath me, my feet suddenly unable to find the earth. I couldn't speak. Couldn't move. Couldn't face the truth, so instead, I lied.

"No," I told her. "I've never heard that name before."

I wanted that to be enough—for both of us. It was bad enough that I had manifested my own Freudian nightmare, marrying a man who was no more faithful to me than Daddy had been to Mama. If I had been foolish enough to spend half my life with someone capable of such deceit, could it have been possible that there were other lies that I had chosen to ignore? Other horrors hiding in plain sight, if only I had the eyes to look? I didn't want to believe it, but Rachel wouldn't allow my mind to rest.

Her harassment continued for weeks, calling me at the office, emailing me strange questions, each one forcing me to contend with facts that I wasn't willing to face. She had even sent me a list of dates, demanding to know whether or not I recognized any of them. Of course, I did, and of course, I didn't respond. Didn't acknowledge that each of them matched the dates of the receipts found buried with the whiskey in Cat's desk drawer.

Between Rachel's questions and Cat's return to work after her release from rehab, life in Williamsburg had become intolerable. And with the latest email sending my thoughts spiraling out of control, not even the promise of Tim's passion in our hotel room had been enough to ease the tension building in my gut.

By the time I had finished up my meetings for the day and made my way back to the Hilton, having sex was the furthest thing from my mind. All I could think about was Mia Davis, those three murdered women, and whether or not the Michael Davies I knew had somehow been responsible for all of their deaths.

"There she is," Tim greeted me as I entered our hotel room that night. He already had two drinks poured, one of which he handed to me as I tossed my purse on the chaise lounge in the corner. I drank deeply from the cup, desperate for the alcohol within to dull my senses, relieve me of the doubt and darkness that was devouring me. "Thirsty, huh?" Tim commented, a coy smile tugging at his lips as he watched me down the gin and tonic in one, long gulp. "I am, too."

I knew he wasn't talking about more alcohol, his greedy hands already pulling at the buttons on my blouse, teeth grazing my neck as he tried to coax me over to the bed. It was the type of behavior that I normally would have been happy to indulge, just as eager to feel his body against me as he was to feel mine against his. But I just wasn't in the mood, and he could sense it.

"What's wrong with you?" he pulled back, the slight annoyance in his voice as soul-crushing to me as the thoughts that were still swirling around in my head along with the gin that had hit much harder than I expected. Maybe it was a bad idea to go the entire day without eating anything other than breakfast.

"Sorry," I muttered, moving past him to place my purse on the floor and take my seat on the chaise. "I've just got a lot on my mind."

"Then let me help take it off," he persisted, kneeling down on the floor in front of me, forcing my legs apart as he wriggled his way in between them, sliding his hands up my skirt. I grabbed him by the wrists before he could reach the top of my thighs.

"Tim, stop," I said sharply. "This isn't funny."

A nefarious expression morphed across his face at my refusal, and for a moment, I thought that he might do the unthinkable, unable to deny himself the thing he so obviously wanted. Just as quickly as it appeared, it was erased, his eyes softening as he removed his hands from beneath my skirt and cupped my face in his palm, stroking my cheek with his thumb. I relaxed a bit, his touch no longer hungry, invasive, but soothing.

"What's the matter?" he pried. "You're not yourself. I know there's something you're not telling me."

"You're right," I admitted. "I'm just... distracted, I guess."

"By what? The project?"

I hesitated, unsure whether or not I should voice the concerns that were threatening to swallow me whole. My eyes fell to my lap and I suddenly felt like a child, the urge to cry mounting in my throat, rendering me speechless. Before I knew what was happening, tears were streaming down my cheeks, giant sobs erupting through my body until I couldn't breathe. It was too much. I couldn't hold it in anymore.

Tim wrapped me in his arms, shushing me against his shoulder like a father calming his screaming child in the throes of a terrible nightmare. He let me cry for several minutes, not daring to push the topic further. But he didn't need to. I had to get this secret off my chest.

"It's Evan," I blubbered, the muffled words falling flat against Tim's shirt.

"What did he do to you?" he demanded, holding me at arm's length so he could search my eyes. "Did he say something? Did he hurt you?"

"No, but he..." I didn't know how to articulate what I needed to say. Where did I even start? How could I possibly make him understand?

"He what?" Tim prodded, wiping the stray tears from my face, his brows pulled together so tight, I thought his skull might tear through his skin.

"I think he might have hurt somebody else," I finally said, breaking down once more, burying my face in Tim's chest.

"Shh, shh," he smoothed my hair with his hand. "Why do you think that? Who did he hurt?"

"Mia," I moaned. I could feel his muscles stiffen at the remark, the name of the girl who had cast a shadow of doubt over our small circle of friends all that he needed to hear to understand. He wasn't immune to the rumors that Rachel and the other students were eager to spread around campus during those last few semesters.

The whole thing had cost him all the prestige he once held over the Sig Nu brothers, his presence at the fraternity no longer welcome after that fateful night.

"Why do you think that?" the words sounded cold, empty. As though he didn't want to know the answer, but couldn't help but ask the question.

"A detective came to the office a few weeks ago," I sputtered. "You remember that girl, Rachel, who lived in the apartment below us? Mia's friend? Well, she's a cop now, I guess, and she cornered me and—"

"Wait a minute, the cops came to talk to you?" Tim's eyes were wild, frightened. "What the fuck, Elaine? Why didn't you tell me this?"

"I'm sorry," I wailed. "I didn't know how to talk about it. It all just happened so fast."

"What did she want?" he demanded. I sucked in a deep breath to calm myself before delivering a response.

"She started asking about when we first came to Charlotte, if Evan was there and all that," I explained. "Then she started talking about dead girls showing up at Holiday Inns near all the student centers we've built, and that's when I knew."

"That's when you knew what?"

"That she was right," fresh tears burned my eyes as I acknowledged aloud for the first time what I didn't want to believe. "Evan's been booking rooms at the Holiday Inn for years without our knowledge."

Tim's eyes widened, his lips parted slightly, struggling to form words.

"H-how do you know that?" he managed.

"Because I found the receipts in Cat's office," I told him. "I thought it was just evidence of their affair, checking in under a different name using that fake ID you made him back in college. You remember, right? Michael Davies?"

Tim didn't move, didn't speak, so I continued.

"Well, whoever's been killing these girls has been using that name to check in, I guess."

"Why do you think that?" his voice was a ghost's as he spoke.

"Because Rachel asked me if I ever heard the name before," I answered.

"What did you tell her?"

"I told her that I never heard of it," I confessed, the guilt of my lie blurring my vision as more tears flooded my eyes. "But I'm scared, Tim. What if he really did this? What if he's been hurting people all this time and I've been so stupid that I couldn't see it happening? I'm such a fucking idiot. Oh God, what if he does it again? What am I going to do? I can't—"

"Hey," Tim gripped me by the shoulders, jerking me out of my slip into madness. "You're not stupid. You did the right thing telling me all this, okay? It sounds to me like Rachel is just trying to put ideas into your head. Make you think things that aren't real. Cops are good at that."

"But what if she's right?" I cried. "What if she's right, and I lied to her, and now someone else gets hurt?"

"That's *not* going to happen," Tim assured me.

"How do you know that?"

"Because I just know," he said. "Evan is a creep, there's no doubt about it. But he's not a killer. I mean, c'mon. He doesn't have it in him. He's not that smart."

"I don't know," I bit my lip, still unconvinced. "I still think there are too many coincidences."

"You wanna know what I think?" Tim brushed my hair behind my ears, swiping tears away with his thumb. "I think you need to calm down. Maybe take a nice, hot bath or something. You've been stressing yourself out about this for no reason. That stupid cop just got in your head. You just need some alone time to decompress."

I sighed. A bath did sound good, and the whirlpool tub beside the walk-in shower in the bathroom was the perfect place for a soak after the long day I had. Maybe Tim was right. I just needed time to relax. Get my head straight.

"Here," Tim crossed the room and headed for the mini-bar, whipping up another gin and tonic in the cup I had emptied moments before. "Drink this. I'll go get the tub going, okay?"

He placed a kiss on top of my head and ducked into the bathroom, the sound of rushing water echoing off the tile walls, creeping out into the bedroom as he worked. After I finished my drink, I stood up on woozy legs and followed him into the bathroom, eager to feel the warm water evaporate my worries away. He watched as I peeled the clothes from my body and let them fall to the floor, his eyes no longer full of desire but a deep sadness as he helped me into the tub, lowering me into the water.

"Just lie back, shut your eyes, and try not to think about all this," he instructed. "There you go."

I rested my neck against the lip of the tub, my head spinning as the warm water opened my veins, encouraging the alcohol to course through my body unimpeded by stress. It was nice to be cared for by him, the loving way he prepared the bath further proof in my mind that he loved me. I closed my eyes and allowed myself to relax for the first time in what felt like years.

"Here, I've got a warm towel for you," he said softly. "Just drape that over your face and let everything go. It'll all be alright, I promise."

I kept my eyes shut as he placed the towel down, the smell of the hotel staff's cleaning supplies more powerful than I had expected. Despite the offending odor, it seemed to do the trick. Within a few moments, my muscles had all but melted away into a puddle. The last thing I remember was the sound of the bathroom door shutting behind my gentle attendant.

***

May 5, 2023

I woke up the next morning in a daze, the need to vomit forcing me from a bed that I hadn't remembered curling up in the night before. I raced to the bathroom, expelling the contents of my fragile stomach into the toilet bowl. *Goddamned gin.* It was a mistake to drink that stuff after a full day of failing to consume anything other than pancakes and coffee. The nausea was unbearable, my retching forceful, seemingly unending. I didn't think that I'd ever stop puking.

What the hell was wrong with me?

I had drunk on an empty stomach before and I knew that I was a lightweight, but the resulting hangover had never been that violent. If I hadn't known any better, I would have guessed that

I had been drugged. It was mystifying. Unsettling. But not as unsettling as the strange soreness that assaulted me as I finally felt able to raise myself from the bathroom floor.

A tenderness invaded me in places that I might have overlooked if the previous night had gone the way Tim originally planned. But I knew that we hadn't had sex. I remembered the look in his eyes when I had refused him. So, why did I feel so violated? The sensation sent a tickle of fear down my spine that I couldn't quite explain. Something was very wrong, but my brain wouldn't let the thoughts come.

I brushed my teeth and splashed cool water on my face, fighting the urge to vomit once more. After all the puking I had just done, I doubted whether I'd be able to drain anything else out of my body even if I tried. As I staggered back into the bedroom, a shock ran through me as though my skin had been touched by a live wire.

The room was empty.

Where was Tim?

CHAPTER 8

May 21, 2023

When the officer came to collect Cat from her cell, the promise of a visitor awaiting her elsewhere in the labyrinthine county jail, I was terrified that it would be Tim joining her on the opposite side of the plexiglass wall. She appeared just as nervous, her body sinking low in the black plastic chair in which she was sat, not at all the image of excited anticipation that her fellow prisoners displayed as they clambered in their cubicles, fighting to see when their own visitors would occupy the empty seats across from them. I was relieved when it was Evan who entered the visitor's center, though the comfort I felt at his presence was tinged with sadness.

He looked as horrible as he had while quivering on the concrete outside of Cat's house the night of my murder. His thick, black hair stood up on end as though he hadn't bothered to comb it since learning the truth of what had happened—or at least, what the police believed to be the truth. The usually clean-shaven face that I had once smothered with affection was scratchy with stubble, making him look gaunt and unkempt. Dark, purple circles decorated his eyes, which were absent of their vibrancy, the bright green pools of his irises appearing as dull and muddied as the moss that framed his father's front porch. He looked gutted, wounded beyond repair. And Cat's reaction to his visit didn't offer any semblance of relief.

She was wicked, full of contempt—the very image of viciousness that I had displayed in his apartment back when I still believed him capable of murder, my mind unwilling to face the truth that my most recent trip to Charlotte had all but confirmed. I couldn't blame her for the way she treated him. If I had been in her position—and I had been—I know I would have behaved in the same manner. But as I watched their interaction, listened as the accusations slipped freely from her lips, I became overwhelmed with heartache, the regret in my soul so profound, I could almost feel it wrapping its icy fingers around my gut.

"If anyone knows what happened that night, it's you," she sneered into the telephone, her confidence no doubt bolstered by the thick pane of plexiglass that separated them. Evan was provoked by the statement, the anger and resentment that he had always struggled to restrain bubbling to the surface in an unfiltered rage.

"What the fuck are you talking about? Why the hell would I know anything?" he spat into his own phone, knuckles burning white as he gripped the handset tighter. Cat let the suspense of her words build between them, intimidating him with promises of legal scrutiny that we both knew weren't true. When he still wasn't getting the picture, she dropped the pretense entirely, choosing a more direct approach.

"I saw you that night," she told him. "I know you were fucking there."

Realization seemed to render him temporarily speechless as he placed the phone back in its cradle, collecting himself as he summoned the strength to face his accuser before grabbing the phone once again. He sounded strangled when he next spoke, as though he were fighting to hold back a flood of emotion tearing at his throat.

"So, you think because I was at your house that night, I must have something to do with Elaine's death?" disgust and devastation seemed to fight for center stage as he formed the words. "Tell me, Cat, what else makes you think I could do this? I'd love to know exactly what the fuck you're thinking right now."

So would I, I agreed, still unable to hear a single thought inside Cat's confused and tortured mind. As Evan waited for a response from the tongue-tied woman who sat before him, an immeasurable sorrow rooted itself in my being. There he was, once again being accused of a crime that he did not commit, the shadow of Mia's untimely death forever hanging over him, defining his very existence. It wasn't fair. For all his anger issues, his unquenchable thirst for alcohol, his bitterness, I knew deep down that none of it was his fault. He was as much a victim in all this as Cat, as Mia and the other murdered women, as *me*. The unfortunate byproduct of a father who never loved him, a mother who never got the chance, a wife who had failed him.

"Evan, baby, I'm so sorry," I knew he couldn't hear me, but it needed to be said. "I should have stayed with you. I should have helped you more. There's so much I wish I could change. So many things I wish I could take back."

I slipped between the plexiglass, hovering at his side, running my hands through hair that remained stubbornly in place despite my efforts to smooth it down.

"I wish you could know how much I truly loved you," I whispered, the ability to shed tears evading me despite my desire to release the emotion swelling in my spectral body. I wrapped my arms around him, attempting a kiss on his bony, unshaven cheek. As my lips found his skin, a shock of sound erupted in my eardrum, his voice consuming my mind. *I could hear him!*

Why is she doing this to me? his pain stitched itself inside of me, his lips unmoving as the words flooded my senses. *Why does everyone do this to me? I made one mistake—one—and now I'll always be a monster. Dad was right. It should have been me. Not Mom.*

"Evan, *no!*" I cried, holding him tighter, my body unable to comply with such mortal displays of affection. I simply sank into him, wearing his skin the same way I imagined that demons might wear the bodies of the poor souls they possessed. But Evan was none the wiser, still demanding a response to his unanswered question.

"Tell me why you think I could do this," he snarled into the phone. "I want to hear you say it."

I watched through Evan's eyes as Cat leaned into the window, her own irises black and unfeeling as she made her true feelings known. Her voice was callous, calculated as it slithered through the receiver.

"Because I know who you really are," she said definitively. "I know what you've done. I know what you're capable of doing."

Evan dropped the phone from his hands, a flash of painful images reeling through his mind. A school bus full of mocking children. A young girl's evil grin, leering out from the crowd. Evan's twelve-year-old fists sinking into her face, over and over and over again. Her swollen, blackened eyes. Disfigured mouth, bloody and toothless in the aftermath of his rage.

He had lived with this horrible act for as long as I had known him, haunted as much by that moment as he had been by Rachel's insistence that he had been responsible for Mia's death. Though he had served his time in juvenile detention, tried his best in anger management, he had never forgiven himself for what he had done to that poor girl. It was an ugly secret—one that, until that moment, I thought he had only trusted me to keep. But Cat's words made it clear that I was not the only one who had helped shoulder his burden.

Evan was deflated, sagging back in his chair, winded by shame. I couldn't stand it, couldn't let Cat sit there and think that she was right.

Come on, Evan, I willed him to pick the phone back up, forced all the energy I could muster into his body before the door to the living was slammed on me once more. In a rush of renewed determination, he snatched up the phone, speaking the words that I had planted inside his throat without his knowledge.

"You're wrong, Cat," my mouth moved in sync with his, the sound of his voice melding with my own. I didn't know if it was the surprise she felt from his change of attitude or if she had somehow heard me speak through him, but the shock that swept through Cat's face left her pallid and shaken. It reminded me of the way she had looked just two weeks earlier as I stood at Evan's doorstep, waiting to be let inside.

***

May 6, 2023

It was always strange to me how big houses could give off the impression of being so grand, so full of promise to the people who didn't live inside them. Envy had that effect, I suppose. The ability to convince others that all their troubles would disappear if only they had a bigger property, a nicer car, more money in their bank account. But having a big house doesn't make its inhabitants free of turmoil. They just have more hiding places to store the skeletons they don't want on display.

These were the thoughts that filled my mind as I lay in bed next to Tim following our return home from Charlotte, my spacious master bedroom stretched out before me, somehow suffocating despite its size and minimalist design. Shadows played off the walls in nightmarish fashion, ghoulish faces matrixing in the darkness, forcing me to see things that I didn't want to see. An early-morning jogger might have stopped to admire the pristine landscape awaiting them at the end of the cul-de-sac where I lived, the polished Audi parked in the driveway, the sandstone façade of my two-story Tudor towering from its place nestled in the center of the two-acre plot of land on which it sat.

What a beautiful home, they might think to themselves, beating at the pavement with bitter feet, wishing they could trade places with whoever they deemed lucky enough to live there. Looks could be so deceiving.

For all its splendor and undeniable style, the truth was that my house afforded me little comfort as slumber's soft embrace evaded me despite the thousand-thread-count sateen sheets that swaddled my skin. My king-sized bed might as well have been a twin, the sleeping monster beside me seemingly oblivious to the claustrophobic effect his presence had on me as I struggled to explain away the feeling that something was terribly wrong.

It turned out that Tim hadn't abandoned me in the hotel room the morning after he had helped prepare my bath. Moments after the prickle of terror had started to creep down my neck in his absence, mind reeling about what had caused my hangover to become so severe, privates pulsing with an unsettling throb that made me feel even more sick to my stomach, he had returned.

"Oh good, you're awake," he smiled, taking me into his arms as he crossed the room, attempting a kiss on my mouth that I refused.

"Sorry," I muttered. "Just threw up a bunch. Bad breath."

"Thought you might be a little hungover today," Tim snickered, settling for a kiss on my cheek instead, the feel of his lips on my skin making my flesh crawl with discomfort that I didn't want to acknowledge. "You've got to stop chugging gin like it's water or you'll end up like Cat. You fell asleep in the tub last night, you lightweight."

I tried to laugh along at his joke, ignore the nagging feeling in my gut that told me to head for the door and run.

"Guess I didn't realize how much I drank," I said, fresh nausea swelling somewhere in my abdomen. I wrapped my arms around my stomach, the feeling of my silk pajamas demanding my attention for the first time all morning. *Had he dressed me?*

"Lucky for you, I was here to keep you from drowning," he grinned before answering the questions I hadn't spoken aloud. "But next time, I'd appreciate it if you could at least stay awake enough to dress yourself."

He left me standing small and uncertain in the center of the bedroom as he pulled open the dresser drawers beneath the flatscreen TV, running his hands along the empty wood as though hoping to find something inside. I realized then that all our clothes had been packed up, a single outfit of mine neatly folded beside our zipped-up luggage on the chaise lounge.

"Hope you don't mind, I left that out for you to change before we go," Tim explained, seeing my gaze fall to the blouse and skirt combination he had selected. He turned over the bedsheets on the mattress, flipping pillows over on their side before opening the drawer to the nightstand. "You haven't seen my phone around, have you?"

I shook my head, the taste of vomit keeping me from opening my mouth.

"Shit," he sighed. "I can't find it anywhere. Tried asking the front desk if they had it just now but no luck. Thought I'd give the room one last look before we head home, but I guess I must've dropped it somewhere while I was out yesterday."

Tim grabbed my outfit off the chaise and handed it to me.

"C'mon, sleepyhead," he chided, "We have to get going. Checkout's in twenty minutes."

I made a move to head towards the bathroom, his hands snaking around my waist from behind, stopping me in place before I could find the door handle.

"You're not going to let me watch?" he purred, the seduction in his voice sending shivers down my spine not at all related to desire. I gulped.

"I'm not feeling well," I told him. "I think I'm gonna be sick again."

"Poor thing," he said, planting a kiss on my neck before releasing me. I darted into the bathroom before he could pull me back in. Though I didn't dare look inside my underwear as I disrobed in front of the mirror, the sensitivity I felt merely stepping out of my pajama bottoms and the light bruising already visible at the uppermost points of my inner thighs were enough to send me over the edge. Horrified and violated, I clamped my hand over my mouth to stifle what I thought was a scream until the burning sensation at the back of my throat told me more bile was frothing to the surface. I leaned over the toilet bowl, a violent tangerine swimming above the creamy porcelain like a runny yolk surrounded by egg whites.

What did he do to me?

A knock came at the bathroom door, reminding me of the oppressive presence still waiting for me in the room beyond.

"You okay in there?" Tim called from the other side.

"Yeah," I squeaked, trying and failing to disguise the terror I felt. I sucked in a sharp breath and pulled myself together.

You can't let him think anything's wrong, I told myself. *Get yourself together.*

"I'll be out in just a second," I promised, shakily pulling the blouse over my head, tucking it into the skirt around my hips, my legs feeling far too exposed, too accessible to the man who had placed his hungry hands all over them the night before.

After I finished changing, I took a few moments to collect myself at the sink, splashing cool water onto my face, giving my teeth another thorough scrub with the toothbrush that Tim had neglected to pack with the rest of our belongings. My nerves felt frayed beyond repair, mind scrambled as I tried to invent innocent explanations for the obvious swelling between my thighs. Maybe in my drunken state, I had made a move on him, led him to believe that I was capable of giving my consent. He had been so sweet, so doting as he helped me into the tub. Was it so far-fetched to think that I had been turned on by his affection? Surely, this was just a misunderstanding. I must have asked him to do this; I just didn't remember.

So, why did he have to dress you? I reminded myself. *If you were cognizant enough to have sex, why couldn't you have put on your own clothes?*

Stop it! I argued silently with myself. *Tim has been nothing but kind to you. He is not a fucking rapist. You probably just fell on your drunk ass while he was trying to change you. It's Evan you should be worried about. Not Tim.*

I shook the poisonous thoughts from my mind and gathered my discarded pajamas and my toothbrush in my arms, forcing a smile on my tired reflection before opening the door.

"I'm a better outfit planner than I thought," Tim's eyes lit up as he took me in. "You look beautiful."

Tears stung behind my eyes inexplicably at the compliment. I hoisted myself up on tip-toes to kiss him fully on the mouth, allowing his tongue to pass over my lips, willing myself to feel safe in his arms. There was no way this man could have defiled me. I was in love with him, after all, and even though he hadn't said as much, I was fairly certain he loved me, too. It wasn't possible to be raped by someone who loved you, was it?

No. I was just being ridiculous, swept up by feelings of misplaced paranoia thanks to a pesky detective with a personal vendetta. First Evan was a murderer, now Tim was a sex-crazed lunatic? Where would the accusations end? Besides, even if the latter was somehow true—and it wasn't, it couldn't be, I wouldn't believe it—but if it was, what choice did I have but to pretend everything was fine? We were four hours from Williamsburg, and he was my only ride home.

And what a long ride home it was. The hours were consumed by silence broken only by Tim's periodic need to confirm that I was, in fact, as alright as I claimed to be. As much as I wanted to be okay, to stop thinking the worst, my mind simply wouldn't let me rest. I blamed it on the hangover, hoping the lie would be enough to convince us both that I would be better by the following morning. But as I sat there in my bed, sleeplessness adding to my building anxiety, I just couldn't shake the sound of Rachel's voice from my mind.

"Three girls dead," she had shouted at me. "Three girls dead in Holiday Inn hotel rooms that just happened to be right next to where *your* team was staying. Where *Evan* was staying."

And she was right about that. Evan *had* been at the Holiday Inn. All those receipts proved that it had been him, the name from his fake ID printed all over each and every one. There was only one Michael Davies—wasn't there? It had to be Evan. So, why did I suddenly feel so unconvinced? Why couldn't I tell Rachel that I had found her killer?

I bolted upright in my bed, untangled myself from the sheets, and crept as quietly as I could across the room into the walk-in closet beside the master bath, careful not to wake Tim in the process. Closing the door to the closet behind me, I flicked on the light and got changed into the first blouse and pants combination I could find, leaving my pajamas in a pile at my feet despite the empty wicker hamper in the corner. I switched off the light and slipped back into the darkened bedroom, tip-toeing past Tim's sleeping form, out the door, and down the staircase into the living room. The clock above the sliding glass door read six-thirty. I knew it was a long shot, but I couldn't take it anymore. I needed answers.

I needed to talk to Evan, however dangerous or stupid that might be.

Swallowing down my fear, I grabbed the keys to my Audi off the hook beside the front door and made my way out to the car. Maybe it was wrong of me to leave Tim without an explanation, not even a note left behind to tell him where I had gone. But the Shady Brooks Apartment Complex where Evan lived was only five miles away, and I didn't need to stay long to get what I was after. Hell, there was a good chance that he wouldn't let me inside at all, meaning there was an even better chance that I'd make it back home before Tim had ever noticed that I had been gone.

The sky looked like rainbow sherbet as I pulled into the parking lot, peachy sun rays poking holes through wispy clouds still sleepy with indigo shadows. I loved how North Carolina sunrises could transform even the dreariest of dumps into a setting fit for a fairy-tale, and Lord knew that Shady Brooks needed all the help it could get in that department. It was a small complex tucked away in one of Williamsburg's less desirable neighborhoods, its brick exterior streaked white with efflorescence, stubby shrubs somehow overgrown yet stunted, carelessly planted with an infuriating degree of asymmetry that gave my perfectionist brain a headache to even look at.

I parked in one of the visitor spaces near Evan's shiny, red Wrangler, its candy apple paint job appearing as out-of-place as my Audi did sitting atop the cracked and faded pavement. He had enough money to buy himself a nice house if he wished; I hadn't been so vindictive as to rob him of his life's savings during our divorce. It wasn't worth it to me to be that petty. Still, he had chosen to live in this pathetic excuse of an apartment complex—in a cramped, one-bedroom unit, no less. I thought about that tiny mobile home masquerading as a ranch where he had grown up in Green Valley. Despite the years he had spent in my company surrounded by fine furnishings, elaborate estates, and immaculate interiors, it seemed he would always gravitate towards the simpler things.

Whatever. I had come there to judge his character, not his living situation. Although, I had to admit that as I climbed the crumbling staircase to reach the second-story apartment unit where he lived, I couldn't help but feel as though the place were made for murderers. The thought sent a tingle down my spine as I stopped short of the front door to his apartment.

What was I doing? Was I insane?

If Rachel was right and Evan was some sort of secret serial killer, what good would it do me to confront him about it in a place as seedy and vile as Shady Brooks? As I raised my fist to knock on the door, my palms began to sweat, heartbeat skipping around in my ribcage like a frantic bird desperate to take wing.

I shouldn't be here, I panicked. *I should turn around and go home. Go back to Tim. Tell Rachel what I know and be done with this.*

But it was too late. The door had already opened.

It was Cat's hand still lingering on the door handle, her eyes stretched wide with the same look of shock and surprise that I'm sure was evident in my own. Her clothes were slightly wrinkled, shirt on inside-out, the smallest hint of a mouth-shaped bruise barely visible beneath the unbrushed curls cascading down her neck. As though I needed further confirmation of what she had been doing there, Evan stood awkwardly to her right, nothing but a pair of boxer shorts and mismatched socks covering his body.

I don't know why I felt so lost for words, so surprised, so heartbroken. After all, I had already found those receipts. I already knew they had been sleeping together. So, why did I feel like screaming all over again? Why couldn't I dislodge the lump from my throat in time to say anything before Cat pushed past me, not a word of apology, of anything on her lips as she bolted to the car and drove away?

"What the fuck do you want, Elaine?" Evan snarled from the doorway.

Shit. What was I supposed to say to that? *Hi, Evan. Crazy story—I think you might be a serial killer. Mind if I come in and poke around, just to make sure?* That wouldn't fly. I needed to think of something quick, but what?

"*Hello?*" his irritation pulled me away from my thoughts. "What're you doing here?"

"I... I'm... I'm looking for something," I blurted out, still trying to figure out a lie that might get me through the door.

"Cool, good luck finding it," Evan said sarcastically, moving to close the door.

"No—wait!" I shoved my foot in the doorway before he had a chance to close me out. "It's Daddy's watch. The one he gave you at our wedding? He wants it back, and I don't have it, so that means it must be here."

"You're shitting me, right?" he balked. "You came over here at the ass crack of dawn to harass me about your dad's stupid watch? You're unbelievable, you know that? Besides, I already gave it back to you."

That was true. In fact, I knew with one hundred percent certainty that Daddy's Rolex was safe and sound around his wrist, if not stored away in his bedside safe. But Evan didn't need to know that.

"Well, I can't find it and he's asking for it, so can I just have a quick look around to make sure?" his eyes narrowed at the sound of my begging. I batted my lashes, trying to make myself appear as innocent as I wanted him to think I was. "Please, Evan? Just five minutes and I swear, I'll be gone."

He let out an exasperated sigh, running a hand through his shaggy mane as he shook his head like even he couldn't believe what he was about to say.

"Fine," he grimaced, widening the door to let me inside. "But I'm telling you, it's not here."

If I thought that Evan's apartment was an eyesore from the outside, the inside of his impossibly small unit somehow left even more to be desired. The floors were covered in this awful, beige carpet that was peeling up at the edges of the yellowed walls, which were completely bare. To the right, a lumpy black sofa was shoved beneath the living room's only window, the glass to which was so smudged with grime, it didn't seem capable of permitting any light to pass through. The kitchen to the left (or was it a closet? It was difficult to say) was barren, except for a coffeemaker and box of Cheerios that sat atop the cheap, laminated countertops.

"Nice place," I commented, not knowing what else to say, the anxiety twisting around in my intestines demanding my full attention, willing me to leave.

"Fuck you," Evan muttered, offended by my insincerity.

"I'm just trying to—"

"Well, don't," he snapped. "Just look around and get the fuck out."

I scanned my empty surroundings in search of a bureau, a filing cabinet, a cardboard box—anywhere that might be used as a secret storage space for a certain fake ID. Aside from looking through the couch cushions (and I was *not* sticking my hands in there), there didn't seem to be many options.

"Is there a box that maybe you haven't unpacked yet or something I can look through?" I suggested.

"Wait here," he growled, moving into the tiny hallway on the other side of the living room where his bedroom door stood just out of view. In a few moments, he returned with an unmarked cardboard box in hand, his torso sporting a plain, white tee-shirt. For some reason, the fabric offended me, as though it was confirmation that he was embarrassed to be seen bare-chested by the same woman whom he had shared a bed with for his entire adult life. He shoved the box in my chest unceremoniously.

"This is all you have?" my eyebrows raised in puzzlement at the small container.

"Not all of us feel the need to live in excess," he spat, looking down his pointed nose at me as I crouched on the ground and began to pick through his meager belongings. The contents of the box were just as lackluster as the rest of his apartment, home to nothing more than a set of shading pencils, some forgotten artwork, a couple of old magazines. I sighed, frustrated by my lack of findings.

"I told you, I don't have it," he repeated. "Can you get out now?"

I couldn't leave. Not without finding that ID. I knew he was annoyed with my being there, and even though I was scared out of my mind that he could snap at any moment, add me to the collection of killings he had accumulated over the years, I decided to press my luck. I was in this deep. There was no sense backing down now.

"Do you mind if I look around your room a bit?"

For some reason, the question made him burst out in laughter, the sardonic tone of his unsuppressed chuckling making me feel queasy as it bounced off the apartment walls.

"Knock yourself the fuck out, Elaine. Honestly, I don't give a shit anymore," he stepped out of my way as I got up from the floor and rushed into his bedroom. It was just as empty as the rest of the place, occupied by nothing but a queen-sized mattress that sat on the floor, not even a proper bed frame to create the illusion of livability. On the far side of the room was a closet door, the only hiding place in an otherwise unobstructed wasteland. I threw the door open and found a black, metal safe stored inside on the floor.

"What's in here?" I spun around to face Evan who had followed me into his bedroom, pointing to the black box on the ground.

"None of your goddamned business," he answered. Adrenaline surged in my body. This was it. It had to be.

"Open it up," I demanded.

"No," he scoffed. "Get the fuck out of my—"

"OPEN THE DAMNED SAFE, EVAN!" I hollered, the sound of my raised voice sending a jolt through each of our bodies. His eyes widened, surprised by the frenzy in my stare. He threw up his hands in defense.

"Jesus Christ, fine," he relented, crossing the room and kneeling down at my feet to enter the combination. The door to the safe gave an audible click as he unlatched the opening and allowed me to take a look. Inside the small, metal locker were two 9mm handguns and a box of ammo, beside which was a flimsy, fabric wallet. Before he could stop me, I snatched the wallet from the box and began to look inside, certain I would find Michael Davies' license staring back at me. But all that was held within was Evan's gun license.

He ripped the wallet from my hands and threw it back inside the safe, slamming the door shut behind it.

"What the fuck is wrong with you, huh?" he was fuming. "What the hell are you—"

"Where is it?" I shouted at him.

"I told you, I don't—"

"I'm not talking about the watch, asshole," I sneered. "Where is your ID?"

Evan's eyebrows pulled together, forming a crease through the center of his forehead.

"My ID?" he said. "You want my driver's license? What the fuck do you want with—"

"Don't play stupid with me, *Michael*," I said, blood pounding in my ears as I struggled to keep my confidence. "I know you still have that fake ID. I know you've been using it at the Holiday Inn. I know *everything!*"

"Holiday Inn?" Evan looked perplexed. Bewildered. Not even a hint of the fear or anger that I had expected to see. "I've never stayed at a Holiday Inn in my life. And if you're talking about that fake you gave me back in college, it's long gone. I got rid of it after those fucking cops brought me in after... after everything."

I searched his eyes, looking for any sign of deceit where none existed, still praying that despite it all, I was right. I had to be right. Rachel had to be right. If we weren't, then what was the alternative?

You know what the alternative is. Stop being so naïve.

Dark thoughts flooded my brain until the only sound I could hear was the dull roar of realization crashing against my eardrum. Fragmented memories burned inside my retinas like a fractured jigsaw that only I could understand. An old yearbook crashing to the floor. Plastic cards scattered across a cigarette-stained porch. Secret orders submitted along with smiling photographs of underaged students hoping to seem older than they were. And at the heart of it all was one mastermind. One person operating in the darkness, evading scrutiny at every turn. One person aside from me and Evan who had known the name Michael Davies. Of course, he had known. He had printed it on the plastic himself.

I felt sick.

"Are you going to tell me what the hell this is all about?" Evan challenged, arms folded tight across his chest. I didn't know where to start. My legs felt like gelatin, stomach filling with acid, eyes burning with tears. "Elaine? Are you okay?"

No, I'm not, I wanted to say. But I couldn't speak. All I could think about was Tim sleeping at home in my bed, slipping his hands all over my body, sticking himself inside me, all the while plotting his next attack. Would it be me, I wondered? If so, why hadn't he seized the opportunity while we were in Charlotte together? While he had already violated me?

Maybe he couldn't risk it. Not in the same hotel room where the staff already knew he was shacked up with me. How long would it be until he'd make me a target? Were there other women waiting on his list as well? Perhaps the one who had broken his heart by cheating on him, or so I had made him believe?

Oh no.

"Cat," I gasped.

"What?" Evan was struggling to follow my train of thought. "What about Cat? What're you—"

"I need a gun," I breathed. "She's not safe. I need a—"

"Woah, are you fucking crazy?" Evan slammed the closet door shut, obscuring the safe from view as though he thought I might be able to unlock it simply by looking at it. "I'm not giving you a fucking gun, Elaine. You need to leave. Right now."

"Evan, you don't understand," I pled. "I need you to listen to—"

"I'm done listening to you," he gripped me by the shoulders, pushing me out of the bedroom, through the living room, and out the front door. Before he closed the door in my face, he gave me a final warning, "I don't know what the hell is the matter with you or why you've got it in for Cat, but you need to leave her the fuck alone, you hear me? And while you're at it, leave me the fuck alone, too."

Without waiting for a response, he slammed the door shut with a thunderous crack that echoed around in my sternum like a heavy rock crashing against the craggy walls of an empty cave. I felt speechless. Powerless. Immobilized by fear. But most of all, I felt completely and utterly alone. There was nothing I could do, no evidence of Tim's involvement aside from a few distant memories and a sinking, hollow feeling tearing away at my gut. If Evan couldn't stand to hear me out, I didn't have a chance of breaking through to Cat. And without anything concrete to give her, I doubted whether Rachel would have listened to the terrified ramblings rattling around in my brain. I had nothing. No one. And I had only myself to blame for it all.

CHAPTER 9

May 12, 2023

"Elaine, darling, you look puffy," Mama commented from her place at the head of the table as I took my seat in the center. "Have you been using that face cream that I gave you?"

"Yes, Mama," I lied through gritted teeth. She raised her thin, blonde eyebrows over her wine goblet, which was brimming with an expensive chardonnay despite the early morning hour. The crystal glass was already stained pink from where her lipstick had smudged repeatedly along the rim. If I had to guess based purely on the richness of the color, I'd say it was probably her third refill of the day. Not bad for nine o' clock in the morning.

"Are you sure?" she continued, her blue eyes scrutinizing my face with unfiltered judgment. "You really ought to take better care of yourself, dear. You're thirty-five, a divorcee, not to mention a homewrecker—you don't need any more reasons to make the men go running for the hills."

"Thank you, Mama," I selected a muffin from off the silver tray in the center of the table and shoved it in my mouth before I ended up saying something that I'd regret.

"Well, now, *there's* your problem," she nodded to the blueberry culprit spilling crumbs across her otherwise pristine king's length dining table. "All those carbs and sugar? Tsk, tsk, tsk. No wonder you look so red and swollen all the time."

Yeah, Mama, that's the problem, I thought bitterly to myself. *I'm sure it has nothing to do with all the crying I've been doing. All the sleep I've not been getting. All the nightmares I've been having...*

"Jesus, Cynthia, would you leave the poor girl alone?" Daddy reprimanded from the opposite end of the table, folding down the top half of his newspaper to cast a warning glance at his wife. She narrowed her eyes at her balding, bespectacled husband, taking a long drink from her glass, nearly draining it empty. When she was finished, she gave a soft sigh and shrugged.

"I'm only trying to help," she shook her head in a defeated fashion as if *she* were the one under attack, not a hair loosening from the French twist in her mane in the process. "If she doesn't get remarried soon, we'll *never* have grandchildren. Don't you want to give us grandchildren, Elaine?"

Bits of muffin stuck to the back of my throat as I choked on the vicious words that I wanted to hurl in her direction. I reached instinctively for my water glass to regain my composure, cradling my head in my hands when I was finished to massage my temples, rubbing away the impulse to scream in her face.

"Elbows off the table, Elaine," Mama snapped. "My goodness, it's like you've got no manners at all!"

Why the fuck did I come here? Oh, right. Because my home was busy being inhabited by a potential killer. Beggars can't be choosers, I suppose. Although, most beggars probably would have jumped at the opportunity to be stuck alongside my parents in their three-story estate. A five-thousand-square-foot riverside mansion complete with an in-ground pool, a guest cottage, a garage full of exotic cars—it probably seemed like a welcome upgrade to any common street dweller. If only they knew what horrors awaited them on the other side of the front door.

***

May 6, 2023

The decision to stay with my parents wasn't one that I wanted to make. But after the confrontation at Evan's house, that's exactly where I found myself. After all, I couldn't go back to my place—not with Tim still there. Not after realizing what he was. I couldn't go to the office, either, the chances of running into him there just as high as it would have been to turn around and go home. With no other options available, I did the only sensible thing and drove the half hour to my parents' place in Edenton.

It was a beautiful little hamlet nestled along the bank of the Chowan River, dotted with quaint shops interspersed between the impressive homes that contributed to the area's decidedly upper-class atmosphere. There was even a lighthouse to complete the idyllic picture. Even when accounting for our bubble of extravagance, Edenton was without a doubt a huge step up from the neighborhood where my childhood home—the home where I still lived—was located. It made sense to me when Daddy retired and decided to sell the house in Williamsburg to me and Evan, heading for greener pastures with Mama.

While the small town was the image of perfection by anyone's standards and was only a short drive away, I refrained from making the trip whenever I could avoid it. No taste of picturesque, waterfront suburbia was worth suffering a visit with Mama, no matter how sweet it truly was. Maybe that's why she and Daddy were so surprised to see me when I showed up unannounced on their doorstep that day. Truth be told, I was surprised myself. But where else could I go? I needed an escape. I needed a plan.

I needed my parents, however infantile that made me sound.

Despite all of Mama's overt criticisms and the constant bickering with Daddy, it was nice to spend the day with them, to get my mind off of everything, to run away. They didn't even pry about why it was that I had shown up so unexpectedly, didn't force me to voice the fears that the morning's events had awakened in me. It wasn't until the sky began to fill with thick, black clouds saturated with the promise of rain that Daddy tried to usher me out of the house.

"There's a storm brewing, honey," he observed from his leather armchair beside the massive windows in the living room that overlooked the choppy river beyond. "You'd better hit the road before you get caught in it."

It wasn't his fault that he didn't realize the irony of his statement. I hadn't told him or Mama about the real reason I was there. About the storm that would be waiting for me back in Williamsburg, regardless of the impending rain. I couldn't tell them; I was still struggling to come to terms with it myself.

Before I left, Mama had pulled me into a cold embrace, her bony arms no more comforting than the thought of driving home to Tim. Yet despite her lack of warmth, the utter absence of any maternal qualities, she was somehow able to detect that something wasn't quite right with her only child. She held me at arm's length before releasing me into the rapidly darkening world beyond her front door, her dilated eyes shrink-wrapped with something love adjacent.

"You know you're always welcome here, don't you, darling?" she had asked me. Her tenderness caught me off guard, my words catching around emotions that I wasn't expecting to feel.

"Yes, Mama," I told her. "I know."

With that, I left the safety of my parents' house behind to face the man whom I had been avoiding. I should have known there would be more trouble than what I bargained for when I pulled into the cul-de-sac to find Cat's car parked on my front lawn. The driver's side door was wide open, engine still purring as I walked cautiously past it, up the cobblestone path to my home. My hand was shaking as I reached for the door handle, my mind fighting off images of Cat's dismembered body lying on my living room floor, Tim standing over her lifeless corpse with a twisted smile on his face.

If he didn't feel safe enough to kill you in that hotel room, he sure as hell isn't killing Cat in your house right now, I tried to convince myself. I shook away the fear from my trembling fingers and gripped the handle firmly, making my way inside.

I crept on feline feet through the foyer, down the hallway towards the living room at the back of the house, straining my ears to hear what was going on. When I reached the end of the hallway, I could hear low voices murmuring to one another. They sounded as though they were coming from the stairwell around the corner from where I stood. I lingered a moment and listened before making my presence known.

"Please don't do this," it was Cat's voice, pleading and desperate, as though she were begging for her life. *Oh shit.* Was I naïve to think Tim wouldn't kill her here? It was starting to sound that way.

"I'm sorry," he muttered back. "It has to be this way."

Over my dead body!

"What's going on here?" I said loudly, hoping the surprise of my arrival would be enough to call off Cat's attacker. "Why is Cat's car on the—?"

I couldn't complete the question as I rounded the corner and discovered the two of them cozied up on the staircase together. It was clear to me that I wasn't interrupting an attempted murder, but rather a tender moment between husband and wife—or at least, what was left of them.

Tim stood up in a hurry, obviously embarrassed that I had caught them in such a compromising position, struggling to locate the right words that might explain his moment of weakness. If he had found the perfect excuse, I never got the chance to hear it. Before he could speak and before I knew what the hell was happening, Cat was lunging at me, grabbing fistfuls of my hair, dragging me to the hardwood floor.

"Get off of me!" I screamed, my scalp searing with pain as strands of my blonde bob ripped loose at the root. For such a small woman, she was much tougher than she looked. She sent a skeletal fist straight into my gut, effectively knocking the wind out of me.

"I should fucking kill you!" her breath reeked of whiskey as she hollered in my face. "HOW COULD YOU DO THIS TO ME?"

My heart ached, and it wasn't just because Cat's surprisingly powerful fists had connected with my sternum, my breasts, my ribs. It was because, in that moment, I knew exactly how she was feeling—cheated, betrayed, heartbroken beyond belief. But it was also in that moment that I realized for the first time that I had lost her. She was no longer my best friend, my confidante, my sister. She was simply a woman who hated me. And I deserved it. I deserved all of it.

"ENOUGH!" Tim snapped into action, wrapping his thick arms around Cat's torso, pinning her own arms at her side as he plucked her off my helpless body and flung her towards the foyer. "Get out of here. Now!"

Cat's big, brown eyes were full of tears as she watched the man she loved come to the defense of the woman she detested.

"After everything I've done, this is really how you want it to end?" her voice was as small and shriveled as an old woman's lying on her deathbed. Tim took no pity as he delivered his ruthless response.

"Get out," he commanded. Cat staggered back through the hallway towards the front entrance, defeat written all over her face. But there was something else there, too. Behind the hurt and the hellfire in her stare was a promise. *I'll be back*, her eyes seemed to say.

No! I fought to catch my breath, find my voice, deliver the warning she needed to hear.

"Stay away from him, Cat," I moaned. "Don't come back here again!"

She paused in the hallway, her back facing me, fists clenched as though she were contemplating the likelihood that she could punch me without Tim getting in her way. For a moment, I thought she might try her luck. But the idea seemed to pass from her mind as her shoulders drooped, her fingers relaxed, and she stumbled without another word through the front door.

"Elaine, are you okay?" Tim knelt at my side, brushing the hair from my face so he could assess whatever damage Cat had caused. His touch made me flinch, which he took to mean that a bruise might be forming somewhere beneath the surface. "Hold still. Let me get you some ice."

He rushed past the marble kitchen island to the stainless-steel refrigerator, pried open the freezer on top to find the ice tray within, and stuffed a few cubes into a paper towel that he had secured from the cabinet beneath the sink. I pressed down on the floor, gingerly collecting myself into a seated position, my back resting against the coffee table beside the tan, suede sectional. As I watched Tim approach me from the kitchen, makeshift ice pack in hand, I caught sight of my laptop sitting open on the coffee table behind me.

That's strange. I hadn't touched my laptop since we had returned from Charlotte the night before. In fact, I hadn't touched any of the things I had brought on our trip. So why was my laptop on the coffee table? Why was my luggage sitting open on the floor beside it?

"Here, leave this on to stop the swelling," Tim attempted to press the towel full of ice cubes against my face, but I recoiled. "I know it hurts," he said, again misinterpreting my body language, "but this will help. Just hold still."

"I've got it," I grabbed the paper towel from his outstretched hand, the frigidity of my movement as cold as the ice that was folded inside, leaving nothing of my true feelings to Tim's imagination. His eyes fell to the floor, jaw muscles flexing as he ground his teeth together, a wolf preparing to devour his prey.

"I'm sorry," he whispered finally. "She just threw herself at me. It didn't mean anything, I swear."

Like I cared about any of that. The only thing I cared about was that Cat was safe—as far away from Tim as was humanly possible. I envied her for that. She had somewhere else to go, whereas I was stuck inside a cage with this terrible beast.

Unless...

"I think I'm going to go stay with my parents for a bit," the words tumbled out of my mouth in a hurry before I had time to overthink them. Tim seemed as surprised to hear what I had said as I had been to say it.

"R-really? Is it... because of me?" he looked crestfallen, as if he couldn't bear the thought of another woman leaving him. It almost made me feel sorry for him. Almost.

"I just need to get away from Williamsburg for a bit," I lied. I didn't want the hurt in his eyes to transform into rage.

"Is that where you've been all day? At your parents'?" he pressed. "I was so worried about you. I didn't have my phone, so I couldn't reach you. You didn't even leave a note. Are you sure you're okay? You've been acting strange ever since yesterday..."

"Yeah, I—I'm fine. I just..." I bit my lip, searching for the right excuse to get the fuck out of my own house. "I'm feeling a little guilty about all this, I think. And tonight didn't help."

"You have nothing to feel guilty about, Elaine," Tim seized my hand in his, those icy eyes frantic with a mixture of despair and desperation. "This can work. It has to work. Please don't leave. I... I love you."

He placed his lips on the hand still clutched inside of his own, the feel of his kiss repulsive, sickening. I winced.

"I'm sorry," I told him. "I just need some time."

He lifted his head to meet my gaze, his grip tightening around my fingers. For a fraction of a second, I saw that look return to his eyes—that same hungry, demonic presence looming behind his iris as was present in our hotel room when I had refused his advances.

Fuck, I thought. *He's going to kill me. He's going to wrap his hands around my throat and—*

"Okay," the fire extinguished from his stare, leaving only smoking embers in its wake. "I'll be here when you decide to come back."

I was glad when he released me, let me collect my things and leave. But I didn't like the sound of his parting promise, or what it might mean for my inevitable return. I gathered up the half-opened luggage, stuffed my laptop back inside, and raced out the door before Tim had time to snap. From there, I made the forty-minute trip back to Edenton. But not before making a pit-stop at the office to collect one very important folder from my desk.

CHAPTER 10

May 12, 2023

I left Mama and Daddy arguing at the breakfast table about the future of their family (or, as Mama had not-so-delicately pointed out, extreme lack thereof) and made my way back out to the guest house. It was irritating to me that Mama felt the need to add to my inner turmoil with her passive-aggressive commentary—if you could classify such blatant assassinations on my character as passive.

I couldn't exactly blame her for all the snide remarks. When I reappeared on her doorstep not two hours after she extended her open invitation, ready to put her rare display of kindness to the test, I knew I needed to tell her some version of the truth to explain away the bruised and battered state in which Cat had left me.

"*Elaine!* What happened to you?" she shrieked, her eyes zeroing in on the small bald spot on my head thanks to Cat's unforgiving fists. I couldn't tell her the real reason I was there, that it had nothing to do with the welt on my head or the contusions forming around my ribcage and everything to do with the fact that the home she and Daddy once held dear was now being inhabited by a monster. I could only tell her a half-truth. The half that made me seem no better in her eyes than the women whom Daddy had gone off to bed with behind her back.

Despite her obvious disapproval over what had landed me back in her home, Mama was kind enough to keep her word and let me stay there for as long as I needed. I took up residence in the guest cottage out back—a cozy two-bedroom dwelling complete with a living room, full bathroom, and a decent-sized kitchenette—not that I needed all that extra space. It was the privacy that I desired. A place where I could conduct my amateur investigation in peace without the prying eyes of my parents to interrupt me.

Even though I felt in my heart that I was right to be afraid of Tim, I knew that I would need to prove it beyond a shadow of a doubt if I was going to tell Rachel—or anybody for that matter. If I had learned anything from being married to Evan, it was that a false accusation of that magnitude had the power to destroy a person. And my false assumptions had caused enough damage as it was. I needed something more substantial than a few decades-old memories and a gut feeling that Evan had been telling me the truth at his apartment. I didn't think it would be that difficult. All I needed to do was prove that at least one of those hotel receipts coincided with a trip that only Tim had taken. But like everything else in my life it seemed, I was hopelessly, unequivocally wrong.

Cross-referencing the dates of the Holiday Inn receipts with the trips that I had arranged over the years was easy. I kept a careful record in my email of all the hotel rooms that I had blocked off for our business trips dating back to the company's founding in late 2009. But as I compiled my findings, it didn't take me long to realize that I wasn't the only meticulous person in the office.

During the week I had spent at my parents' place, I printed out receipts of all the hotel reservations I had made for Burg Interiors, pairing each one with a Holiday Inn receipt from the folder I had found in Cat's office. By the time I was finished, the interior of the charming country cottage behind my parents' mansion had transformed from a nautical-themed bed and breakfast to a chaotic paper trail reminiscent of a disorganized librarian's office. In between fielding calls and emails from prospective clients (yes, I still had to keep the business going just in case I ended up being wrong about everything), I called every single hotel from the past fourteen years to double- and triple-check that what I was seeing was real. And, to my utter dismay, it was.

Every pair of documents seemed to magically align with trips for client presentations that required the presence of the entire team. All of us—including Evan. It was as if Tim had intentionally selected such occasions, knowing that should anybody grow suspicious, there would be an unsuspecting scapegoat ready to shoulder the blame.

I had to admit that knowing Evan was there did make me second-guess whether his fervent denials of ever staying at the Holiday Inn had been genuine. Had he simply been trying to throw me off his scent? Get me out of his apartment before I found any evidence of his involvement so he could plan his next attack?

No, I thought to myself. Despite how terrible things had become between us over the years, I still felt deep down that I knew Evan better than anyone. Perhaps even better than he knew himself. We had been married for twelve years, together for sixteen. Throughout our relationship, there had been plenty of times when I had caught him in a lie, but that day in his apartment had not been one of them. I could feel it. But I knew that gut instinct wasn't going to be enough. I needed something more. Something concrete that proved beyond a reasonable doubt that he was innocent.

But what?

I spent most of the day trying to find an answer to that very question to no avail. By the time six o' clock rolled around, all I had to show for my efforts were a pile of damning documents and a consult with a prospective client two and a half hours away in Fayetteville booked for the following day. *Perfect.* Just what I needed. The cherry on top of a fantastic fucking week.

Frustrated and emotionally drained, I sank into the camel-back sofa in the living room, papers crunching beneath my weight as I snatched my laptop off the wooden coffee table and began to peruse the folders in my email once more. Maybe there was something I had missed. Some glaring piece of evidence that would make Evan's guiltlessness undeniable. Or maybe I was wrong. Maybe all of this—the hotel receipts, the business trips, the affair, Tim's strange behavior in Charlotte—maybe it was all a crazy coincidence. Just my imagination gone wild thanks to Rachel's obsession dredging up old memories from a time in my life that I had worked so hard to put behind me.

As I mindlessly flicked through my email, a loud buzzing disrupted my thoughts. It was my cellphone vibrating against the coffee table, signaling the arrival of an incoming text message. I waited for the notification to appear on my laptop screen; Evan had helped me configure everything so that my texts got forwarded to my computer back when we were still married, frustrated by the fact that I kept missing his messages thanks to my preoccupation with work. *How rude of me.* But as I waited for the text to show, it never appeared.

What the hell was wrong with this thing?

I rolled my eyes, annoyed by yet another needless aggravation in a week full of irritating and unnerving disappointments. I knew that I was a bit computer illiterate—I didn't even bother to use the Mail app on my laptop, preferring to use a web browser to navigate my email instead—but I didn't remember screwing around with any settings that might prevent my texts from coming through.

Dragging my finger across the trackpad, I moused over the dock of applications hidden at the bottom of my MacBook screen to access the Messages app. An angry, red badge glared at me from the corner of the green speech bubble icon, indicating a total of six missed messages. I opened up the application to view the texts that had somehow eluded me.

It was Cat.

But none of these messages were meant for me. As I scanned the contents, it became very clear that they were all somehow meant for Tim:

> **Monday, May 9, 3:42 p.m.:** I can't believe you're giving up on ten years of marriage.

> **Monday, May 9, 6:03 p.m.:** Are you proud of yourself?

> **Monday, May 9, 6:14 p.m.:** ANSWER ME!
>
> **Tuesday, May 10, 5:21 p.m.:** I miss you so much it hurts.
>
> **Tuesday, May 10, 7:34 p.m.:** Please, Tim... I can't do this.

I didn't understand what I was seeing or, more importantly, why I was seeing it. How was it possible that I was intercepting Tim's messages? My mind wandered back to the sight of my laptop sitting on top of the coffee table in my living room beside my half-opened luggage. Had Tim changed my settings over to his account? If he had, why would he have done such a thing?

I was so worried about you, his words echoed around in my eardrum. *I didn't have my phone, so I couldn't reach you.*

Had he simply used my laptop as a way to get in touch with me? Was this all just an innocent misunderstanding? I wanted to believe that it was, but something about it just felt off. Like waking up in a bed that I didn't remember falling asleep in. Or feeling the pain of pleasure that I couldn't recall enjoying. I couldn't explain why, but I felt deeply unsettled by it all—and that feeling was only compounded by the sight of the most recent message staring back at me from my screen:

> **Wednesday, May 11, 9:11 p.m.:** Can you please come over this Friday? Please. I want to fix this. I need to fix this.

My heart dropped to my feet. *Fuck*. Friday was tomorrow. Friday was the day I'd be in Fayetteville.

Friday was Cat and Tim's wedding anniversary.

Shit, shit, shit!

Though I felt oddly comforted by the fact that I knew Tim had been too smart to implicate himself in any of the killings on Rachel's radar, I couldn't shake the sinking feeling that seeing Cat might set him off. He had seemed so heartbroken when I last saw him, so frayed and fragile—like a tree branch splintering in the wake of a violent wind, dangerously close to snapping. Would seeing the woman who had broken his trust on a day that should have been a celebration of their love be enough to break him? To make him do something irrational? Unthinkable?

I couldn't sit back and let it happen without at least trying to deliver some kind of warning. I thought about calling her or sending her a text, but decided against it, the memory of our fist fight still fresh in my mind. Maybe if I sent her an email instead, she would believe the message was work-related somehow and have a better chance at actually acknowledging what I had to say. She might not listen to me, but I had to try. My fingers flew over the keyboard as I typed out an email that I hoped might be enough to get her to back off:

Subject: *Stay Away*
Sent: *Thursday, May 12, 6:18 p.m.*
Cat,
I am telling you for the last time, you need to stay away from Tim. I know you're hurt and confused, but one day you'll look back and realize it was for your own good. I'm warning you—leave him alone.
—Elaine

It would probably end up getting deleted on arrival, but at least I had done *something* to intervene. As I watched the message fade from my outbox, praying that she would take the hint, my phone buzzed violently against the coffee table once more, this time signaling a phone call. I snatched it off the table and slid my finger across the screen to answer.

"*What?*" I snapped.

"Don't you take that tone with me, missy," Mama reprimanded me. "When you're staying at my house, you live by my rules. It's suppertime—come eat with your family. Or do homewreckers not care about such trivial things as family?"

I jammed my finger down to end the call, fresh fury building in my abdomen at her latest insult.

Fuck you, Mama.

***

May 13, 2023

The last day of my life was a blur. A hectic, nightmarish blur. It began like every other day at my parents' place: Mama nitpicking every aspect of my appearance, my manners, my life choices; Daddy attempting to come to my rescue even though it only made matters worse. Though I wanted to scrub my computer clean of Tim's account, erase that creep's digital footprint off my laptop, there was no time for me to waste on overcoming my technological incompetence. I was due in Fayetteville for the client consultation by two o' clock, which meant I would have to leave no later than eleven if I wanted to be on time (or as I called it, fashionably early).

Apparently, I was the only one who operated by such a code of professional conduct. I booked the meeting at an Italian eatery downtown and arrived promptly at one-thirty, giving myself plenty of time to get settled. It was an intimate little bistro tucked away within the brick façade of Fayetteville's historic district. The dining area consisted of a dozen or so round tables, each adorned in red linen tablecloths which were accentuated by the warm glow of amber lamplight that dangled from the shaded pendants overhead. Black-and-white photos of various crooners decorated the walls like a shrine to the voices that sang out from invisible speakers somewhere in the restaurant.

I got to know the place well as I sat impatiently at a table set for four closest to the establishment's only window. I could tell the wait staff was beginning to get annoyed, perhaps even taking a bit of pity on me as they assumed (like I did) that I had been stood up. It was two-thirty by the time the bastards finally walked through the door.

A pair of sharply dressed gentlemen in fitted charcoal suits were accompanied by a curvaceous redhead clad in what I deemed to be an entirely inappropriate navy blue dress. I could almost feel Mama's pursed lips and upturned nose creep across my face at the sight of the woman's cleavage bursting through her low-cut neckline, a sparkling pendant dripping down her porcelain skin, daring anyone not to look. The man to her left seemed happy to oblige the challenge, his brown eyes so glued to the jewel between his coworker's breasts that he nearly tripped over a nearby table as the hostess led the group to the table where I was seated.

On her right was a different story entirely. I could tell from the feminine way his hips swayed as he sauntered to the table that the thin, blonde man with the wide, apologetic grin on his face wouldn't have been the least bit interested in the beguiling businesswoman at his side even if she had been fully naked.

"Oh, Ms. *Reid*, honey, I am *so* sorry we are late," he said to me as he made his approach. "You know how it is at the end of the week. The mind just gets set on the weekend and well... I'm afraid I can't give you a better excuse than that."

I fixed a tight smile to my lips, clamping down on the long lecture about wasting other people's precious time that was tickling my vocal cords like an oncoming cold.

"That's alright... Mr. Walker, I'm assuming?" I settled on a more polite response, standing up to accept his outstretched hand and make his formal acquaintance as I guessed his identity. As we had only corresponded via email up until that point, I couldn't be sure if he had been the same person with whom I had scheduled the meeting.

"*Please*, Mr. Walker is my father, sugar. You can just call me Nathaniel," he gripped my hand with surprising vigor considering his flamboyance, gesturing with his free hand to the companions at his side, "This here is Austin, and this little tart is Carolina."

The redhead's hair color seemed to stain her cheeks as she blushed at Nathaniel's introduction, whacking him on the shoulder with an open palm.

"Watch your mouth, Nathaniel, or I'll have to smack that, too," she warned with a smirk before offering me her hand next. "Pleased to meet you, Ms. Reid, and apologies in advance about these two morons."

She rolled her eyes in feigned aggravation as if to say, *Men—am I right?*

"Who're *you* calling a moron?" Austin piped up, his biceps bulging slightly as he folded his arms across his broad chest.

"We're so glad you could join us here today, Ms. Reid," Carolina continued as though she hadn't heard a word that her partner had said. "We were really impressed by the portfolio you sent over to us. Burg Interiors has certainly done some outstanding work over the years."

"Oh, you can call me Elaine," I told her, thanking her for the compliment as I nodded to Austin and the four of us proceeded to take our seats at the table.

"I'd love to learn more about what it is you're envisioning for your project," I prompted, wanting nothing more than to get on with the consultation that was already a half hour behind schedule.

"Oh, we'll have plenty of time for all *that*," Nathaniel waved away the remark with a flick of his wrist before grabbing for the menu situated on top of his place setting. "Food first, then business. Have you ever been here before? The lasagna is absolutely *to die* for!"

"I can't say that I have," my cheeks hurt with strained diplomacy. *First he's late, now he's delaying the inevitable? What gives?*

"Well, now, we'll just have to fix that then won't we, sugar?" his blue eyes twinkled as he winked at me. "Oh, and the tiramisu? *Lord almighty*, you simply *must* have a taste. I will not take no for an answer, no ma'am, I will not."

I forced a laugh at his theatrics, setting my phone down on the table to keep my eye on the time. It was already a quarter to three. If it had been any other week, any other day, I might have enjoyed his friendliness, been more willing to sit and chat for a while. After all, Burg Interiors was renowned for our personal touch. But my mind was preoccupied by other, more pressing matters. Like whether or not Cat had read my email. Or what Tim was doing. Or how I was going to prove Evan's innocence.

Nathaniel's need to steer the conversation away from the details surrounding his property development plans for a local townhouse community continued at an infuriating rate throughout the entire consultation—if you could still call a four-hour lunch-turned-dinner a consultation. I suspected that whatever had caused the group's tardiness in the first place was more related to his insatiable thirst for the spotlight than it was to any daydreams over weekend plans as he had suggested. He was undeniably charming and funny, but I had little patience for his antics, my finger hovering above my phone screen, tapping it periodically to see how much more of my time he had wasted. All I wanted was to head back to Edenton, continue my investigation, check on Cat—if she'd let me. But the longer the consultation stretched on, the more impossible that seemed to achieve.

By the time the so-called meeting was finished, it was nearly two hours into dinner service, a long line protruding out the door as the Friday rush of hungry restaurant-goers swarmed the front entrance. The young, dark-haired waitress who had served us so well didn't seem to mind that we were keeping her from turning over another table, but I sure did. Just as I was about to speak my mind on the subject, Nathaniel beat me to the punch.

"Well, I am *stuffed*," he announced, patting his tight little torso as though it held any substance whatsoever. "And I'm afraid I must apologize to you again, Elaine. As I'm sure you've gathered, I can be a bit... distractible at times."

"Ha! *That's* putting it lightly," Carolina barked. Nathaniel's eyes narrowed on her.

"Bless your itty-bitty little heart, honey," he quipped before turning back to me, "I know we didn't get to talk much about our project, but I do want you to know that we would love to use Burg Interiors for the work. And as a thank-you for being so gracious with your time today, please allow me to pay for our meal. I promise next time to let *you* do all the talking."

"Better bring some duct tape, just to make sure," Austin chimed in.

"Oh, *hush*, you!" Nathaniel laughed. "So, honey," he turned to me again, "can we count on y'all to help us out, then?"

I grinned and shook his hand, eager both to close the deal and to get the fuck out of the restaurant. With his promise to settle the check and my heart set on making it out to my car, I began to collect my things and excuse myself from the table, assuring each of them that I would reach back out to schedule a follow-up once I got back home. Before I could walk away from the table, Nathaniel's voice sang out.

"Oh, Elaine?" my heart dropped. *What the fuck did he want now?* I turned around to see him holding the cellphone that I had somehow left behind on the table. "Wouldn't want to forget this now, would we?"

"Oh you are a *lifesaver*," I said emphatically. "What an idiot I am. Thank you!"

"It's nothing, honey," he assured me. "Those things are easy to track anyway. I'm sure you would have found it on your own eventually."

I paused, my curiosity piqued.

"How do you mean?"

"Oh, it's *easy*, sugar!" he smiled. "As long as you're logged into your account, you can just use the Find My app on your computer to find your phone."

All the blood in my body seemed to evaporate at once.

"Thank you, Nathaniel," I said again. "You have no idea how much you've helped me just now."

He tilted his head in my direction, eyebrows raised as if he were seeing me for the first time.

"Ain't no thing, honey," he shrugged. "Glad I could help."

More than you'll ever know, I thought as I whipped around and headed back out through the throng of customers to climb inside my car and race back to Edenton as fast as I could. I still hadn't switched the account settings on my laptop back to my own—I didn't know how. But maybe that was a good thing. If all I needed to do was open up this "Find My" app or whatever the hell Nathaniel had called it, then maybe I could use it to find Tim's missing phone. To prove once and for all where he had been.

It was almost ten-fifteen by the time I had made it home, the Friday night traffic from the city adding an unnecessary half hour more to my trip. I skipped the pleasantries with Mama and Daddy, choosing to go around back to the guest cottage rather than through the main house. I would suffer the consequences from Mama later for that egregious display of terrible manners. There were more important things at hand than satisfying her constant need for propriety.

As soon as I made it into the guest house, I grabbed my laptop off the coffee table. I had to do a quick Google search to even know where to find the damned application that Nathaniel had mentioned.

When this is all over, I told myself, *you're taking some computer classes.*

Opening up Finder, I navigated to my Applications folder and scrolled until I found the words "Find My" next to a little green icon that looked like a radar screen. I held my breath as I waited for the application to load, praying this would be the moment I had been waiting for all week. On startup, the application prompted me to enable notifications to "find my friends and lost items," which I ignored, as eager as I had been at lunch to just get to the point already. There was a thin, dark-green menu on the left which was labeled "Devices," beneath which was a little picture of a smartphone that was simply named "iPhone." Under the word "iPhone," I could see a location listed: Charlotte, NC.

I clicked on it instinctively, and as I did, the map on the right side of the screen zoomed in on the device's location, showing me precisely where the phone would be found—just like Nathaniel had said. Disappointment swirled in my gut. There on the screen, the phone appeared at first glance to be located at the Charlotte Hilton.

But that can't be, I thought. He had searched the hotel room before we left and claimed to have gone down to the concierge to find it to no avail. It had to be somewhere else. I tilted my head onto the back of the sofa, letting out a heavy sigh. I thought for sure that his phone would be at a Holiday Inn. It's not like he would have had to go very far to get there. There was a Holiday Inn right across the parking lot from the Hilton where we had stayed.

Right across the parking lot!

I snapped my head back to the screen and scrolled over to the plus sign at the bottom right-hand corner of the map, zooming in as far as the application would permit to see if my epiphany would be proven correct.

It was.

As I zeroed in on the cellphone, I could see that Tim's phone hadn't been at the Hilton at all, but was hovering somewhere in the depths of the Holiday Inn—right across the parking lot.

I raced around the room, stuffing receipts into a canvas bag that I had lying around, snatching up my cellphone and my car keys as I headed back out the door to make my way to Williamsburg. Again, I chose to evade my parents. There was no time to explain the gravity of what I had just confirmed. I needed to get to the office so I could grab Rachel's number from my desk. She had given me her card the day that she had initially stopped me in the parking lot.

"Here's my number," she had said to me. "Call anytime."

Of course, I dumped the thing in my desk drawer like an idiot and had zero intention of calling her. At least I knew that it would still be there for me. Even so, I wished I hadn't added an unnecessary stop between me and Cat. I wanted to get to her, to tell her everything that I knew, to apologize for how wrong I had been about everything over the past few months. She had to listen to me now that I had all the proof in my hands—didn't she?

It was ten forty-five by the time I got to the office, an eerie quiet settled over the place in the absence of my business partners. Rachel's number was sitting in the long, thin drawer along the top of my desk, just where I had left it. I reached for my cellphone and began to punch in the number on my way back to the car, my fingers sweaty and trembling as they struggled to enter each digit. My heart thumped around in my chest like an angry rabbit as I walked across the parking lot, listening to the phone ring without answer in my ear, fumbling with my car keys, which I dropped on the pavement in a brilliant display of unwanted clumsiness. *Fuck me.*

"You've reached Detective McGowen," I heard her answering machine inform me. "I'm not available to take your call right now, but leave a message and I'll get back to you as soon as I can."

Shit, shit, shit!

I plucked my keys off the ground and unlocked the car.

"Detective McGowen, it's Elaine," I said, climbing into the driver's seat as I rushed to get out the words. "I need to see you right away," I brought my Audi to life, not even realizing that doing so had taken over my phone speaker as the car's Bluetooth kicked in. *Fucking technology.* "I think there's something really wrong with Tim—not Evan—and I have the proof. Meet me at Sally's Diner tomorrow at nine."

I didn't even know if she was still in town, didn't know if she'd even hear my message in time to meet me there. But none of that mattered anyway.

Fifteen minutes later, I was dead.

PART 2
CATHERYN

CHAPTER 11

May 24, 2023

"I'm Detective Rachel McGowen, and I think I know who really killed your friend," the words almost didn't seem real to me, like I had imagined the way they might sound and mistaken my daydream for reality. A heavy silence filled the air as she waited for me to say something in response, her hazel eyes unblinking, thin hands still folded on top of her small stack of dossiers.

"Mrs. Clark?" she prompted when I remained quiet.

"It's Cat," I corrected her.

"Cat, do you understand what I just—"

"Who?" I interrupted, my mind reeling. "Was it Evan? Did you talk to him?"

The detective cast a sideways glance at Owen, who hadn't spoken a word since the two had arrived at the county jail. He seemed to squirm in the seat across from me, giving an almost imperceptible shake of his head in Rachel's direction. She refocused her attention back to me, unfolding her hands and laying them flat against the metal table that separated us.

"We'll get to that in a moment," she decided. "I have a few questions to ask you first if you don't mind."

I leaned back in my own chair, resting my restrained hands in my lap. My leg jiggled with impatience, the sound of chains tinkling through the concrete room as I bounced my knee against the handcuffs at my wrists. I watched as Rachel opened one of the manilla folders on the table and extracted a sheet of paper from within. She slid it across the surface, tapping it with her index finger.

"Can you take a look at this and let me know if anything jumps out at you?"

I leaned forward in my seat to get a better view of the paper. It was glossy, the fluorescent bulbs overhead refracting against its surface, causing a slight glare to form across the page. From what I could tell, it looked as though it were a page pulled from a yearbook, except instead of different student photos, there was a single face smiling back at me twenty-five times in a row. She looked young—younger than she had been when I first met her—with full lips stretched around a set of pearly white teeth, blue eyes shimmering against the camera flash, blonde hair tucked behind one ear. I didn't need to look at her for very long for the blood in my veins to go numb. No one who had gone to Green Valley University at the time could ever forget that face.

"This is Mia Davis," I said, sliding the paper back across the table. Rachel stopped me in my tracks, pushing the page back in my direction.

"Yes," she confirmed, her voice sounding a little strained. "But I need you to look a bit closer. Specifically at the names. Are there any names on this page that catch your eye?"

I raised an eyebrow in confusion, not at all understanding what it was that I was meant to see. The sound of metal scraping against metal grated against my nerves as I traced my finger across the sheet of paper, reading each name in order: Jordan Carmichael, Alison Conley, Brittany Cooper, Chase Crenshaw, Morgan Dabney, Leslie Dalton, Matthew Daniels, Mia Davis, Michael Davies, etcetera, etcetera. Though I knew it wasn't the answer Rachel wanted from me, the only name I recognized out of the list that lay before me was Mia Davis's. I slid the paper back across the table and told her so. She gave a slow nod in return, accepting the yearbook page and stuffing it back inside the folder from where she had first removed it.

Before closing the file, she grabbed another sheet of paper, tilting it slightly in Owen's direction before placing it in front of me. Owen's face turned pale, his dark eyes lingering on the paper as it slid across the table. His mouth fell open as though he wanted to say something, but Rachel never gave him the chance.

"Tell me if there's anything different about this page," she instructed. I was starting to get a bit annoyed with the dramatic buildup. *If you know who killed Elaine, why won't you just fucking say it instead of playing these stupid mind games?* I bit my tongue and decided to just play along, casting my gaze down at the new page before me.

This paper was different than the one she had presented before. Rather than a glossy finish, it had a matte, gritty texture, with black-and-white photos spread across it instead of the colored photographs of Mia that I had just seen. There was a dark, black mark lining the left-hand side of the paper, telling me this was not the original document but rather a scanned copy. Aside from the color, there was one other glaring difference between the two pages.

"Mia's face is only on here once?" I guessed, hoping I had passed Rachel's stupid test. She sighed.

"Look closer," she said. "Who else do you see? Anyone you recognize?"

I looked down at the first few names on the page: Jordan Carmichael, Alison Conley, Brittany Cooper...

"I already told you, I don't fucking know these people," I snapped.

"Just humor me, okay?" she nodded with her chin at the page on the table. "Do you recognize anyone—*aside* from Mia?"

I rolled my eyes and turned my attention back to the paper, skimming each row with all the confidence in the world that I would not see a single face that I recognized. But as I moved past Mia's portrait in the center of the page, my heart stopped beating.

It was a little hard to tell at first with the photo being black-and-white, but the longer I stared into the picture, the more difficult it became to deny what I was seeing. To the right of Mia's photograph was the face of a young man, his lips unsmiling, long, light-colored hair in a shaggy mess across his face. I almost didn't recognize him at all, but it was the eyes that confirmed it, the grayscale imagery accentuating the icy stare that I had fallen in love with at the Sigma Nu house all those years ago. There was no mistaking it. It was Tim.

But it wasn't Tim. It couldn't be—not if the name beneath the photograph was correct. *Michael Davies*. Whoever the hell that was. And even if it had been a misprint, even if it was Tim, after all, what did it matter anyway? What did it have to do with—?

I think I know who really killed your friend, Rachel's earlier words seemed to harden in my stomach, arresting my thoughts at once. A cold sweat began to creep down my neck, settling in the base of my spine as I steeled myself to speak.

"This is Tim's face," I whispered, pointing to the unfriendly portrait staring back at me, "but that's not his name. I... I don't understand what this is. I don't know why you're showing me this."

Yes, you do, a sinister voice inside my mind caressed my ear. *You know exactly why she's showing you this.*

Rachel reached across the table, mercifully removing the paper out from beneath my fingertips. She placed it back inside her folder on top of the yearbook page she had shown me, then dragged her metal chair across the linoleum floor, reaching under the table for something.

"Detective? I think that maybe—"

"Look, Mr. Strong, I appreciate your concern, but please. Let me do my job," Rachel interjected, giving Owen a sharp look as she lifted a plastic bag with a big, red label marked "EVIDENCE" and a box of rubber gloves onto the table. She grabbed a pair of gloves from the box before sliding it across to me. "You'll need to put these on for this next part."

I did as I was told, awkwardly pulling the blue rubber over my fingers, the handcuffs making what should have been a simple process clumsy and inelegant. Once my hands were covered, I lifted my gaze in time to see Rachel extract the contents of the evidence bag. My breath caught in my throat as my eyes landed on the bloodstained tote bag in the center of the table, crumpled papers peeking out of the opening, instantly transporting me back to that night in my kitchen.

"That's Elaine's bag," I breathed. "She had it with her the night I... the night she was..."

I let the meaning of my unspoken words hang in the air rather than give them a name. Rachel smoothed a stray piece of auburn hair behind her ear and proceeded to remove the papers from Elaine's tote bag.

"Do you know what these are, Cat?" she laid the papers out side by side, some of them no longer legible through the deep, brown bloodstains that had soaked into the surface. I counted seven total, the meaning of their existence making me nauseous with anger.

"They're hotel receipts," I croaked around the lump in my throat. "Elaine and Tim were having an affair."

"Why do you say that?" Rachel prodded. I closed my eyes, images of Tim's visit to the rehab center burning in my retinas, forcing me to remember.

"He told me everything," I shuddered, the memory of Tim's wedding ring missing from his finger like a black hole sucking the life right out of me.

"What exactly did he tell you?" my heart lurched at Rachel's words. I didn't want to think about that day. I couldn't think about that day. "Cat? This is important. I need to know what—"

"He told me he was fucking her, okay?" I shouted, tears streaming freely down my cheeks.

"And by 'her,' you mean...?"

"Elaine," I spat the name out like snake venom.

"Did he say how long the affair was going on?" I shook my head in response. It wasn't something that I allowed myself to think about since learning the truth of what had happened between them. There were black stains of rage in my mind where recollections should have been. All I remembered from the day Tim had come to confess his sins to me at the rehab center was the stabbing sensation that his admission had ripped through my chest, and the tight grip of the nurses' hands around my wrists as they dragged my screaming, thrashing body back to my room.

"I don't know how long," I whispered. "But I think it might have been a long time."

"How long have you and Tim been married, Cat?" my veins turned to ice at the question.

"Ten years," I answered. "May 13th was our anniversary."

"I see," Rachel nodded, glancing down at the papers in front of her until she found the one she wanted and plucked it off of the table, pinching it between her rubberized fingertips. "That would have made your wedding day May 13, 2013, then, right?"

"Yes," my voice was tight, broken. I tried not to think about how happy I had been, the smell of the bluebells in my bouquet, the feeling of Tim's hand holding my own at the altar, sliding a golden band down my ring finger, vowing to love me forever. *For better or for worse.*

"And you were married in Green Valley, correct?" I raised an eyebrow in response.

"How did you—?"

"I want you to take a look at this receipt for me," Rachel interrupted before I could finish, placing the paper down in front of me and pointing to the top right-hand corner. "Read me what it says there."

I squinted at the receipt on the table, Elaine's blood making it difficult to make out what was printed in the place that Rachel had indicated. But once my eyes adjusted, I could feel the room begin to spin.

"Green Valley Holiday Inn," I read aloud, "May 12, 2013."

I looked up at Rachel, her eyes boring into mine.

"Let me ask you something, Cat: Do you believe your husband was having an affair with Elaine the night before you got married?" I could feel the vein in my jugular lunging out from my neck, threatening to burst through my skin, stain the room red with my blood. The day before our wedding was the same day that Tim had asked me to marry him. Elaine had helped us plan the entire thing in less than twenty-four hours, her event planning prowess put to the test as she coordinated every last detail right down to Tim's wedding ring.

Tonight, we'll all meet up in the hotel lobby by eight, then go our separate ways for the bachelor and bachelorette parties, I could still hear her voice excitedly plotting out every step we'd take leading up to the altar. She and I had spent that entire night together, drinking and chatting well into the early morning hours, giddy with the rush of matrimony on the horizon. There was no way that she had slept with Tim that night. I knew it for a fact.

"No," I finally answered. "Elaine was with me that night. She... he wasn't... they couldn't have. It wasn't possible."

"I want you to look back at the receipt," Rachel commanded. "Tell me who it's addressed to."

I looked down at the paper as I was told, my eyes rapidly trying to locate the place where the recipient's name was listed. Above the explanation of charges was a brief message that had somehow been unscathed by bloodshed:

> *Dear Mr. Michael Davies,*
> *We hope you enjoyed your stay at the Holiday Inn.*
> *Please find a summary of your expenses outlined below*
> *for your convenience.*

A ringing noise echoed around in my ear, mouth and nose smacking of metal as though someone had poured iodine into my sinuses.

"I don't understand," I fumbled for the right words. "Who is this person? Why was this name under Tim's photo?"

Rachel straightened in her chair, her eyes like steel as they pierced through me—cold, unflinching.

"I want you to listen very carefully to what I'm about to say to you," she began. "I don't believe your husband is who he claims to be."

I gripped the edge of the table, knuckles turning white as I held on for dear life.

"What do you mean?" the words seemed to form without my knowledge, expelling from my body like vapor. It was impossible to pluck them out of the air. Impossible not to hear Rachel's response.

"Tim Clark is not your husband's real name," she said. "His name is Michael Davies."

"What the hell are you talking about?" I shot back. "Why would he change his name?"

"I'm not exactly sure," Rachel admitted, "but I think it has something to do with these."

She pointed to the receipts that were still scattered across the table before continuing.

"These receipts you're looking at? They aren't from an affair that he's been having."

Her statement dangled in front of me, a carrot spinning on the end of a stick. Like the jackass I am, I chanced a bite.

"What are they then?" I ventured.

"Trophies," Rachel replied, "for all the victims he's taken over the years."

Victims? Was she honestly suggesting that Tim was some sort of deranged serial killer? There was no way I could believe that. Despite everything that he had put me through with the affair, I still remembered the man he had been before we were torn apart. The man I had seen at the frat party, quiet and reserved by the bar. The man I had rescued from certain death, the madness in his mind urging him to take his own life. The man I had fallen in love with, the scars of his past embedding themselves in my skin. He was tender, wholesome, caring, albeit a bit troubled. But that didn't make him a monster.

"I don't believe you," I said. "Tim would never—"

"Michael," Rachel corrected me.

"I'm not fucking calling him that!" I snapped. "I don't give a fuck what you think you know. *Tim* is not a killer."

I sat back in my chair, tears stinging my eyes as I avoided Rachel's stare, choosing to count the cracks in the concrete wall rather than face her scrutiny. She gathered up the bloodstained receipts from the table and placed them back inside Elaine's tote bag, resealing everything back inside the evidence bag before removing the rubber gloves from her hands. When she was finished, she placed the contents back at her feet and reached for one of her manilla folders.

"Do you like poetry, Cat?" the question disarmed me, forcing me to look in the detective's direction.

"What the fuck are you—?"

"Do you know what an acrostic is?" Rachel said, pulling a sheet of paper out of her folder. She didn't wait for my response before continuing, "It's a kind of poem where the first letter from every line combines to form a word or phrase. You ever do one of those when you were a kid?"

"I don't… know what the hell you're talking about," I snarled.

"That's okay," she said. "You'll understand soon enough. I want you to take a look at this and tell me what you see."

I was getting very tired of this exercise. It gave me the odd sensation of being herded, trapped into a pen, guided to my own demise. Before I could protest, she placed two sheets of paper down in front of me. The paper to my left looked like another scanned document, except whatever had been scanned had been isolated so that only a single, handwritten sentence fragment showed. All that it said was, "Maybe in another life," but the words weren't what made my stomach churn with dread. It was the fact that they had been written in Tim's handwriting. I would recognize that chaotic pen stroke anywhere—it had appeared on every birthday card, every shopping list, every love note left on my nightstand since the time we had first started seeing one another.

I peeled my eyes away from the words to read the paper to my right. At first glance, it almost looked like some sort of to-do list, a brief sentence occupying each individual line. But as I read closer, I could tell that it wasn't a list at all, but rather some sort of stream-of-consciousness ramblings with the first letter of each line bolded. It read:

> **M**aybe in another life, things could have been different.
> **I** could have made you love me.
> **C**ould have made you see that we belong together.
> **H**ow many years I've wasted, hanging on the promise that I was all you needed.
> **A**nd in the end, it was all lies.
> **E**very last word of it.
> **L**ies, lies, lies.
>
> **Do**n't pretend like you didn't see this coming.
> **A**fter all, you promised you would always be mine.
> **V**ery soon, it'll all be over, and I'll finally be at peace.
> **I**'ll finally have you—one way or another.
> **E**nding it was not an easy decision, but it's too late now.
> **S**orry I couldn't find another way.

"I typed that out myself to make it a little easier for you," Rachel commented when I looked up from the page. Her eyes were glossy, as though she were fighting to hold back tears. "It took me a long time to realize what it said. Kind of stupid, actually. Do you know what it says?"

I screwed my brows together in frustration, rolling my eyes as I tilted my head back down and began to read, "Maybe in another life—"

"No, not that," she stopped me before I could continue. "It's an acrostic, remember? You have to use the first letter from each line to see what it means. Look at the bolded letters. What does it say?"

I glanced back down at the paper, still fuming and irritated and wishing that Rachel would fuck off and leave me alone to rot in my cell in peace. But as I pieced together the puzzle before me, a small seed of panic began to force its way through my intestines. It went in perfect order, unmistakable to anyone who saw it: M, I, C, H, A...

"It spells Michael Davies," I muttered. Suddenly, a shock of lightning bolted down my back as I realized the significance. It wasn't just the fact that this poem spelled out what Rachel believed to be Tim's true identity. It was the sinking realization that the first line of the poem and the words in my husband's handwriting were exactly the same. I clung hopelessly to my denial, a child unwilling to admit that she could be wrong. "Who cares?" I huffed, "What does a stupid poem prove anyway?"

"Because that's not a poem, Cat," Rachel said softly, her voice almost inaudible. "That's Mia Davis's suicide note. And that handwriting sample? It came from a note found at the site of a recent homicide."

The ringing in my ears grew louder, deafening. Black patches formed at the edge of my vision, the feeling of dizziness so profound, I thought that I might sway out of my seat. I gripped the table tighter, my palms sweating, slipping along the slick, metal surface.

What the fuck is going on?

"Cat?" I could hear Owen's voice, his figure nothing more than a shadow in my peripheral as he leaned in my direction. "Cat, are you okay?"

I was breathing heavy, nostrils flaring out, hungry for oxygen that seemed in painfully short supply. Stomach acid burned in my throat, gurgling to the surface. I started to gag, clutching clammy hands over my mouth, eyes darting around the empty room, desperate to find a trashcan. Just as I was certain that I was going to spew bile all over the table, I felt a gentle hand press against my curls, guiding my head into a plastic bin.

"Easy," Rachel rubbed the space between my shoulder blades as I retched into the receptacle that I had failed to locate. I heard Owen's chair screech across the linoleum as he stood up from the table.

"I'll ask them to bring some water," he mumbled before knocking on the door to get the guard's attention. Within a few moments, Owen returned to the table with a bottled water and a box of tissues, placing each at my side before sitting sheepishly in his chair, running a nervous hand through his salt-and-pepper hair. I heaved a few more times before dabbing my face clean with a tissue and taking a few sips of water. When she was satisfied that I had regained my composure, Rachel returned to the seat across from me, collecting the papers that were still on the table back into her folder. *Thank God.*

"I know this can't be easy for you," she said slowly. "But I need your full cooperation so we can stop more innocent women from getting hurt."

"I don't understand," I whispered. "This doesn't make any sense. Tim wouldn't..."

I trailed off, a terrible awareness washing over me. It didn't matter what I thought Tim would or wouldn't do. I didn't know him. Nobody did. He wasn't real.

But Michael Davies was.

"Cat, I know I'm asking a lot of you here today," Rachel spoke with the careful gentleness of a lion tamer approaching a spiraling beast, "but I need to ask you some questions, and I need you to be completely honest with me, okay?"

I snapped my head in her direction.

"What the fuck could I possibly tell you?" my eyes welled with tears, pressure building in my throat, a kettle bubbling on a stovetop, ready to scream. "I didn't even know his name! I don't know anything! I can't remember anything! I CAN'T FUCKING REMEMBER ANY—"

A sensation like being submerged in ice water stopped me mid-scream. I could feel my body still seated in the metal chair, the pain in my wrists from the handcuffs digging into my skin. But I could no longer see the world around me. It was as if a veil had been dropped down around me, blocking out every noise, every image of the physical world that I could still feel was there. I was standing in my kitchen, Elaine's hand tight around my wrist, her eyes frantic with fear.

"Just stay away from Tim!" the sound of her screams bounced around the room. "He's a monster, Cat. He's done horrible, horrible things, and he's going to do it again."

I pushed her off of me, her nails ripping through my flesh as she resisted. She staggered back against the counter, the yellow glow of streetlights trickling in through the window behind her golden hair. I reached for the butcher's block, grabbing for the biggest knife I could find, ready to cut her open. As I turned to face Elaine, I could feel a pair of hands reach out from the shadows, wrapping themselves around my nose and throat. The smell of cleaning supplies or some kind of powerful chemical overpowered my senses, making me go weak at the knees. But there was something else, too. Something familiar.

Like spiced pine and worn leather.

"I remember," I gasped, the memory instantly dissolving from my vision, the buzz of the fluorescent lights above replacing the sound of Elaine's blood-curdling screams. "He was there. He did something to me. He... he killed Elaine."

"What do you remember?" Rachel prompted, clicking a pen that seemed to materialize in her hand. "What did he do to you?"

"I... I don't know exactly," I confessed. "He put something over my face. Like, a rag or something. It smelled awful—like that stuff they use at nail salons, but worse. But I know it was him. I could... I could smell his aftershave, too."

My voice cracked as I let the tears run rivers down my cheeks. I didn't even bother to sop up the mess with the tissues in front of me. I wanted to drown. I wanted to go numb. He had drugged me. He had brutalized my best friend in front of my unconscious body. He had framed me. My own husband had framed me.

"I'll talk to the evidence department," Rachel's voice broke through the darkness clouding my mind. "Maybe there's something there that got overlooked. One way or another, we'll find out what happened to you, Cat. I promise. But I need you to be brave right now, okay? I need you to answer some questions about your hus—about Michael."

I shuddered, the sound of the stranger's name haunting, unnerving.

"What do you want to know?" I croaked.

"For starters, where did you first meet?" Rachel began.

"It was at a frat party in college," the words were hollow, absent of the fondness they once possessed whenever I thought about that night.

"At Green Valley University?" the detective confirmed. I nodded and she continued, "Did he ever mention anything about Mia Davis? About the fact that they went to high school together?"

"No," my voice quivered. "He didn't talk much about his past. All he told me was that he was forced to live at his grandfather's ranch in Red Rock when he was young. He said he was abused there. He had all these... scars on his body."

Goosebumps raised on my arms as I remembered the sight of Ti—the sight of *Michael's* puckered, mangled flesh on his back.

You don't have to do that, he had said to me as I lay naked in the bed beside him, caressing his exposed scars. *Pretend I'm not a monster.*

"Where were they?" Rachel ripped me from the memory. "The scars, I mean?"

"All over his back," I answered. "He had them on his wrists, though, too. He told me he did something... I thought he meant to himself. I thought he was in pain. Oh God, I'm such an idiot."

"You're not an idiot," Rachel reached across the table, pushing the tissue box closer to the edge. "People like Michael are good at hiding in plain sight. None of this is your fault, you understand me?"

I nodded feebly, accepting a tissue and blowing my nose before the detective continued with her questions.

"Did he ever show signs of odd behavior?" she asked. "Mood swings? Unexplained absences? Anything like that?"

I froze, the Greene Street Bridge flickering like a hologram in my field of vision.

"Yes," I whispered. "The day after Mia... the next day, he was at that same bridge, leaning over the railing like he was going to jump off. I saved him that day. He's been in therapy ever since."

"Do you have the name of his doctor?" she pressed.

"Dr. Browning, I think," I said. "At least, that's who it was back then. I don't know if it's changed. We... we didn't really talk much about that stuff."

I hung my head in shame at the admission. I wondered how many lies of omission I could have caught if I hadn't been so busy drowning myself in rivers of whiskey.

"Do you know if he was on any medication?" Rachel went on.

"Yeah, actually, he was," I confirmed. "These little blue things I saw him take sometimes. I'm not sure what they were, though."

Rachel nodded her head as if she already knew the exact medication to which I was referring. I didn't push the subject. I didn't want to know what had made her look so confident on the matter.

"I've got one last question for you and then I'll leave you alone," she lifted her gaze from her notes and looked me in the eye, "Do you have any ideas about where he might be now? Any family he might have had that'd be willing to take him in? Anything at all?"

"Is he... missing?" for some reason the concept caught me off guard. Of course he had to be missing. Rachel would have arrested him already if he had been nearby. She wouldn't need to talk to me about it.

"Yes," the detective voiced the answer I already knew she would give. "Can you think of anywhere that he might be? A mom? A dad? A sibling's house maybe?"

"All I know about Tim... about Michael's family is that his mom died years ago, his grandfather abused him, and he had a half-brother that he never talked to—all in Red Rock," I answered. "I'm sorry, but that's really all I know."

Rachel nodded, collected her notes and her folders into a neat pile, and began to stand up from the table.

"Thank you for your time here today, Cat," she walked around the table and patted me on the shoulder. "You've been a big help."

My heart sank to my stomach.

"You're *leaving?*" I half-yelled. "What about me? I need to get out of here! I need to—"

"I'm sorry, but it doesn't work that way, Cat," Rachel said solemnly. "All the evidence we have in Elaine's case still points to you. Until I'm able to track this fucker down and prove that he's behind this, I'm afraid you'll have to stay here."

The heat rose to my cheeks, burning behind my eyes until the tears flooded my vision.

"Please... please don't leave me here," I begged.

"I'm sorry," Rachel said. "There's nothing I can do."

A crippling loneliness suffocated me where I sat, sending pinpricks of hysteria deep inside my gut. My best friend was dead. My husband had murdered her. And now I was stuck in this hellhole, serving time for a crime I didn't commit, with nothing and no one left in the world. Except—

"Evan," I breathed. Since I had been arrested, I had spent all my time convincing myself that he had been somehow responsible for all this mess. That he had been the one that framed me. I had told him as much during his visit just three days earlier.

I know what you've done, I had said to him. *I know what you're capable of doing.*

My heart twisted at the sound of my own words echoing around in my skull. I had been so vile, so full of hate, so completely wrong about everything. And because of that, I had pushed away the only person in the world who might have given a damn about me.

"Rachel, you have to help me," I pleaded. "Evan was here the other day and I... I said such horrible things to him. Please, I need you to talk to him for me. Tell him I'm sorry. Tell him... tell him I need him. I need to see him again."

She hesitated a moment, contemplating whether or not to agree to my request.

"Okay," she decided. "But if he comes here, you can't discuss what we talked about today. This is an open investigation. I can't have anyone compromising that—not at this stage."

"I won't," I promised. "Please just... just let me see him again."

CHAPTER 12

May 28, 2023

When I was a kid, I remember knowing everyone's phone number by heart. Granted, there weren't very many that I needed to memorize—just my home phone, my parents' work numbers, and the number to Elaine's house. If I was feeling sick at the nurse's office, I didn't have to guess which ten-digit sequence to dial before finding a ride home to safety. When I bounded up the porch steps to my childhood home at the end of the school day, homework abandoned on the kitchen island as I rushed through the back door to pluck the corded phone from its cradle, I didn't hesitate over a single button, Elaine's number like a tattoo printed on my fingertips. But as soon as cellphones entered the picture, all that changed.

There was only one other phone number that I had bothered to memorize since technology had made such practices irrelevant, its imprint on my brain as sickening to me as the knowledge of who it belonged to. But I had no desire to speak to Tim or Michael or whatever the fuck that monster wanted to call himself. The only person I wanted to talk to, the person I needed more than anyone else in the world, was nothing but a contact in my cellphone, which was likely sitting somewhere in the evidence department, as dead and unreachable as his ex-wife.

Maybe that's what made the days following Rachel's visit so insufferable—the complete uncertainty, the unknowing, the taunting glare of payphones lining the walls of the common area in the county jail, mocking the blank spot in my mind where Evan's number should have been.

She said that she would talk to him for you, I reminded myself each day. *You can trust her. You have to trust her.*

But when Saturday arrived and visiting hours came and went, I began to lose hope that I would ever have the chance to rectify the damage I had caused. Even if Rachel had kept her word and passed along my message, what difference would it make? It wasn't just the memory of what I had said to him during his visit that made me question whether Evan would ever grace me with his presence again. It was everything that had happened between us before Elaine wound up stabbed to death in my kitchen.

When I needed a shoulder to cry on after getting released from rehab, no husband at home to return to, Evan was there to pick up the pieces. And what did I do? I slept with him, then proceeded to pretend like the whole thing had been some terrible mistake, vowing to never do it again. Then when I broke that promise repeatedly and found myself back in his bed, I got annoyed with him for falling in love with me, too hung up on a man who I thought I knew, who had done everything in his power to hurt me, to give a proper shit about the one who actually cared for me. I rejected him, slammed my door on him, cursed him out on my front lawn. And as if that weren't enough, I accused him of the worst thing imaginable, my only supporting evidence being the knowledge of a terrible secret that he had trusted me enough to keep.

Your secret's safe with me, I had told him that night, drying his tears and absorbing his pain only to throw it back in his face not even a month later. He had been nothing but honest with me, revealing the demons of his past with only good intentions to guide him, and I betrayed him in the most deliberate and disgusting way possible. If he never wanted to see me again, I couldn't blame him. I could only suffer the consequences, knowing there was no one but myself to thank for the gaping void his absence left behind.

By the time Sunday afternoon arrived, I had all but given up on the idea of seeing Evan in person. So, I settled on writing him a letter instead, planning on passing it on to Owen or Rachel when I next saw either of them (the jury was still out on when that might be). Nothing I wrote seemed adequate enough to express how truly sorry I was, the apologetic ramblings sounding cheap and inauthentic rather than heartfelt and genuine. I was busy scribbling out the latest paragraph that I had written from the confines of my concrete prison when I heard the guard enter the cellblock.

"You've got a visitor," she barked, sticking her key in the iron and sliding the bars back to enter the cell I shared with Luisa.

"You talkin' to me or the *gringa?*" my cellmate jutted her chin in my direction as she tossed out the Spanish insult that she thought I was too ignorant to understand. And I was. Despite all the Latin landscapers whom my parents had hired to tend to their acreage, I never did learn to speak their language. I had no idea what it meant, only that it gave me the strange sensation that I was being disrespected.

"Clark," the guard clarified, my flesh wriggling off of my body in response to my married name.

"It's Cat," I corrected her, not even realizing the significance of why my name was being mentioned in the first place.

"Whatever the fuck your name is, let's go," the officer snarled. "Visitation's starting soon."

My heart floated from my chest, lifting me from my cot in an instant. Rachel had kept her word. *Evan was here!*

As quickly as my spirits soared, they came crashing down to the ground, exploding in a thousand tiny pieces at my feet. *Evan was here.* And if our last conversation had been any indication of what would be waiting for me in the visitor's center, I knew it wouldn't be good. But I had to see him, no matter how small or scared it made me feel to do so. I needed to apologize. I had to make this right.

The officer slipped her cuffs around my wrists and the two of us headed upstairs, through the maze of hallways until we arrived at the visitor's center. There were already several other prisoners seated at their cubicles situated along the length of countertop that separated the cinderblock wall from the plexiglass window which peered into the visitors' side of the room. I was placed into a black, plastic chair near the front of the line that had a perfect view of the visitors' door so I'd be the first to see who came through.

My heart felt like a fist beating against the inside of my ribcage as I waited for the flood of visitors to make their way inside. I didn't have to suffer the suspense for very long—as soon as the door buzzed, permitting the visitors to enter their side of the room, my gaze locked on a pair of pale green eyes that I was certain I'd never see again.

I snatched up the phone in my cubicle before Evan had the chance to settle in his seat. Rather than do the same, he leaned back in his chair, his arms folded tight across his chest as he looked straight through me, not an ounce of kindness visible in his stare. I deserved that.

It seemed like hours passed beneath his icy gaze, my body too frozen with a combination of fear and regret to do anything other than sit in awkward silence with my ear pressed against a dead telephone line. He looked even more hollow and haunted than the last time I had seen him, with bloodshot eyes and an unruly, black beard dulling the edges of his angular features, making him appear wraithlike, diminished. For a moment, I thought that the entire visit might pass by without a single word uttered between the two of us, but Evan unraveled himself and reached for the phone, proving me wrong in the process.

"Mind telling me why the fucking cops are up my ass?" there was a slight tremble in his voice as he struggled to contain his rage. I swallowed around the tightness in my throat before answering.

"Evan, I'm sorry. I can—"

"Fuck your apology!" he hissed. His eyes were glassy, pupils like little black pinpricks drowning in a sea of green. I couldn't tell if it was anger or alcohol that had made them appear so fragile, as if they might spill out from their sockets and onto the countertop. "They think I had something to do with this now. It's Mia Davis all over again. I can't believe you would do this to me."

My heart sank. *What does he mean they think he has something to do with it?* All I had told Rachel was to pass on my message of apology. Why would that have led Evan to believe that he was a suspect in Elaine's murder case?

"I don't understand," I proceeded with caution. "What did Detective McGowen say to you?"

"Like you don't fucking know," he spat. "You're the one who sent her there to harass me."

He had me there, but he was wrong about the reason why.

"Evan, I didn't send her there to *harass* you," I searched his eyes, imploring him to believe me. "All I wanted was for her to convince you to come see me again, so I could... so I could apologize. For everything."

He barked a bitter laugh in response.

"You're so full of shit, you know that?" he sneered. "I've been through this before. I know when cops are just trying to build a motive, make their stupid fucking connections like they mean anything. *Oh, Evan,*" he pantomimed with open disdain, "*when did you first suspect an affair between Elaine and Tim? Why were you at Cat's house the night Elaine was killed? Have you ever heard the name Michael Davies before?*"

My heart slammed against my sternum at the sound of Michael's name, but not because of what Rachel's last visit had shown me. It was the way in which Evan had said it, as though he *had* heard the name before and was already convinced it held no significance.

"Have you?" I whispered.

"Have I what?" Evan snapped.

"Heard that name before?"

"You're kidding, right?" he forced an ironic laugh. "I don't know what game you're trying to play bringing that shit up or what it even has to do with Elaine, but I'm getting really tired of people—"

"Bringing what up?" I stopped him before he could finish his tirade. "What does that name mean to you?"

"Oh please," he waved a dismissive hand. "Don't insult my intelligence. You and Elaine shared everything with each other. You're honestly going to try and tell me that you didn't know *anything* about the fake ID she got me in college?"

I shook my head cautiously.

"What fake ID?"

"The one she got for me at the end of sophomore year?" he said the words as if he were speaking to a toddler. "Some guy was selling them out of the library or some shit, and she had one made for me with a fake name so I wouldn't get in trouble with my record. Michael Davies bought me a lot of liquor that year."

The world seemed to come to a stop around me, the panicked blood rushing past my ears stuck in a dull roar, crashing against my skull like an unrelenting ocean. I was no longer sitting in the visitation center. I was miles away at Green Valley University, following a handsome stranger to the eighth floor during my shift, wondering how he had been able to gain access to the restricted section without raising a single eyebrow of suspicion.

"She bought it in the library?" I repeated. "In the restricted section? Did she say who she got it from?"

"I don't know where the hell she got it or who she got it from," Evan said. "All I know is she handed me some old yearbook at the end of sophomore year and out popped a fake ID with my face and Michael Davies' name on it."

My mouth felt dry, palms glistening with sweat. I was still stuck inside that elevator, the real Michael Davies explaining away his trip to the restricted section as though it had all been some innocent misunderstanding.

I was hoping to take a look through some of the old yearbooks, he had lied without hesitation when I caught him there. Months later, he admitted that there had been an ulterior motive for his secret trip to the eighth floor that day, feeding me a story about selling homework answers to our peers. But even that had been a falsehood. A distraction to keep me in the dark. I felt sick with stupidity. How could I have been so completely blind?

"I don't even know what the fuck that has to do with what happened to Elaine anyway," Evan pulled me out of the elevator cart in my mind back to the visitation room. "What the hell does my fake ID from fifteen years ago have to do with anything?"

I could only think of one answer, but of course, I couldn't verbalize it.

You can't discuss what we talked about today, Rachel's words forced my teeth down on my tongue until I was sure I could taste blood. I didn't know how much longer I'd be able to keep my promise to stay quiet about what I knew. Not with Evan still thinking he was a prime suspect. He deserved to know the truth.

"I told her you were the reason, by the way," Evan continued, oblivious to my internal struggle. I shook my head, failing to understand what he was saying.

"Reason for what?"

"For being at your house that night, or did you forget again?" he jeered. "If it hadn't been for your desperate text, I would have never left my apartment that night."

I gripped the phone tighter, unnerved by the same revelation that Evan had supplied during his last visit. Despite what little I could recall about that night, I felt confident that I hadn't been the one to invite Evan to my house. After all, I hadn't been alone—the olfactory memory of my husband's aftershave burning in my nostrils along with the scent of whatever chemical he had used to drug me. I was but a marionette, dangling by a thread through the darkness while some unseen puppeteer mapped out my every movement from the shadows.

"Evan, that wasn't me," I told him.

"Really?" he straightened in his seat, ready to challenge me. "Then why is it *your* name on my phone at ten-thirty at night, begging me to come over?"

"That might be the case, but I'm telling you, I didn't write that message," I bit my lip, fighting the urge to blurt out what I wanted to say but couldn't. Evan wouldn't settle for the quiet.

"If you didn't send it, then who did?" he demanded.

"It was… someone else," I avoided his stare, letting my gaze fall to my lap rather than land in the pool of sea foam green before me.

"Who?" his voice growled against my ear through the phone. I could feel the words burgeoning in my throat like vomit, fighting to erupt out of my mouth.

"I—I can't tell you," I whispered. "But it wasn't me. I swear to you, it wasn't."

"What the fuck do you mean you can't tell me?" he was seething, and rightfully so. "You owe me this, Cat. I deserve to know why the cops are barking up my tree for some shit I didn't do for the second time in my life. *You* did this to me."

The crack in Evan's voice forced me to look in his direction. Pain seemed to strip away the years that had passed since the cops showed up at our apartment looking for answers about Mia's death. I was no longer staring into the face of a thirty-five-year-old man, but that of a scared and misunderstood boy masquerading as an adult. The same boy whom we had all watched shrink away from the world, the rumors of his possible involvement as damning and debilitating as if he had been arrested on the spot. The same boy whose name had become a taboo so ominous, so disturbing, that to speak it aloud was an offense akin to invoking a demon. All while the devil himself leered undetected in the darkness, too close, too seemingly benign for any of us to see.

What was it that Rachel had said? *People like Michael are good at hiding in plain sight.* They're even better at it when there's someone like Evan nearby, ready to absorb whatever accusations might otherwise land on their shoulders.

It wasn't right. I couldn't let Evan spend another moment of his life living in the shadow of a monster. He needed answers, and no matter what Rachel had said about it potentially jeopardizing the investigation, I wanted to be the one to give him the peace he deserved. I wanted to be the one to save him from a life of agony that never should have been.

"Evan, I... I need to tell you something," my voice trembled around the heartbeat that was pulsing through my throat. "But if I tell you, you have to swear that you won't say anything. Detective McGowen made me promise not to tell you, but I can't do that to you. Not after everything. You deserve to know the truth."

Evan swiped a palm over each of his cheeks, clearing the tears that had involuntarily glided down his pale face.

"Just tell me what's going on," he said miserably. "I can't take this anymore."

"I know," I breathed out long and slow before continuing. "Detective McGowen came to visit me last week to discuss what happened with Elaine. She said she knew who really murdered her, and at first, I... I thought she was talking about you."

Evan's eyes flashed with anger, his lips curling back as though he were preparing to launch into a fresh outburst. I started to explain before he could say a word.

"I was wrong," I told him. "I know that now. *She* knows that now."

"If she knows that, then why is she still trying to pin this on me?" he challenged. "Why is she asking me all these stupid fucking questions like I had anything to do with it?"

"I don't think she was asking you those questions because she thinks you're guilty," I said. "I think she was trying to do her job, get some answers about... about the real Michael Davies."

I let the statement hang in the air, watched it work knots in Evan's brow as confusion replaced resentment. He shook his head, shaggy, black locks falling over his eyes as he did so.

"What do you mean the real Michael Davies?" he said finally.

"I don't really know how to explain it," I admitted. "I'm still trying to wrap my head around it all. None of it makes much sense to me."

"Ten minutes left!" the guard's announcement cut through me like barbed wire, my mind racing to come up with the words that would accurately express what I still needed to tell Evan.

"You'd better hurry up and spit it out," he muttered. "We're running out of time."

"Okay just... listen to me," I scrambled, rushing over my words with unsophisticated urgency. "Detective McGowen showed me this high school yearbook page with Mia Davis's photo on it. Right next to her picture, there was a student named Michael Davies. Only it wasn't Michael Davies in the picture. At least, that's not the name I knew him by..."

"Cat, you're not making any sense," Evan's voice was strained with frustration. "Who cares about some yearbook with a guy's name you don't even know?"

"Because I *do* know him," tears were welling in my eyes, my throat tangled with emotion. "We both do. We just didn't realize it was him."

"*Who?*" Evan barked.

"Tim," I wailed. "Tim Clark *is* Michael Davies. Evan, he's not who he says he is. He went to high school with Mia. His fucking name is in her suicide note and everything. I think he... I think he killed her. And she's not the only one."

Every muscle in Evan's body seemed to slacken at once. His shoulders sagged as though the skin and bones might slide right down his arms, lips parted like a fish pulled from the water, gasping for breath. He sank back in his chair, eyelids stretched wide around two pistachio-colored saucers. Watching the wave of realization crash over him was like witnessing a tsunami erase all evidence of civilization from a once-bustling shoreline. His voice was so faint and muted when he next spoke that I almost didn't hear him at all.

"What do you mean she's not the only one?"

"I'm not really sure," I admitted. "But there were all these receipts in Elaine's bag when she came to my house that night. I thought she was gloating about the affair, but she wasn't. I think she was trying to warn me. And he killed her for it. Oh God, Evan, I'm sorry. I'm so, so sorry."

Grief blinded me as rivers of regret spilled down my cheeks. A chasm deepened in my chest, the desire to collect Evan in my arms so overwhelming that I thought my veins might burst. I wanted nothing more than to break through the plexiglass, rest my head in his lap, beg for his forgiveness. But all I could do was watch my words shatter him beyond recognition.

An uncomfortable silence stretched between us broken only by the guttural sobs that shook my chest. With mere minutes left to spare in our visit, Evan regained the courage to speak.

"Where is he?" his voice was ragged, like loose gravel crunching beneath the weight of steel-toed boots. The sound of it turned my blood to slush.

"I don't know," I said. "I don't even know who he really is."

"You have to know *something*," he asserted, his eyes piercing through my flesh, pinning me in place.

"I th-think he m-might be in Red Rock," I stammered. "He mentioned growing up on a ranch there, but I really don't know if that's where he is."

"Red Rock," Evan repeated, his demeanor relaxing a bit as he spoke the words. Though it was nice to see him letting go of the initial hurt that had come from such a life-altering revelation, I detected something sinister somewhere beneath the surface. Something dangerous.

"Evan, you can't—"

"Don't worry," he interrupted. "I'm not going to tell anybody."

Though his words were meant to be reassuring, I couldn't unsee the gears grinding away behind his eyes.

"What're you going to do?" I breathed.

But I never got to hear the answer. Visitation was over. It was time to go back to my cell.

PART 3
RACHEL

CHAPTER 13

May 16, 2023

It's not an easy thing to admit fault. At the academy, I wasn't trained in the art of apology. I was trained to follow my instinct, to stick to my hunches. I never stopped to think about what the consequences might be if my intuition turned out to be incorrect. It wasn't an option. But everything I thought I knew about being a detective changed the day I was forced to acknowledge that Evan Summers was innocent.

I stayed in my motel room for a long time, staring into my cellphone, unable to pull my gaze from the yearbook entry that had been hiding in plain view for nearly two decades. How many times had Mia's sisters and I stayed up late together, making fun of her poor editing skills, trying to fill the void of her absence with liquor and laughter? We must have mentioned that very yearbook page a thousand times over the years—how she had somehow swapped out the photos of every student with her own senior portrait—but not a single time did any of us bother to read the names that were listed beneath her photograph. Why would we? It was painful enough to see her smiling face frozen in time, trapped in a state of perpetual youth for all of eternity. Maybe if grief had been kinder, we would have dared to linger a bit longer with her image, peered beyond the hurt to find what our heartache would not permit us to see. But once I saw Michael Davies' name matched to his high school portrait, I couldn't erase it from my mind.

He didn't look the same as the man I had seen sobbing in the lobby at Burg Interiors. He didn't even have the same name. Despite his obvious anguish, Tim Clark was polished, poised, with close-cropped sandy hair and smooth skin—a far cry from the long, shaggy blonde locks swept across a pockmarked face in Mia's senior yearbook. If it hadn't been for his eyes—an arctic steel like the threat of a snowstorm mirrored in the glassy surface of a glacial pool—I probably wouldn't have realized that the person in the photograph and the man I had seen at the design firm were one in the same. But there was no mistaking it: Tim Clark *was* Michael Davies.

The more I thought about it, the more it made sense to me. I knew that Tim had gone to Green Valley University, had lived in the apartment above mine—the same one that I shared with Mia for months before she died. And I also knew that he was part owner of the design firm that just happened to be building student centers nearby when Laura Talbot, Joan Chickless, and Stacy Dunlap had died. He had the opportunity—there was no doubt about it. But what about the means? The motive? I needed more answers, but with the way I had left things at the Green Valley Police Department, I wouldn't have the luxury of police resources to back me in getting them. Thankfully, I still had Nick's support to guide me.

"Hey, kiddo," the sound of the nickname he had given me while we were still dating disarmed me, filling my heart with fresh agony that had nothing to do with my investigation. "Any luck tracking down Elaine yet?"

The room around me blurred, throat strangled with rage and sadness. *Elaine.* Just another in a long line of victims that I had failed to protect. Suddenly, I was speechless again.

"You there?" Nick prompted, the sound of department chatter from where he was stationed in Charlotte consuming the cellular space between us, reminding me of the job I no longer had yet still felt an obligation to perform. I cleared my throat, shook away the stabbing sensation in my chest.

"I'm here," I said. "But Elaine isn't. She... she's gone, Nick. He killed her. I was too late."

"*What?*" if I closed my eyes, I could almost see Nick's dark brows knit together, forming deep creases in his forehead. "When did this happen? *How* did it happen?"

"She was killed on Friday night," I whispered. "That's all I know."

Silence pressed against my eardrum as I waited for Nick's response. It was a long time before he found the words to speak.

"But you were watching Evan that night... weren't you?" I bit my lip, fighting the urge to scream or vomit or some combination of the two. I had spent so long trying to prove that Evan was to blame, had lost my position at the department because of it, sacrificed the only romantic relationship that I had ever had, all in pursuit of a myth. A fallacy. And now I was forced to say it out loud for the first time to the very person I had pushed away with my dogged persistence. The tears fell like a heavy rain, sudden and inescapable.

"Rachel, breathe," Nick tried to calm me down. "C'mon, kiddo, don't do this to yourself. Talk to me. Tell me what—"

"It's not him!" I shouted. "It's not Evan. It's Tim. Michael Davies is Tim Clark."

"Wait a minute, slow down," Nick said. "Who is Tim Clark and why do you think he's Michael Davies?"

I took a deep breath, dabbed my eyes with the back of my hand, and proceeded to tell Nick all about the man I had met at Burg Interiors, how he was an exact match for the photograph of Michael Davies sitting in the center of Mia's botched yearbook page, how he had been present for every one of the killings throughout North Carolina. He had to have been. Elaine said so herself.

It was an initial presentation, so we were all there.

The same words I had used to justify my suspicions about Evan now seemed to confirm that it was someone else entirely. My mind wandered back to Sheriff Kane's office the day he had asked me to resign.

I recognize tunnel vision when I see it, he had said. At the time, I thought that he was wrong, but now? All I could see were the walls I had built, every brick laid perfectly in place to fit a narrative that I had convinced myself to be the truth. I was sloppy, careless, reckless. And it had cost me everything.

Nick was quiet for a long time after I finished telling him everything that I had discovered. I wondered if, like me, he had also been thinking about all the time I had wasted, all the love we could have shared if I hadn't been so focused on all of the wrong things. If he had, he didn't mention it when he next spoke.

"We need proof," was all he said. "Don't get me wrong—I believe you. You know I do. But this is still too circumstantial. We need physical evidence. Like a—"

"Like a DNA sample?" I suggested.

"Exactly," he agreed. "You need to stay on top of him like you did with Evan. Get a sample that we can link to the Dunlap case. Can you stay in Williamsburg a bit longer?"

I thought about my dwindling bank account, about the paycheck I no longer had coming in from the department. My heart sank.

"I'm getting kind of broke," I admitted. "I don't know how much—"

"Don't worry about the money," he assured me. "I'll figure something out, okay? Just stay put and do your thing. We have to catch this fucker."

After I hung up with Nick, I raced back to Burg Interiors so I could keep my eye on my new target. But by the time I made it back to the office, there was no sign of his silver Nissan Altima in the parking lot, no trace of the bright-red Corvette that belonged to the lawyer who had been there with him, either. I staked out Elaine's house, remembering how they had been sleeping with one another for weeks before her murder, hopeful that he might show up there.

Nothing.

It seemed that in the short amount of time it took me to learn his true identity and formulate a plan to link him to his crimes, Michael Davies had seized the opportunity to leave town without a trace. Two days passed before I finally had to admit to myself that he was gone. That I had failed. Again.

"I've looked everywhere," I complained to Nick after failing to locate my suspect. "He's not at the office or Elaine's house. His wife's place is an active crime scene, so he's definitely not there. I have no idea where to look, Nick. I... I'm scared. He's going to kill again, and there's nothing I can do about it."

"Yes, there is," Nick comforted me. "You can't get discouraged. Someone has to know where he might be. You said he was sleeping with Elaine, right? Maybe she was killed because she found something out that she wasn't supposed to know."

"What good does that do me?" I moaned. "She's dead! It's not like I can call her up and ask her about it."

"Did you find anything out about her case?" Nick tried to keep me focused rather than engage with my sarcasm.

"How the hell am I supposed to do that?" I complained. "I'm not a cop anymore. I can't just walk into the station and go demanding answers."

"You can't," he agreed. "But I can. Why don't you head back home for a few days and get some rest while I see what I can find out, okay?"

I sighed.

"Okay," I said.

With that, I packed the few belongings I had lying around my motel room back into my duffel bag, checked out, and made my way back down to my townhouse in Green Valley.

***

May 21, 2023

After spending so much time in a motel, splaying out on the queen-sized mattress in my townhouse felt like a luxury retreat. But even with the pillow-top surface cradling my body, the down duvet swaddling my skin, finding the peace to sleep seemed like an impossible dream. Each time I closed my eyes, Mia's face was burned into the back of my lids, her features glowing brighter and brighter until they were no longer hers at all, but an amalgamation of all the other women whom Michael Davies had taken. Laura and Joan and Stacy and Elaine and who knew how many others—all of them erased from existence, their light extinguished with the swiftness of a blown-out birthday candle. And all I could do was lay in bed and wish for a different outcome.

My phone buzzed against the wooden surface of my nightstand, demanding attention that I didn't want to give. But as soon as I saw the name emblazoned across the screen, I bolted upright, suddenly eager to take the call.

"Took you long enough," I griped.

"I know, I know," Nick apologized. "It's been a bit crazy over here and that Podunk excuse for a sheriff's office they've got over in Williamsburg took their sweet time getting back to me, but I finally got some answers."

"What'd you find out?" I held my breath, hoping to hear some good news.

"Well, for starters, they've got Catheryn Clark in custody for Elaine's murder," he answered. I couldn't contain my surprise.

"They're pinning this on his wife?" I couldn't believe it. "But why?"

"Apparently, she was found at the scene covered in the victim's blood. She was even holding the murder weapon," Nick said. "They seem pretty confident that it's open-and-shut, but I was able to get the contact information for Mrs. Clark's attorney. It's strange, though. He doesn't even practice criminal law. Some business lawyer out of Green Valley. I've got his contact information if you want to give him a call, see what you can find out."

"Please," I insisted. "I'll contact him right away."

"I'll text you the name and number after we hang up," Nick agreed. "Good luck, kiddo. Let me know how it goes."

As soon as we hung up the phone, Nick sent me the contact information for one Owen Strong, Esquire III. I punched in the number right away and, within moments, had Mrs. Clark's attorney on the line. It wasn't long before I learned that his client had started to suspect that someone else was to blame for what had happened to Elaine. But like me, her tunnel vision was targeted at the wrong person.

"She thinks one of her business partners was at her house that night and drugged her," Owen had said when I called him. When I asked him which one, he responded quickly, "Evan Summers. I'm headed over to his apartment to ask him some questions this afternoon."

"Don't," I urged him. "I'd like to talk to you in person about all this first if you don't mind. There are some things I think you need to see."

Owen's office wasn't far from my place, so he agreed to meet with me at the Starlight Café in Green Valley to review what I had found. When he entered the small eatery, I was surprised to learn that we had already met. Even if he hadn't parked his bright-red Corvette outside of the café window, his salt-and-pepper, slicked-back hair and chocolate-brown eyes were enough for me to recognize that he was the same lawyer at the Burg Interiors office the day that I had gone looking for Elaine. But my surprise paled in comparison to the look of shock on his face as I revealed the truth of what I had discovered.

"This can't be," he insisted, gaping at the image of the man he knew as Tim Clark staring back at him from the snapshot of Mia's yearbook that her sister had texted me days earlier. "Tim is a good guy. He's so mild-mannered. Barely says a word. It can't be him."

"It's not," I agreed. "It's Michael Davies."

Owen rubbed the back of his neck, unsure what to make of my assertion. He wasn't ready to admit it—not to himself, and certainly not to Mrs. Clark.

"Let me ask you something, Mr. Strong," I began. "When's the last time you spoke to the person you know as Tim Clark?"

He nibbled on his lip, his dark eyes avoiding my gaze as he struggled to find an answer that wouldn't cast further doubt over the man he thought he knew. When he could think of nothing favorable, he was forced to admit defeat.

"I haven't seen or heard from him since the Monday after Elaine died," he confessed. "That was almost a week ago. Come to think of it, I've reached out a few times and he hasn't responded."

"Does that seem normal to you?"

"Like I said, the guy barely says two words," he argued. "Maybe he's grieving? I mean his lover *was* just murdered by his wife."

"Maybe," I conceded. "Or maybe he's avoiding you for a reason."

"But *he's* the one who called *me* to take on his wife's case," he retorted. "Why would he do that if he was responsible for Elaine's death?"

I considered that for a moment, took a sip of the coffee I had ordered from the barista who was not-so-subtly eavesdropping on our conversation from the counter. It did seem like an odd thing to do. But if there was one thing I had learned about Michael Davies, it was that he was great at covering his tracks, at blending in, at avoiding suspicion. Maybe the decision to get Owen involved wasn't as benign as the lawyer believed. Maybe it was an act of self-preservation, another layer of deceit to throw everyone off of his scent.

"I don't know the answer to that," I decided. "But I do know that Tim Clark isn't who he says he is. And I know that Michael Davies has been checking into hotel rooms all over North Carolina—nearly all of which have had a dead woman found inside shortly after his stay. So, you can either help me get to the bottom of this, or you can try and stand in my way. Either way, Mr. Strong, I'm going to be talking to Mrs. Clark about this, so you'd better decide what part you want to play in that conversation."

Of course, I was bluffing. Without his help, it wasn't likely that I'd be able to barge into the county jail in Williamsburg and speak to his client on my own. How could I? I wasn't a police officer anymore. I didn't have that kind of authority. But Owen didn't need to know that. For one horrifying moment, I thought he had seen through my lie, the long pause following my empty threat causing bursts of panic to explode inside my stomach like a thousand angry firecrackers. Finally, he released a sigh.

"Fine," he relented. "When are you planning to see her?"

"The sooner the better," I told him. "But before we go, I'll need to review the details of her case along with whatever evidence was collected at the scene. With the affair that Elaine had going with him, there's a good chance that Michael Davies was involved with her death, and I'm going to need to confirm that first."

"Why?" Owen challenged. "If you're so sure based on what you have already, what difference does it make?"

"Because your client is the only person who might know where he is," I reminded him. "And last I checked, spouses aren't usually keen on ratting each other out to the cops. If I'm going to approach her about this, then I need her to see as much as I do who her husband really is."

"Okay," he nodded, putting his hands up in forfeit. "I'll see what I can get together."

***

May 24, 2023

Three days after my conversation with Owen, I was sitting beside him in the attorney visiting room at Monroe County Sheriff's Office with a bag full of evidence from Elaine's murder case that he had helped secure for the occasion. Nick had been kind enough to take photocopies of Stacy Dunlap's suicide note, which I had tucked away in a manilla folder along with Mia's. It wasn't until I had typed it out to prepare for the meeting with Catheryn that I realized there was a hidden message contained within each note. When laid out line by line, I couldn't help but feel embarrassed that I had missed such a significant clue: The first word of every sentence combined to spell the name *Michael Davies*, the sight of it so brazen, so full of confidence, it was as though he actually wanted to get caught.

Though I was confident that I had enough evidence to convince Mrs. Clark (or Cat, as she had been so quick to correct me) of her husband's guilt, I was still nervous about what her reaction might be. Would she be stuck in a state of denial, unwilling to speak ill of the man she still loved? Or worse—would she be so overcome with disbelief that it would render her speechless, unable to provide any helpful information whatsoever? It seemed as though the latter might be the case when my revelations had caused her to vomit.

I raced to collect a trashcan from the corner of the cold, callous concrete tomb that was the attorney meeting room (Nick was certainly right about his assessment of the sorry state of the Monroe County Sheriff's Office; it was abysmal). As she relieved herself into the bin, I tried to be as gentle as I could, rubbing her back and soothing her, hoping that suffering the stench of her bile would be worth it in the end. Maybe if I showed her that I really was there to help, she wouldn't go into a state of shock and get quiet on me. I was so close to getting what I had come there for; if I had to get splashed with stomach contents in the process, so be it.

To my delight, my plan seemed to work: Despite the fact that she didn't think she had been helpful, Cat's responses to the questions that followed her persistent retching had been more eye-opening than even I expected. She had admitted to me that her husband was on medication. From her description of the "little blue things" she saw him take from time to time, I was willing to bet my life on the fact that they were Valium—the same medication found in the hotel rooms next to many of his victims. I made a note of the psychiatrist's name that Cat had mentioned so I could follow up with them later. But even more compelling to me was the answer she provided to the final question I had asked.

"Can you think of anywhere that he might be?"

"All I know about Tim... about Michael's family is that his mom died years ago, his grandfather abused him, and he had a half-brother that he never talked to—all in Red Rock," she had spoken the name of the town as though it meant nothing. Just a random combination of words that some colonists had jumbled together decades before either of us had been a thought in our parents' minds. But I didn't need a map to know the significance the place held.

I knew well the cattle ranches that surrounded the suburbs of Sudbury, had passed the sign to Red Rock dozens of times during my trips to the Davis's sprawling mansion. I had seen it again the following day as I made the long drive to their house once more, confident that I would find the person responsible for robbing their youngest family member of her life. But before I left Williamsburg, there was one last thing I needed to do at Cat's request, and not one part of me was eager to do it.

I needed to face Evan.

***

May 25, 2023

I had been to the Shady Brooks Apartment Complex countless times during my stakeout, had committed its rundown brick exterior to memory. With its lopsided landscaping, its cracked asphalt parking lot, its menacing tenants loitering around every corner, it wasn't a welcoming environment by any stretch of the imagination. But in all the hours I had spent there in the shadows tracking my target in secret, I had never felt more scared or unsettled than I did as I climbed the stairs to Evan's unit and prepared to speak to the man whom I had once believed to be Mia's killer. All I could think about were the words Elaine had said to me the day I questioned her outside of Burg Interiors.

He never got over all those nasty things you said about him. He's been a miserable drunk ever since and it's all your fault.

At the time, I didn't think anything of her remarks. If anything, I took a bit of pride in being responsible for causing Evan's misery. But that was before I realized who the real Michael Davies was. Before I knew how wrong I had been. How much hurt my persistence had caused. Part of me wanted to get back in the car and drive straight to Sudbury in search of Michael's relatives without ever confronting the man whose life I had ruined. But I couldn't do that—not to Cat, and not to Mia or any of the other victims. I owed it to each of them not only to acknowledge my role in delaying justice for so long, but to get any answers that Evan might have that could help me right my wrongs.

It was early on Thursday morning when I arrived at Evan's doorstep—well before his daily departure at eight-thirty to arrive at the office by eight forty-five as I had watched him do so many times from my post in the parking lot. Despite the early hour, the air was already thick with heat and humidity, which did nothing to stop my palms from sweating as I brought my fist to the door and knocked. Within moments, he was standing in front of me, not at all the image of the man I had been following for weeks on end.

He wore a loose tee-shirt and worn, gray sweatpants that flared out around his skinny frame, giving him the illusion of having no legs at all. His normally clean-shaven face was consumed by a wild mess of black facial hair that made his striking, angular features disappear into obscurity. But the most jarring aspect of his appearance was the look of pure hatred radiating from his eyes as he drank me in.

"Evan Summers?" I broke the glacial silence with caution. "I'm Detec—"

"I know who the fuck you are," he growled. "Why are you here?"

"I was hoping I could talk to you," I explained, "about what happened to Elaine. Do you mind if I come in?"

"Yeah, actually, I do mind," he folded his arms and squeezed his body in between the doorframe, blocking the view into his apartment. "Anything you have to say to me, you can say right here."

"Fair enough," I agreed. "Listen, I spoke to Cat about what happened that night."

"That fucking bitch," he muttered to himself. "So, I guess you're here to ask me all about why I was there, then? Gonna try and pin this one on me, too?"

"What? No, I..." I trailed off, the meaning of his assumptions slowly sinking in. "Wait—why *were* you there?"

I watched his fingernails dig into his skin as he clenched himself tighter.

"She texted me," the words came through gritted teeth, reluctant and rigid. It was clear that he wasn't going to offer any further detail without my asking, so I continued.

"What did she say exactly?"

He pressed his lips together into a deep frown as though he were contemplating what would benefit him more: answering my question or telling me to fuck off as it was clear he wanted to do. After what felt like a full day of hesitation, he reached into his pants pocket and extracted his cellphone, tapping away at the screen until he found the message in question.

"Read it yourself," he said, shoving the device into my hand. I scanned the message briefly, careful not to let my emotions get the better of me as the familiar words danced before my eyes:

> **Friday, May 13, 10:35 p.m.:** Maybe in another life, it could have been us. It could still be. Can you come over? Hold me. And everything will be alright. Everything will be like it should be. Like it was meant to be all along.

The message was shorter than the suicide notes that I had found, but I didn't need to copy it down onto a separate sheet of paper to realize that the first letter of every sentence spelled out *Michael*. It didn't matter that the number on Evan's phone indicated the message had come from Cat. There was no way that text had been composed by her.

"Do you mind if I take a screenshot of this and send it to myself?" Evan shrugged in response, which I took to be his nod of approval. When I was finished sending the screenshot, I handed the phone back to him and attempted to continue our conversation, "What do you think she meant by all that?"

Evan shuffled his weight, visibly uncomfortable by the question. A strange anguish seemed to absorb the anger in his eyes, forcing his gaze down to the floor.

"She was just drunk, I guess," he mumbled. "And lonely. I thought that maybe... it doesn't matter what I thought. It was a hard day for her, and me and Elaine got caught in the middle of her shit."

"What makes you say that?" I already knew the answer, but I wanted to get his side of the story, see if there were any differences in his timeline of events.

"Because it was her wedding anniversary," he said. "And she just found out her husband was cheating on her with her best friend. She wasn't in good shape. I was... I was really worried about her."

"Do you know when the affair started?" When I had spoken to Cat, she seemed to think that Michael and Elaine had been together for years. I was curious to know if Evan had a different understanding.

"I have no fucking clue," he crossed his arms in front of his chest, resuming his defensive posture. "If I had to take a wild guess, I'd say it probably started around the time Cat went to rehab back in March. They started acting weird around each other after she was gone, but I didn't know for sure that they were together until Cat told me when she got out."

I nodded carefully, debating how best to phrase my next question so he wouldn't shut down.

"You and Cat were also having an affair, though, weren't you?" I pointed out. "Could that have been what caused Mi—what caused *Tim* to be unfaithful?"

"What? No!" Evan balked. "Cat and I didn't get together until *after* she found out about Elaine and Tim. She was crushed by it all. I was just trying to help her. I... never mind. It doesn't matter anymore."

Evan reached back into his pocket and removed his phone, checking the time on the screen.

"Look, I need to get ready for work," he said. "We done here?"

"Almost," I promised. "The night that Elaine died, she was carrying a bag full of hotel receipts—all with the name Michael Davies on them. Do you know why she might have had those with her? Have you ever heard that name before?"

A ripple of fear shimmered behind Evan's eyes at the question—not at all the reaction that I had been expecting. He looked nervous as he ran a bony hand through his long, unruly hair, grappling with what his response should be. I waited patiently for him to provide it.

"Fuck," he whispered. "Yeah, I've heard that name before, but I don't know anything about any hotel receipts, okay? I swear to God, I have nothing to do with that."

My breath caught in my throat. *How did he know that name?* More importantly, who did he think it belonged to?

"Where have you heard that name before?" I asked him.

"It's so stupid," he mumbled. "Elaine got me a fake ID while we were in college, and the name on the card was Michael Davies. This was almost twenty years ago, though, okay? I don't even have the fucking thing anymore. I got rid of it after the cops started questioning me about Mia—thanks again for that, by the way."

The ground seemed to spin beneath my feet, stomach churning with acid aching to be expelled. I knew that Evan couldn't be guilty; no serial killer who had spent the better part of two decades evading capture would admit to having a fake identity that was linked to his crimes so easily. Besides, I knew from having read Mia's case file that what he said was true: During his interrogation, the police had asked him about how it was that he had been able to get so drunk so often despite being underaged. Even then, he had confessed to having a fake ID. And he wasn't the only student who had one.

There was a fake driver's license found in Mia Davis's wallet when her body had been discovered on the bank of the Tar River. Had she gotten it from the same person as Evan? If she had, who could it have been? And why would they have created a fake ID with the name Michael Davies on it?

I could think of someone who had gone to Green Valley University during that time. Someone who ran in the same circle as Evan. Someone who was practiced in the art of masquerading through life with someone else's name. Maybe making that ID for Evan was some sort of a test. A way to shed his true identity, to hide in plain sight, to run away from his past. But why?

There was only one way to find out.

"Thank you for your time, Evan," I told him, my mind already miles away in Sudbury, hoping to find more answers.

"Whatever," he grumbled, moving to close the door. Before he could slam it shut, I stuck my hand out to stop it from closing, almost forgetting why it was that I had come to his apartment in the first place.

"Cat wanted me to tell you that she wants to see you again," I said.

"Why the fuck would I go to see her?" he snarled. I thought about passing on Cat's words of apology, about offering my own statement of regret for the hurt I had caused the innocent person standing before me, but my mouth wouldn't budge. I was paralyzed by cowardice, too frightened by the consequences of admitting fault to say what needed to be said, so instead, I left the hard work to Cat.

"Just talk to her," I told him. "She really needs to see you right now."

I left Evan at the doorstep and scurried back down the decrepit concrete staircase into the parking lot below. As soon as the car door slammed shut behind me, I pulled up Nick's contact card on my phone and pressed "Call."

"Hey, McGowen," he answered formally. My chest felt tight. *What happened to kiddo?* I could hear a woman's voice somewhere in the background, answering my unspoken question, telling me the reason why he had abandoned his affectionate nickname for a more formal greeting. "How'd it go at Monroe County yesterday?"

I swallowed hard around the golf ball that had somehow lodged itself in my throat.

"It went okay," I managed to get out. "The wife said that she thinks Michael has relatives in Red Rock—that's right outside of Sudbury. Where Mia lived?"

"You think he could have gone to stay with one of them?" Nick pondered.

"Maybe," I said. "His wife seemed to think that he and his family were estranged, but I can't shake the feeling that there's something there. Something that might help us understand where he might be now. I have to go find out what it is."

"You heading over there now?"

"Yeah," I confirmed.

"Okay, well, just be careful," he warned. "Give me a call if you—"

"Baby, who are you on the phone with?" the sweet sing-song of that woman's voice hardened in my stomach, turning my insides to stone. I didn't wait to hear his answer. Didn't have the strength to say goodbye. I jammed my finger on the "End" button, pulled out of the parking lot, and drove away, not daring to shed a single tear.

CHAPTER 14

May 25, 2023

After a quick pitstop at my townhouse in Green Valley to gather more clothes into my duffel bag, I was back on the road to Sudbury. It had been over a week since I last spoke to Mia's sister, Sarah, too bogged down by the complexity of my investigation to explain why it was that I had called her, screaming out my demands to see a twenty-year-old yearbook page.

Though she had texted and called me multiple times since then, I didn't have the energy to answer her. I had already robbed her of her sanity for so long, forced her to keep the secret of her sister's possible murder—all while she navigated the first five years of her daughter's life. The next time I spoke to her, I wanted to be completely certain that I knew who was responsible for causing her agony. As I left Green Valley behind, I felt that I was finally able to give her the answers she deserved—the answers that all the Davises deserved.

"You'd better have a good fucking reason for avoiding me," she snapped as she answered the phone. "You scared me half to death, and then I don't hear from you for almost two weeks? What the hell, Rachel?"

"Hello to you, too," I quipped. "Look, I'm sorry for leaving you hanging, but I'm actually on my way to your parents' house right now. Any chance you'd be able to meet me there with Beau, Leah, and Josh? I think the whole family should be around for this."

I heard a sharp intake of air carry across the phone as Sarah sucked in a breath.

"Did you... did you find who did it?" her voice was small, quiet. If I listened hard enough, I thought I could hear the tears as they trickled out from the creases of her crystal eyes, gliding down her tanned skin.

"Yes and no," I told her. "I'll tell you everything once I get to town. Can you get everyone together before I get there? Should only be a few hours from now."

"Yes," she sniffled. "Yes, I can do that. Oh Rachel, thank you. Thank you for not giving up. Thank you for—"

"Don't thank me yet," I told her, my throat tightening around the urge to cry. I swiped away the stray tears that had managed to slip free from my eyes. "I'll see you soon, okay?"

I had been to the Davis's house countless times over the years, the beauty of their antebellum mansion greeting me like an old friend with each visit. Each drive through the yawning pines that lined their brick driveway was like a warm welcome I didn't feel I deserved. But as I puttered up to their wraparound porch and parked the car, there was something different in the air. A stillness that made me feel strangely unsettled—like I had stepped into a sleeping forest only to hear the loud snap of a thick tree branch cracking beneath the weight of some terrible creature.

I shivered the thought away, tried to tell myself that it was nothing. I was just nervous about what I had come there to do. After all, no one aside from Sarah and her husband, Beau, had known anything about my investigation into Mia's murder. For all her family knew, Mia had committed suicide—there was nothing more to the story than that. But what I was about to tell them would change their lives forever, and even though I felt it was the only way that I would get to the truth about Michael Davies, I still didn't feel good about doing it.

"Aunt Rachel, Aunt Rachel!" the sound of tiny feet stampeding down the wooden porch thundered through the air as Emma raced to greet me. I scooped her up in my arms, my back groaning out in pain as I straightened to a standing position.

"What'd you gain, like, eighty pounds since the last time I saw you?" I teased, pinching a plump, pink cheek between my fingers. "You're a monster, kid!"

"*Rawr!*" she spread out her hands and wiggled her fingers as she growled triumphantly in my face, her little nose scrunched up with mock intimidation. I planted a kiss on top of her chestnut curls before placing her back down to the earth, ignoring the way her big, blue eyes reminded me of the real aunt she never had the chance to meet.

"Where's your mama?" I forced a smile at the five-year-old beauty who bumped her shoulders in response to my question as if to say, *Beats me*.

"She's inside with everyone," a deep, southern drawl consumed the air as Beau stepped down from the porch to join me and his daughter. The afternoon sun sparkled in his cerulean stare like a diamond glimmering beneath a sea of sorrow. Despite the broadness of his shoulders, his powerful build forged from years of manual labor, he seemed deflated, meek. It wasn't the Beau that I was used to seeing, the confident bravado that once seemed etched into his being now noticeably absent. As he approached, a wide grin spread across his face that appeared at odds with the sadness in his eyes.

"It's good to see you, Rachel," he greeted me with a half hug, the tone of his voice not at all conveying the affection of his words. It wasn't good to see me. How could it be? We both knew the real reason I was there. That there was nothing *good* about it.

"You too," I gave him an extra squeeze before releasing him.

"Daddy's taking me to get ice cream!" Emma announced proudly, beaming up at her father with expectant eyes. He ruffled her hair affectionately and nodded.

"That's right, baby, we'll be leaving soon," he assured her. "Gotta give the grown-ups some space while Aunt Rachel has a talk with them all."

Emma didn't seem to notice the way her father's voice grew tighter with every word he spoke, but I did. A pit formed in my abdomen, its icy tendrils snaking out to grip my intestines. If Beau was this emotional about my visit, I didn't want to think about what was waiting for me on the other side of the Davis's front door. I sniffed, coaxed the corners of my mouth to climb higher up my cheeks as I gazed into Emma's hopeful, oblivious face.

"What flavor are you gonna get?" my attempt at distraction seemed to do the trick.

"Pink! Pink!" she yelled, forcing a genuine laugh from both me and her father.

"You mean strawberry?" I corrected her.

"Nooooo," she shook her head from side to side, her soft, brown hair flailing around her delicate features. "Pink!"

Beau snatched her up and threw her on top of his shoulders, shrieks of glee breaking through the humid air as he did so. For a moment, I almost convinced myself that everything was normal. I was just there for a family barbecue. There was no darkness looming in the background, no heartbreak to be had, no old wounds to open.

"Everything's pink these days," Beau rolled his eyes, steadying his giggling daughter with a pair of beefy hands. As she settled on his shoulders and quieted down, a heavy silence fell between us. He cleared his throat and said, "Well, I'll leave you to it then. We'll talk later, I'm sure."

With that, Beau carried his daughter down the driveway, placing her into the back of a white minivan before climbing into the driver's seat and driving away. Part of me wished I was sitting in the passenger seat alongside him, promises of Rocky Road melting across my tongue rather than the words I wasn't sure I had the courage to speak. But I couldn't afford such childlike luxuries. I had a promise to keep.

The Davis's foyer looked as impressive and lavish as I remembered it being the first day that I had followed Mia through the front door. Mahogany floorboards stretched out in every direction, bathed in floods of natural light that trickled in through the frosted windows that flanked either side of the entrance. The staircase railing gleamed with fresh wood polish, taunting me with its elegance, as though the house itself knew my presence was an unwanted blemish on its perfection.

"Rachel, honey, is that you?" a matronly voice called out from the room to the right of the staircase. I crossed the threshold into the front parlor to find the Davis family sitting around the empty fireplace, Mrs. Davis standing up from the antique sofa to greet me as I entered. She looked as prim and proper as ever with her signature hair twist and pearl necklace draped around her collarbone. With a warm smile, she gathered me into her arms and whispered, "What a wonderful surprise. It's so great to see you."

My heart dropped into a pool of acid at the words. I knew it wouldn't be long until her opinion on my impromptu visit would change.

As she released me from her embrace, I looked nervously around the room to find a group of smiling faces staring back at me. There was Mia's oldest sister, Leah, and her husband, Josh, nodding at me from their place on the leather armchair beside the unlit fireplace. Mrs. Davis reclaimed her seat on the sofa beside her own husband whose lips quirked up in a soft grin that told me he was just as unaware of the reason for my visit as his wife had been. But there was one person in the room who didn't have the bliss of ignorance to keep an even composure.

Sarah sat ashen-faced on a tufted ottoman between the sofa and the armchair, her eyes vacant, haunted, teeth working absently at her fingernails like a worried patient awaiting the results of her biopsy. The rims of her eyelids were red and puffy, evidence that she had been crying likely since the time that I had called her to request the family meeting. I walked over to her, bending down to meet her gaze, the suddenness of my presence snapping her out of her trance.

"Oh Rachel," she squeaked, collapsing into my arms, allowing the dam to break down around me as she sobbed into my shirt. I smoothed her soft, brown curls and held her tight, trying my best not to let my own walls come crashing down. As we held each other, I could feel the atmosphere in the room begin to shift.

"Sarah!" Leah gasped, her eyes bouncing back and forth from her sister to her mother. "What is the matter with you? You've been acting strange all morning. What the hell is going on here?"

Sarah pressed away from me, hiding her face in her hands, unable to answer her sister's question. I took a staggered breath and rose to my feet, wiping my face with the back of my hand to dry the few tears that had managed to break through my defenses. Sarah's whimpers filled the room as all eyes turned to me, demanding answers. I hung my head and said a silent prayer.

Here goes nothing.

"You're probably wondering why I asked Sarah to gather you here today," I began.

"You can say that again," Leah's blonde eyebrows creased together with concern as she gazed at her sobbing sister. "What's going on, Rachel? Is everything okay?"

"No," I said flatly. "No, it's not okay. It's... it's about Mia."

The room became so quiet, so still at the mention of Mia's name that I was sure I could hear the hum of humidity sighing against the window pane. Josh flung a strong arm around his wife, gathering her to his side instinctively as though preparing to face a heavy wind. From the sofa, Mr. Davis spoke first.

"What about Mia?" he croaked. I fixed my eyes on the floor, too overwhelmed to meet the stare of a father still mourning the loss of his youngest daughter.

"What I'm about to tell you is not going to be easy to hear," I whispered. "But I need you to understand that it's the truth."

"Honey, please just tell us," Mrs. Davis said. "You're giving me a fright."

I nodded, sucked in a long, slow breath, and spoke the words that I had been waiting fifteen years to say.

"I'm so sorry," my voice sounded miles away from my body, a ghost drifting at sea. "I don't know how to tell you this, but Mia didn't commit suicide. She... she was murdered."

A loud scream punctuated my statement as Sarah burst into fresh tears. Leah clamped a hand over her mouth, stifling an outburst of her own, Josh stroking the length of her golden hair from his place on the armrest as his wife shook violently in the center of the chair cushion. I dared a glance at Mr. and Mrs. Davis, their silence as ear-splitting as their daughters' cries of anguish. They looked like two shells of human beings, devoid of spirit. I clutched my sternum, my chest feeling as though it might cave in on itself. This time, Leah was the first to speak.

"How can this be? How do you know this?" she wailed. As soon as the question left her body, a fresh realization danced across her face. She whirled toward her sister, "You knew about this, didn't you? How long have you known? How could you keep this from us?"

I put up my hands, coming to Sarah's defense.

"Don't be angry with Sarah," I begged. "It's not her fault. She caught me questioning Beau at Mia's ten-year celebration of life, and I asked them both to keep quiet about all this until I was absolutely certain of the facts."

"Beau knows about this, too?!" Leah shrieked, turning on her sister once again, "You kept this from us for *five years?* I can't believe you. I can't believe—"

All at once the anger seemed to evaporate from her being. She tilted her head slowly back in my direction, horror dancing behind her eyes like a flickering flame, "Why were you questioning Beau? Did he... was he—?"

"*No!*" I shouted, putting a stop to her reasoning. I collected myself and started again, softer this time, "No. But I had reason to believe at the time that he might have been involved. He wasn't. I can promise you that."

"Who?" Mr. Davis's voice was as fragile as a death rattle as it washed over the room. For the first time since revealing the truth to him, I met his gaze. "Who did this to my baby?"

"I believe your daughter was killed by a man named Michael Davies," I answered, knees threatening to buckle beneath the weight of Mr. Davis's grief. Confusion and anger deepened the wrinkles in his forehead, aging him rapidly before my eyes.

"Michael *who?*" Leah verbalized the question on her father's lips before he had the chance to speak.

"Michael Davies," I repeated, launching into an explanation of how it was that I had made the connection. The strange wording in Mia's suicide note. The similar messaging in notes found alongside Michael's laundry list of victims. The hotel check-ins with Michael Davies' name. The photograph in Mia's yearbook with Michael's portrait situated right next to hers. It was difficult to distill fifteen years of investigation into a single conversation, but I did the best I could to make them understand the truth that I had known all along. To see what I had seen since the moment Nick had arrived at my apartment to tell me my best friend was dead.

"I know this is extremely difficult to take in," I continued, "and if you need more time to process, I completely understand. But I can't give you all the time you need. Michael is out there right now, and there's going to be another victim—I'm sure of it. Unless I can get to him first. But I need your help to try and find him."

"*Our* help?" Leah gaped. "How could we possibly help you? We don't even know who this person is!"

"Yes, you do," I reminded her. "You, Sarah, and Mia all went to school with this person. There's got to be something you remember about him."

"Mia was younger than us," Leah argued. "And even if she wasn't, even if we were all magically in the same grade, it wouldn't change the fact that high school was twenty years ago. How the hell are we supposed to remember—?"

"I remember something," Sarah whispered, forming words for the first time since her tears had rendered her speechless. All at once, the room's attention turned to the ottoman, waiting for an explanation. She dabbed at her tear-stained face with the back of her hand and continued, "I was a year older than Mia, so I was in college when it happened, but I remember reading about it in the paper."

"Reading about what?" I prompted. "What do you remember, Sarah?"

"That name—Davies—that's the family whose house burned down the summer after Mia graduated high school," she clarified. "I don't remember there being anything about Michael's name in the article, but I remember the name Davies for sure. It was terrible. I think the whole family died if I remember correctly."

I furrowed my brow, perplexed by the revelation. If Michael had a half-brother like Cat had said, then how could the whole family have perished in the fire? Something wasn't adding up.

"Are you sure?" Sarah nodded her head slowly in response.

"I'm pretty sure," she confirmed. "But I could be wrong. It was a long time ago, and I don't really know all the details. There's probably an article about it somewhere online. It was a pretty big deal."

Something about Sarah's words tugged at my mind, like a loose tag digging into the back of my neck, niggling into my skin. *An article about it somewhere online.* Why did that sound so right to me? So familiar? I logged the thought for later contemplation, painfully aware that the Davises still had their eyes fixed firmly on me.

"I'll look into it," I promised. "Is there anything else you remember? Anything at all? Maybe Mia mentioned Michael from class at one point?"

The room went silent once more, both Sarah and Leah shaking their heads, unable to produce a single memory that might prove helpful. Mr. and Mrs. Davis seemed like ghosts of themselves, there but not, the shock of my words still stitched into each of their faces. The sight of them made me feel horrible. Responsible somehow. Maybe if I hadn't been trapped inside a tunnel of my own making, I could have had this conversation years ago. Could have had a better chance at bringing the man to justice who had robbed them of their daughter. Now I was standing in the same parlor where we had gathered to mourn her loss before the funeral, grasping at straws, hoping to form connections that seemed too far out of reach—and they could see me flailing. Could see me failing them once again.

I looked around the room, the aftermath of my words shaking me to my core. In all my years coming to the Davis's house, I had always felt like part of the family, their warmth and acceptance more inviting to me than my mother's house in Glendale had ever been. But as each of them flinched away from my gaze, too stricken by the distress I had caused them with my words, I began to feel like an outsider.

"I should go," I announced. "I'm going to be staying in town for a couple of days, though, so I'll be around if you—"

"Don't be ridiculous," Mrs. Davis's voice was brittle and broken as it cracked through her strained vocal cords. "You aren't going anywhere. You're family. You'll stay here with the rest of us."

My lip quivered, eyes misted over with gratitude. I rushed over to her place on the sofa, sank to my knees, and gathered her into my arms.

"Thank you, Mrs. Davis," I whispered. "I'm so sorry. I tried so hard. I really wanted to—"

"Hush, child," she murmured. "You've nothing to be sorry for. None of this is your fault."

"I'm going to find him," I promised. "I'm going to find him, and I'm going to make him pay for what he did if it's the last thing I do."

"I know you will," she said. "I know you will."

***

That night, I stayed in Mia's room—just like I always did when I slept at the Davis's house. But despite the fact that I had been invited to stay there, despite the deep familiarity I felt at the sight of the French doors that led out to the second-story balcony, the floor-to-ceiling windows that framed the fireplace in her room, the feeling of the trundle bed beneath my body, I felt like a stranger. An intruder. Each time I tried to fall asleep, I was jerked awake by the image of Sarah's quaking shoulders, Leah's unrelenting anger, Mr. Davis's waning life force evaporating from his body like water vapor.

It didn't help that Sarah and Leah hadn't made their usual appearance at Mia's balcony door, tapping on the window pane to invite me onto the terrace so we could take turns pulling swigs from a bottle of scotch, drowning our sorrows together as we had done so many times before. I knew that the knowledge of their sister's murder wasn't going to be received lightly, but part of me couldn't help but feel disappointed. It's not like I was expecting to be lauded as a hero. How could I be? I hadn't actually caught the killer—yet. But Leah's anger with me was palpable. No matter how many times I tried to explain to her that I couldn't jeopardize my investigation by telling her my theories before I had any proof, she didn't want to hear it.

"She just needs some time," Josh had said to me after a quiet, uncomfortable dinner. "You know how she can be. She's a little stubborn. She'll come around."

"Sooner than later, I hope," I said miserably. "I can't stand her hating me."

Josh placed his hands on each of my shoulders, forcing me to look into his face. If I hadn't known any better, I would have said that he was a blood relative to the Davis family with his dirty blonde hair, tanned skin, and perfect nose. It was his eyes that gave it away, though—two pools of hazel where blue should have been, an exact match for my own.

"No one hates you, Rachel," he told me. "Trust me. I'll talk to her. She'll come around."

It was an early night for the family, the emotional exhaustion from our conversation making the need for sleep more urgent, more necessary than usual. After spending so much time in Williamsburg, I was especially tired, my vision gone pixelated and foggy with fatigue, shadows deepening in the creases beneath my eyes. But no matter how hard I tried to succumb to slumber, it never came.

My mind was racing with thoughts about Michael Davies, Mia and her sisters, and the mysterious circumstances surrounding the house fire that had supposedly wiped out the entire Davies family. I tossed and turned well into the night, flames licking the inside of my eyelids any time sleep drew near, jolting me awake in a panic, the taste of smoke somehow coating my tastebuds. Kicking the sheets off of my body in frustration, I decided to give in to my anxiety, reaching for my phone to see if I could find any articles on the Davies family fire as Sarah had suggested.

I hadn't bothered to check my cellphone since arriving at the Davis's house, too preoccupied with what I had come there to do and the aftermath that followed to give a damn about any calls or texts that I had received. When I entered my passcode and arrived at the Home screen, I was surprised to see that I had three missed text messages—two from Nick asking if I had arrived at the Davis's house and how the conversation had gone (I decided I would answer those in the morning. Best not to give his girlfriend the wrong idea by texting him back so late in the night); the other was from an unfamiliar phone number.

At first glance, the sight of the strange number made the hairs on the back of my neck stand on end. I never received messages from numbers I didn't recognize, had avoided giving out my personal information to any online services, placing my name and number on the National Do Not Call Registry to eliminate the possibility of such intrusions into my personal life. It was an anomaly to receive even one robocall from an unlisted phone number during the course of an entire year, let alone a text message. But as soon as I tapped on the unread message, every ounce of panic that had swelled inside slowly dissipated. It was from Evan—the screenshot of the text from Cat that I had sent to myself earlier that same day.

I saved the image to my iPhone Photos, opening it up to view its contents once more, the unusual wording sending rivulets of terror surging down my spine.

Maybe in another life, it could have been us.

There was a sense of desperation in the words that felt all too familiar, reminding me of the messaging that I had seen in Stacy Dunlap's suicide note.

All I wanted was to be with you, to have you forever, hers had read. But before that, an even more terrifying inscription: *Denying it only makes it stronger.*

That statement was proving to be more ominous with every passing day. Since Stacy's life had been claimed in the Holiday Inn in Charlotte, two more women had died—another young girl found a few short blocks away from the same hotel where Stacy had been discovered, and Elaine. How long would it be before Michael felt the need to release the "darkness inside" as he had so eloquently put it? I didn't want to know. Didn't want to think about the ticking clock counting down to my next failure. But I didn't have that option. The sand was being drained from the hourglass, and if I wasn't careful, I would get buried beneath the granules right along with every victim that I had been unable to protect.

I navigated to the web browser on my phone and began punching different combinations of the same key phrase into the search engine: Red Rock family tragedy; Davies family fire in Red Rock; Davies house fire in Red Rock, NC. When I hit enter on the last combination, a tingling sensation tugged at my insides, working its way slowly from my scalp down to my tailbone. At the top of the search results page was a headline for an article dated May 16, 2018—one that I had already seen just five years earlier:

Years After Deadly Fire, Davies Family Matriarch Dies at 63
Sudbury, NORTH CAROLINA—May 16, 2018—Thirteen years after a horrifying house fire that shocked the Sudbury community, Carolyn Davies died on Wednesday night following a long battle with chronic lung disease. As one of only two family members who made it through the devastating events of 2005, Carolyn is survived only by her remaining son, Matthew Davies. A memorial service will be held on Sunday, May 27, at St. Augustine's Southern Baptist Church in Red Rock, North Carolina. In lieu of flowers, the family asks that donations be made to PhoenixRise: Advocates for Burn Survivors.

* This article has been updated for accuracy to reflect the correct timeline of events.

Once again, it seemed that I had overlooked a piece of pertinent information, mistaking it for something insignificant since it didn't align with my preconceived notion that Evan was to blame for Mia's death. If the details in the article were correct, then Sarah was mistaken when she said the entire Davies family had perished in the fire. But there was one thing in the article that made my gut churn with ice, one glaring error that I knew wasn't true—not if this was the same Davies family that I had been searching for.

Carolyn is survived only by her remaining son, Matthew Davies.

My mind was reeling. Why would this article suggest that Carolyn had only one son who survived the fire when Michael was still alive and well? Was it a simple mistake, an oversight from a novice journalist? Or did everyone believe that Michael was dead? If they did, was that intentional?

Was that why he chose to change his identity?

I peered into the screen, searching the spaces between each sentence as though the answers might magically appear. Cat's voice tickled my eardrum, the words she had spoken during our conversation taking on new meaning in my mind.

He had all these... scars on his body.

I wondered what kind of scars she had meant, cursed myself for not thinking to ask in the moment. Cat had suggested that they might have been caused by some sort of abuse incurred by Michael's grandfather, but given the content in the article, I wasn't so convinced. Perhaps they weren't relics of physical torment at all but were from something far more sinister. Like surviving a house fire—or setting one.

I shot upright in the trundle bed and tossed my phone on the mattress, making a beeline for the window seat beneath the giant panes of glass peering out into the Davis's front lawn. It was clear to me that if I was going to find where Michael was, I would need to do more digging around in the past. I had found my first big break in the case hiding in one of Mia's yearbooks—perhaps there were other answers to be found lurking between the pages of the others she had tucked away within her secret storage space.

One by one, I lifted the pile of yearbooks from Mia's academic career out of the window seat, splaying them across the hardwood in chronological order. There were thirteen total—one for every grade from first through twelfth. Already familiar with the icy stare that awaited me on the page that held Mia's senior portrait, I skipped over the twelfth-grade yearbook and started with the one from her junior year. I flipped through the pages until I found the one with Mia's photo, her big, blue eyes and infectious smile framed by her signature blonde bob. But when I moved from her portrait to the student next in line behind her, Michael Davies wasn't there. Justin Deagan had taken his place, the pudgy, curly-haired student's affable smile nowhere near the empty, haunting stare that I had been expecting to find.

I moved on to the yearbook from Mia's sophomore year, her freshman year, her days in middle school, each time finding zero evidence of Michael Davies. Sudbury was a close-knit community not known for having many transplants—a fact that was reflected in the sea of familiar faces that I had seen as I hunted for the one portrait that eluded me. It seemed strange that Michael had seemingly materialized out of thin air during his senior year of high school in a town where most students had gone to school together for the duration of their lives. It seemed even stranger that he would hold some kind of bizarre grudge against a girl whom he had barely known at all aside from their single shared year of high school.

By the time I had made my way halfway through Mia's elementary school yearbooks, I was ready to call it quits. Michael Davies hadn't made a single solitary appearance in any of the pages that I had scanned since twelfth grade. But I wasn't about to fall victim to my own assumptions once again. I resolved to make my way through each and every one, even if the results yielded nothing but more unanswered questions.

It was well past one o' clock in the morning by the time I cracked open the pages of Mia's second-grade yearbook, moonlight spilling in from the windows, casting a ghastly glow across the glossy pages that made my discovery within even more disturbing. Towards the middle of the yearbook at the top of the page was a heading in large, bubble letters that read "Ms. Martin's Class of 1996," beneath which was a group photo of all her happy second-graders. My hands began to shake as my gaze fell to the center of the photograph to find the unmistakable image of Mia flashing a toothy grin at the camera. And standing right beside her, clutching her hand inside of his own was a sandy-haired child with icy blue eyes fixed adoringly on his classmate, not at all concerned with directing his attention to the front of the room with the rest of his peers.

Suddenly the room felt too hot, too heavy, too oppressive. I snapped the yearbook shut and stumbled over to the French doors, flinging them open and bursting out onto the balcony, gasping for fresh air. My hands gripped the railing, searching for balance in the white-lacquered woodgrain. It wasn't until I heard a low voice call out to me from the darkness that I realized I wasn't alone.

"Can't sleep either, huh?" Beau observed, the sound of his drawl making me jump. His lips quirked at my sudden movement, a small chortle escaping his lips. "Didn't mean to scare ya."

"Sorry," I said, still gripping the railing. "It's just... been a long day."

"Yeah, I know what you mean," he agreed solemnly, turning his gaze towards the moon.

"Did... did Sarah tell you about... you know?" Beau hadn't come back from his trip to the ice cream parlor with Emma until well after I had discussed everything with the family. With his daughter close by for the remainder of the evening, I hadn't had the opportunity to tell him everything myself.

"Yeah," he nodded, still looking into the sky. "Yeah, she told me."

We remained in quiet contemplation on the balcony, neither of us daring to acknowledge the reason why we each found it impossible to face one another. In the distance, I could hear crickets chirping, crooning out their melancholy chorus from the fields below. I wondered if they could sense our sadness, if they could feel the way our hearts thrummed out the same sorrowful tune that their tiny legs squeaked out between the blades of grass.

"I knew him, you know," Beau broke the silence first, turning away from the moon to face me. "Michael, I mean."

My pulse seemed to disappear from my body entirely, no longer able to hear the insect symphony below over the sound of the blood rushing past my ears.

"What?" I faltered. "What do you mean you knew him? How? When?"

"It was a long time ago, back when we were just kids," he answered. "I was a couple of years older than Mia, but when I was in fourth grade, me and the rest of the kids in my class had to be Peer Partners for the second-graders. We each got matched with a younger student to help show them the ropes, you know? Give 'em a little more confidence and all that. That's how I met Mia. She was my Little Learner—that's what the teachers called it."

I remained quiet, biting my tongue around the mountain of questions that wanted to erupt from my mouth like a volcano. Something inside told me to let Beau tell his story on his own terms.

"Even then, she was sweet as could be," his voice was even as he spoke, but I could see the tears twinkling in his eyes beneath the starlight. I turned away, embarrassed, giving him what little privacy I could muster while still listening. "All the other kids were jealous I got paired with her. She was... special, you know? Everyone thought so. Especially Michael."

He cleared his throat then, and I pretended not to see as he rubbed his face on his sleeve, clearing away the evidence of his grief.

"They were best friends, those two," he continued. "Shit, I don't think you ever saw one without the other. Mia and Michael, Michael and Mia. It was kind of annoying to be honest with you. Some of the other kids would get real ornery about it. *Ms. Martin*," he adopted a child's voice, "*Mia and Michael won't let us play with them!* They were always leavin' others out. I kept tellin' Mia, you know, you gotta open up a little more. There are lots of other kids in school, and it's great to have a best friend, but you can't leave everyone else out. It ain't right. She didn't wanna hear about none of that. But it didn't make a difference anyway. At the end of second grade, Michael moved away, and none of us ever saw him again.

"I remember Mia was real upset about it. She just couldn't wrap her head around losing her best friend like that. But, you know, the summer came and went, and by the time third grade started back up, she was back to her usual self," his lips danced upward at the image in his mind that only he could see. I imagined a bright and bubbly nine-year-old Mia laughing in the schoolyard, skin kissed bronze from the beating summer sun.

But what about Michael? Was he able to recover from losing his friend in the same way that Mia had? Or had he let the ashes of their friendship smolder, stoked his anguish with a hot poker until the embers became an insurmountable inferno?

"What do you know about the fire?" I pressed. "Sarah had mentioned that there was a fire at the Davies' house. You hear anything about that?"

Beau nodded his head slowly.

"Yeah, I know about it," he said. "That's the weirdest part about all this. I've gotten to know the survivors pretty well—well, *survivor*, now. My HVAC company does a lot of community giving, you know, so we donate pretty regularly to that nonprofit—"

"PhoenixRise?" I interjected. Beau tilted his head quizzically.

"Yeah, that's it," he confirmed, impressed by my foreknowledge. "Anyway, we give to the organization every year, and they always do a little ceremony to acknowledge the Davies family. But it was just Carolyn and Matthew who survived. Michael Davies died in that fire, and so did Carolyn's fiancé, Steve. It doesn't make any sense. How can a ghost be responsible for...?"

He trailed off, unable to complete the thought. His words hovered in the air, lulling us into an uncomfortable quiet once more. I decided to break the silence first.

"You said you know the family pretty well?" I ventured. He gave a nod and I continued, "What're the chances you could put me in touch with Matthew?"

"I'd say they're pretty high," Beau said.

"High enough to get me his home address?" I pushed. Beau frowned, leaning his head to one side as though trying to work out a difficult calculation.

"Yeah," he decided. "Yeah, I think I can pull that off."

CHAPTER 15

May 27, 2023

That Saturday, I found myself fifteen miles south of Sudbury in an unassuming mobile home community standing outside of Matthew Davies' ramshackle trailer. True to his word, Beau had tracked down Matthew's address for me with relative ease, the HVAC company's history of community giving providing a paper trail of correspondence that proved especially useful for my investigatory needs.

I left the Davis's house that morning sailing on a wave of renewed confidence that I hadn't felt in years, eager to speak to someone who might finally have some answers about the man I had been chasing. But as soon as I parked my car outside of the yellowed, filthy manufactured home that belonged to Michael's half-brother, reality began to set in once more.

Don't do anything stupid, I could almost hear Nick chastising me all the way from Charlotte, begging me to play it safe. As much as I wanted to pretend that I was being cautious, deep down I knew that I wasn't. I had shown up unannounced to the relative's house of a suspected serial killer with no real plan, no backup, no one aside from the Davis family aware of my whereabouts (a lot of good that would do me if something went awry). For all I knew, Michael could be hiding out inside, ready to ambush me, add me to his never-ending list of victims.

Of course, I still had my gun and my badge—I hadn't handed in either like Kane had asked me to before heading back to Williamsburg to continue my stakeout. I didn't even want to think about what Nick might say if he found out that I was carrying what was essentially a stolen firearm from the Green Valley Police Department, or that I planned to get Matthew to talk to me by flashing my inactive badge.

What he doesn't know won't hurt him, I had convinced myself. But as I drank in the tiny, dilapidated structure that stood before me, my self-assurance began to wane. I took out my phone and decided to shoot Nick a quick message letting him know where I was. Not that it would matter; he was still an hour away in Charlotte. But at least he would know where to come looking to find my body if things turned sour.

I gulped.

The wooden steps on the side of the trailer creaked beneath my weight as I climbed to the top of the landing in front of the screen door. Cigarette butts littered the ground beside an old lawn chair to the left of the porch area—if you could call a two-by-two stretch of decaying wooden planks a porch. Paint peeled away from the siding, which was caked with unwashed dirt and grime. An uneasy feeling settled in my stomach as I steeled myself and proceeded to knock on the door.

I strained my ears, listening for the sound of life stirring somewhere within the building but heard nothing. Maybe he wasn't home? I looked around to see a beat-up old Chevy Silverado parked halfway on the front lawn.

No, I thought, *there's definitely someone here.*

Midway through my musings, I heard the door unlock, sending my nerves into overdrive as a young man appeared in the doorway. My mouth fell open as I took him in. He looked to be in his late twenties and was much thinner and frailer than the tall, muscular man I had seen at Burg Interiors. But everything else about him was an exact match for the photo I had seen printed next to Mia's senior portrait.

His sandy hair was long and unkempt, sweeping over his face in a manner that suggested I had just spurred him awake from a deep slumber. Though I could tell he was well beyond his teenage years, his skin was angry with acne that decorated his jawline like a family of fire ants. Through the stretched-out neckline of his tee-shirt, I could see a mess of mottled, puckered skin that seemed better suited to an eighty-year-old's body rather than the young person who stood before me.

But the thing that made the hairs stand up on the back of my arms had nothing to do with the deep scars creeping up his collarbone. It was those eyes—the same powder gray irises that I had seen shrink-wrapped with grief at the interior design firm days after Elaine was found stabbed to death in Cat's kitchen. The same frozen tundra that I had seen staring back at me from Mia's yearbook.

"Can I help you?" his voice was quiet, timid as he spoke. I fumbled for the badge in my pocket, flipping it open more clumsily than I had intended, too distracted by the similarities he shared with his sibling to keep my composure.

"I'm Detective McGowen with the Sudbury PD," I lied, snapping my badge shut before he had time to realize that the words "Green Valley Police Department" were engraved on its surface. "Are you Matthew Davies?"

He paused, muscles gone rigid with apprehension.

"I am," he admitted. "Sorry... what's this about?"

"I'm investigating a homicide that happened in Sudbury," I told him. At least that part wasn't a lie. Matthew's eyebrows pressed together across his forehead, his body jerking back as though my words had physically pushed through him.

"I-I don't know anything about that," he stammered.

"I'm not accusing you of anything, Mr. Davies," I assured him. "But I would still like to ask you a few questions if you don't mind."

"I don't get it," he argued. "If you don't think I'm involved, then what the heck's this got to do with me?"

I paused, thinking over my response. He didn't seem willing to speak with me unless I could provide a substantial reason for my being there. My gaze fell to the scars peeking out beneath his shirt, the sight of his damaged skin forcing a cruel yet crafty falsehood to take shape inside my mind.

"We think it could be a case of arson," I said. "It could even be connected to what happened to your family. Please—can we talk?"

Though I didn't feel good about all the dishonesty, my words seemed to have the desired effect. Matthew ran a shaky hand through his unkempt hair, craning his neck around to peer back into the darkened room beyond the front door.

"It's kind of a mess in here," he confessed.

"That's okay," I forced a tight smile. "It'll only take a second."

After a brief moment of hesitation, he pushed open the screen door and allowed me to cross the threshold. The inside of the trailer was as dirty and dingy as its dismal exterior, with a cramped living area decorated only by empty pizza boxes, stray cigarette cartons, and discarded beer cans. A lumpy, pinstriped sofa was crammed beneath the window on the far side of the room, beside which sat a metal folding chair not unlike the one I had sat in at the Monroe County Sheriff's Office. Matthew gestured towards the sofa, allowing his guest to take the more comfortable of the two available seats. He flicked a switch, bathing the room in a hazy, yellow light that swam out from overhead.

"Sorry it's so..." he waved his hand around, grasping for the words that might adequately describe the sorry state of his living situation.

"No need to apologize," I tried to ease his obvious embarrassment, though I had to admit that the surroundings made me feel a bit squeamish. He took a seat in the metal chair, wringing his hands in his lap, his body radiating anxiety. I cleared my throat and extracted my notepad and pen from my pants pocket. "Like I said, Mr. Davies, we think this case might be connected to what happened at your house in 2005. Can you tell me a little bit about what happened?"

"You can call me Matt," he mumbled nervously. "And I don't really know what to say about that. I was only ten when it happened. It'll be nineteen years ago this summer."

"That must have been scary to go through as a kid," I commented, bringing my hand to my clavicle with a grimace. "Is that how you got those scars? Were you inside the house when it happened?"

Matt's fingers flew to his neckline, tugging his shirt up instinctively to cover the marks to which I was referring. His cheeks flushed red as he nodded.

"Yeah, I... I guess I was," he said cryptically.

"You guess?"

"Like I said, it happened a long time ago," he explained. "It was weird, you know? Everything happened so fast. One minute I was asleep in my bed, the next I was laying on the grass outside, watching my house burn down."

His eyes went wide, as though he had been transported back in time, forced to watch the flames engulf his home once more. He blinked away the memory, joining me once again in his living room.

"How did you end up outside?" I tilted my head, unsure what to make of his story. "Was it a firefighter that rescued you?"

He shook his head, eyes welling with tears.

"No," he said. "I just... woke up out there. All I remember thinking is, *Why does my chest hurt so bad?* Everything burned. It hurt to breathe. I kept looking around, trying to find an adult, but there was no one around. That's when I heard them..."

He drifted off again, those icy irises filling with smoke and ash as I forced him to relive what was likely the worst day of his life.

"Who did you hear?" I pressed gently. His lips contorted into a pained expression that made me regret asking the question.

"My mom and dad," he whispered. "They were trapped in there and I... I couldn't..."

He brought his hands to his face, his shoulders heaving as he allowed the hurt to pass through his fragile body. I felt awkward sitting there, watching a grown man, a perfect stranger sob in front of me. The only thing I could offer in the way of comfort was one of the many crumpled napkins that lay scattered around the room. I decided against it, choosing instead to use my words.

"I'm so sorry that happened to you," I told him, biting my lip as I tried to regain control of the conversation, search for something more positive to say that might help him recover his composure. "Your mom survived, though—didn't she?"

Matt brought his tee-shirt up to his face, drying away his tears. As he did so, I could see the whole of his torso shared the same wrinkled pattern as was visible from his neck. I winced.

"I guess," he whimpered. "I wouldn't really call that surviving. She was wrecked after that. Her body was completely burnt to a crisp. Her lungs were totally ruined from all the smoke. It was a miracle they were able to pull her out of there, but it still killed her in the end. She died a few years back. Body just... gave up on itself."

"I'm sorry to hear that," I said. "What about your dad? Did he...?"

Matt shook his head grimly.

"When the firefighters went in to grab my mom, the roof caved in as they were trying to save her," his voice was strangled as he fought the urge to cry. "There was no hope for him after that. It took them all night to put out the fire. By the time they were done, there were only pieces of him left. Not even enough to fill a casket."

He hung his head low, tears dropping with audible thuds into his lap—the only sound permissible in the wake of his harrowing tale. If I had known him better, I might have placed a soothing hand on his back, rubbed the space between his shoulder blades like my mom used to do when I was young and the kids at school had been too mean. But all I could do was absorb his pain from afar, wait until he seemed strong enough to handle another question. When he finally lifted his head, I didn't waste any time.

"You had a brother, too, didn't you?" I held my breath as I awaited his response, careful not to put my emotions on display.

"Yeah," he answered. "Michael was my half-brother. He... he didn't make it, either."

My stomach flipped. So, even Matt was under the impression that Michael had perished in the fire—but why? As though he could hear my thoughts, he continued.

"There wasn't much to find in the rubble," he explained. "All they could find of both my dad and Michael were a few bones here and there. It was... awful."

I bit the inside of my cheek until I could taste blood, trying not to let the questions in my mind spill out of my mouth. How could there have been bones left behind for a person who I knew for a fact was still living? I had seen Michael Davies with my own eyes standing in the Burg Interiors lobby not even two weeks ago. But if what Matt said was true and they had recovered his brother's bones at the site of the fire, then Michael couldn't be alive—could he?

A loud ringing chirped out from my back pocket, pulling me away from my thoughts in an instant. It was my cellphone signaling an incoming call. I put up an apologetic finger to Matt, excusing myself as I extracted the phone from my pocket to check who was interrupting us.

It was Nick.

"Excuse me," I murmured. "I have to take this."

I hoisted myself up from the sofa and moved to the front door, stepping out into the sticky, southern heat.

"Hey, can I call you back?" I answered. "Now's not a—"

"Rachel?" Nick's voice was urgent, the sound of it sending shockwaves through my stomach.

"Nick, what's wrong?"

"We just got the autopsy results for Charlie Hamlin—the vic found in the alley near the Charlotte Holiday Inn?" his words seemed to tumble out of his mouth faster than he could articulate them. "There was male DNA found on the body. We ran it through the database, and you're never gonna believe what came back."

My breath caught in my throat.

"Don't tell me it was Evan all this time," I groaned. "I swear to God, I will fucking—"

"It's not Evan," Nick assured me. "But it is a match for the DNA that was found at the Dunlap scene."

"Oh my God," I breathed. "So that means—?"

"Yeah," he cut me off again, his excitement palpable. "Whoever killed Stacy also killed Charlie."

I let the weight of his words sink in. Of course, I already suspected that to be the case, as did Nick. But having the physical proof to support it made everything seem more real. I felt vindicated, justified in every action I had taken since first learning about Mia's death. But I also felt frustrated. We had a match, yes, but without a sample to cross-reference, we still didn't have our killer. And with Michael nowhere to be found, getting my hands on such a sample was going to be impossible. I puffed out a frustrated sigh, turning my head towards the earth, nothing returning my gaze but a pile of cigarette butts scattered across the ground.

Wait a minute.

An old episode of *Criminal Minds* played on a movie screen inside my head. I could see the Behavior Analysis Unit agents stepping in to save the day, solving a string of ritualistic killings in Tallahassee by using an ancestry DNA website.

"What do you know about ancestry?" I blurted, pulling the thread in my mind.

"Umm... what?" Nick replied.

"Like, if I got a DNA sample from someone related to the suspect, could it help confirm who we think is the real killer?" I stepped down the rickety staircase, toeing a few of the discarded cigarettes at my feet.

"Well, yeah, it could," Nick said. "But we still don't know where Michael's family is, so we'd need to—"

"I'm at his brother's house right now," I interrupted.

"Whose brother?"

"Michael's," I answered.

"You're *what?*" Nick was furious. "Rachel, do you have any idea how fucking dangerous that could be? You said yourself that he could have been hiding out there!"

"Yeah, well, luckily, I was wrong about that," I gave a nervous laugh.

"Rachel, this isn't fucking funny," he griped. "You could've gotten hurt. You could've gotten *killed!*"

"Well, I didn't," I pointed out. "So, do you want this DNA sample or not?"

Silence.

If I closed my eyes, I could see Nick's jaw pulsing impatiently as he ground his teeth together, his dark brows looming low over the storm swirling somewhere in his copper eyes.

"Collect what you can," he grumbled finally. "Then come straight here."

CHAPTER 16

May 29, 2023

The traffic heading into Charlotte was insufferable that Monday, making the hour drive from Sudbury take even longer than expected. Weaving through rush-hour traffic in the Queen City's bustling Uptown area would have been bad enough on a normal day, but with the Memorial Day parade shutting down Tryon Street, finding my way to the precinct where Nick was stationed proved to be downright exhausting.

I had left the Davis's house that morning at seven o' clock sharp, eager to get the DNA from Matt's cigarette butt into the hands of the lab technicians. In an ideal world, that would have placed me through the department doors no later than eight-thirty. Unfortunately for me, I didn't get there until ten.

From the outside, the Charlotte-Mecklenburg Police Department was more impressive than any station that I had ever seen, with large, ivory columns towering overhead, flanking either side of the front entrance. It looked more like a building that belonged on the campus of some Ivy League institution rather than situated in the heart of urban North Carolina. Once I crossed the threshold into the front lobby, however, I was thrown into a cacophony of chaos.

Throngs of officers and their detainees buzzed about the station, a disgruntled arrestee declaring his innocence as I pushed my way into the busy reception area to find the front desk. I should have expected such a scene what with the citywide celebrations underway—if being an officer had taught me anything, it was that even the smaller holidays were subject to bringing out the worst in humanity. But with my mind focused on delivering the DNA sample, it hadn't dawned on me that it was Memorial Day weekend until I was already in the thick of parade traffic.

"Can I help you?" a stout, bespectacled woman peered at me above the rims of her thick-framed glasses in a manner that communicated helping me was the furthest thing from her mind.

"I'm looking for Officer Gildan," I explained, holding up the plastic bag containing Matt's discarded cigarette. "He's expecting me. I've got a DNA sample connected to the Hamlin case that needs testing."

The woman raised a skeptical eyebrow, appraising my lack of police uniform with the incredulity of a schoolteacher pondering the likelihood that her student's dog truly did eat her homework.

"Take a seat over there," she motioned toward the waiting area, which was noticeably devoid of such accommodations—every seat in the house was occupied by one person or another. I chose a length of semi-private wall space to lean against while I waited for the officer manning the reception desk to notify Nick of my arrival. It seemed like hours passed before he came bursting through the wooden door that led into the bullpen, a harried expression on his face as he scanned the room.

"Nick," I waved in his direction as I joined him by the door where he had just materialized. Once his gaze landed on mine, he broke out into a grin, the dimples deepening in his cheeks enough to make my heart jump to my throat.

Despite the frazzled look on his face as he entered the room, he still appeared handsome as ever, his eyes catching sunbeams that danced through the colossal windows lining the front of the building, glistening like two pennies at the bottom of a wishing well. I wanted nothing more than to melt into his arms, feel his hands find the familiar path along the small of my back as they had done so effortlessly once upon a time. But that part of our lives was over. He was spoken for, and even if he hadn't been, it wouldn't have been appropriate given the current climate in the lobby.

"Hey, kiddo," he greeted me. I allowed one corner of my mouth to pull upward in a coy half-smile, twisting it back down in an instant to keep my cheeks from glowing red.

"I've got the sample," I held up the plastic bag for him to see, reminding him of the reason I had come there. For a moment, his face changed, a flicker of what looked to be concern or heartache flashing behind his copper eyes. Before I had time to pinpoint the emotion stippled across his features, it morphed back to the casual calm I had seen him wear as I first approached.

"Great," he reached out to take the bag from my hands, "I'll get this over to the lab right away. You didn't do anything too stupid to get this, did you?"

I rolled my eyes.

"Give me some credit," I griped. "The damned things were laying all over his front lawn. It's not like I had to snatch it out of his mouth."

Nick's dark brows ruffled together.

"You're sure it's his, though, and not a neighbor's or something?" he squinted at the bag, as though he could tell just by looking at it whether the sample belonged to the right person.

"Positive," I affirmed. "I thought about just grabbing one off the ground while I was there, but I was afraid of the same thing. So, I decided to stake him out for a bit, wait until he took a smoke break so I could make sure it was really his."

Nick grimaced, wrinkling the bridge of his hawkish beak as he did so. He let out a short sigh and shook his head.

"Well, I'm just glad you're alright," he said finally. "Did you find anything else out while you were off pretending to be invincible?"

"Yeah, a lot actually," I nodded. "It's a lot to explain... can we maybe sit down somewhere and talk it over?"

"Normally, I'd say yes," he craned his neck around, observing the general disarray of the lobby, "but this place is a madhouse. It's not even noon, and we've already had to process half a dozen drunken and disorderlies, not to mention all the domestics. You know how the holidays are."

"Yeah, I completely forgot about Memorial Day," I admitted.

"It's probably going to be a long day for me here at the station," he said. "Might not get home until late tonight."

I nodded, ignoring the way his words twisted around the chambers of my heart. I don't know what I was expecting, but it certainly wasn't a simple drop-and-dash. We had been working the case together for months—was it really so much to ask for us to have a proper debriefing that wasn't done over the phone? My shoulders sagged.

"Well, I guess I'll leave you to it then," I gave a curt nod and turned to leave, but Nick caught my hand before I could take a step away.

"Hang on," he commanded, his fingers sending electric currents through my skin. "I want to see you—about the case, I mean. Can you stay in town for a few more days—at least until the lab results come back? We can grab dinner or something after my shift tomorrow to talk more about what you learned. Shouldn't be as hectic."

I frowned, my heart sinking to the bottom of my embarrassingly empty bank account.

"I can't," I told him. "I'm broke, remember?"

"That's okay," he assured me, his dimples making yet another devastating appearance. "I'll spot you."

"I don't know," I hesitated. "You've been doing that a lot. I don't want to put you out. Plus, your girlfriend can't be—"

"Don't worry about it," he said. "Just get yourself settled and shoot me a text to let me know where you're staying. I'll pick you up tomorrow night when I get off work."

I chewed my lip, conscious of the fact that his hand was still holding mine.

"Okay," I decided. "I'll let you know where I end up."

With that, I reluctantly released myself from his grasp, pressing through the crowded precinct until I found myself back on the streets of the Queen City in search of a place to stay.

***

May 30, 2023

Maybe it was morbid of me to choose the Charlotte Holiday Inn. Even more so to request the same room where Stacy Dunlap had spent her final night. I don't know why I did it. Perhaps I was hoping that being there might help me access the mind of the madman who was still out there somewhere, avoiding capture. As though he had left behind remnants of his darkness, a trail of shadows for me to follow that might lead me to his hiding place.

The room was exactly as I remembered: A dated blur of beige and taupe that bled together until the walls were no more distinguishable from the carpet than they were from the boxy furniture that populated the space. Everything looked the same as the day that I had inspected the crime scene with Nick. Well, everything except the bathroom, that is. Whatever cleaning crew had tackled the bloodstained tub basin where the victim had been recovered did an excellent job. If I hadn't known any better, I would never have guessed that the shower walls had once been coated crimson with Stacy's blood.

While I didn't find any traces of evil that might have pointed me in Michael's direction, being in the room reminded me that I still hadn't done any research into the psychiatrist that Cat had mentioned. My eyes scanned the nightstand where Stacy's suicide note was discovered beside an empty prescription bottle, the Valium within spilled across the counter. Though the label had been ripped off, I knew in my heart that the medication belonged to Michael. If I could just speak to his doctor, maybe I could confirm those suspicions.

I spent hours tapping away at my cellphone, trying to locate the office of Dr. Browning to no avail. It seemed that the therapist had been just another in a tangled web of lies that Michael had intricately woven together like the ignominious arachnid he was.

I thought about making cold calls to various psychiatrists' offices throughout the Green Valley area but decided against it. Without a warrant or police credentials to provide, I knew it was unlikely that any doctor would be willing to speak to me about their patients, and they'd be well within their rights to deny me such information. There was such a thing as doctor-patient confidentiality, after all. I decided it was best to text Nick the information so he could follow up on the lead instead.

It was half past five when he finally called to let me know that his shift at the station was ending, his voice tired, drained of its usual easy charm no thanks to the Memorial Day madness that had ensued the previous day. A thrill rushed through my body at the thought of his arrival, which was quickly followed by soul-crushing humiliation as I realized that I had been forced to wear the same clothes that I had worn when I met with him at the station. I hadn't been expecting to stay in town, leaving my duffel bag at the Davis's house rather than taking it with me on my "quick trip" to Charlotte. At least I had thought to take a shower and make myself appear halfway presentable.

He's not interested in you anyway, a nefarious voice called out somewhere inside my mind as I gazed into the bathroom mirror, wishing to see something other than the purple shadows under my eyes, the frizz of humidity curling my hair at awkward angles. *He's moved on. This is strictly business.*

A knock at the door to my hotel room pulled me away from my misery. I peered through the peephole before unlatching the security chain and finding Nick in the hallway, still dressed in his uniform.

"Dunlap's room, huh?" he smirked, nodding at the room number next to the doorframe. "You do that on purpose?"

I rubbed the back of my neck, feeling the heat rise to my cheeks, embarrassed by my own superstition.

"Yeah, I just... thought it might help," I said. "Kind of stupid, I know."

"Hey, I'm not judging," he smiled a bit wider, the mischievous glint in his eye telling me something else entirely. "Okay, maybe I'm judging a little."

"Shut up," I nudged him on the shoulder, checking my back pocket for my room key before joining him out in the hallway. "So, what's for dinner?"

"Chinese?" Nick suggested. A pang of nostalgia ripped through my chest, the memory of paper containers littering the floor of my apartment as we wrestled each other on the ground forcing me to look away from his expectant eyes.

"Sure," I agreed. "That sounds good."

"Great," he grinned. "There's a place right around the corner from here that's really good. We can just walk there if you're okay with that?"

I shrugged and nodded.

"Lead the way," I told him.

The balmy twilit evening created a thin sheen of condensation on my cool skin as we exited the air-conditioned hotel lobby and stepped into the southern heat. Vibrant pink and orange hues painted the sky, reflecting off the mirrored glass of the skyscrapers that surrounded us as we navigated the city streets. With the sunset filling the air with a rose-colored haze, the smell of Nick's aftershave wafting in my direction, I began to feel dizzy with yearning. Romantic thoughts swirled with stubborn persistence through my head, the impossibility of their fruition forcing me to remain quiet for the duration of our walk.

Before long, we arrived at a nondescript brick storefront, the words "China Star" printed across the front window in big, red letters. A sharp bell rang out overhead as we entered through the glass door. The place was objectively unimpressive, reminiscent of an outdated pizza parlor with its dark-paneled walls and yellowed linoleum floors. It was clear from the absence of a formal dining area that the restaurant wasn't accustomed to accommodating many sit-down orders, with only a few small tables filling the tiny room in front of the cashier's counter.

An elderly Chinese woman not much taller than the height of the countertop where she was stationed waved excitedly over to Nick as we selected a table by the window.

"Good to see you again, Mr. Nick," she spoke in her broken English as she joined us at the table, placing a set of napkins and chopsticks down in front of us. "I see you have pretty friend with you tonight."

Her eyes crinkled at the corners as she smiled in my direction, bowing her head slightly. I blushed at her compliment, brushing a loose piece of hair behind my ear.

"Hi, Mei," Nick greeted the woman like an old friend. "This is Rachel. She's in town for a couple of days, so I figured I'd treat her to the best Chinese food in the Queen City."

Mei's hand flew to her chest as though Nick's words had stopped her heart. She bent at the waste, diving down for a deep bow.

"Oh, *thank* you, Mr. Nick," she gushed. "I make sure it come extra special just for you. You want usual order, or you want see menu?"

Nick glanced my way before answering.

"Up to you," he said. "But you should know, the Szechuan chicken is pretty amazing."

"I trust your judgment," I smirked.

"Two Number Fours it is, Mei," Nick announced to the delight of our waitress. "And a couple of waters, too, please—unless you want something else?"

"No, water's fine," I assured him.

Mei gave a wide smile, bowed her head once more, and walked away to provide our order to the kitchen. Within a few moments, she returned with our waters, then made her way back to the counter to give us our privacy. As I took a sip of my water, I caught a glimpse of Mei stealing surreptitious stares in our direction from the corner of my eye, as an excited mother might do when meeting her son's girlfriend for the first time. I groaned inwardly at how misguided her assumptions about our relationship had been, how desperately I wanted them to be true.

"I sent the DNA to the lab on rush order," Nick's voice jerked me away from my wayward thoughts, reminding me of the true nature of our outing. "Should have the results back by tomorrow or the next day."

"Wow, that's fast," I commented.

"Yeah, well, the sooner we get an ID, the sooner we can get a warrant and put out an APB to catch this guy," he took a sip of his own water and continued, "I got your text about the psychiatrist angle, too, but so far, no luck yet."

"Keep after it," I encouraged. "There's got to be something we're missing. Someone is filling those Valium prescriptions, and whoever it is might be able to tell us something that can help us find our guy."

"You don't have to tell me twice," Nick set his elbow on the table, resting his chin in the palm of his hand. "So, what'd you learn at the brother's?"

I folded my hands on the table in front of me and leaned back in my chair as I recounted the story that Matt had told me about the fire, how he had watched his house burn down in front of him, how he had listened to his parents' screams.

"Jesus," Nick shook his head. "To go through all that... and he was only ten?"

I gave a solemn nod.

"It's weird, though," he mused. "How was he able to make it out but his parents couldn't?"

"That's what's bizarre about it," I agreed. "He says he can't remember how he got out of the house. Just that he was asleep in his bed one minute, and the next, he's waking up on the front lawn. The firefighters hadn't even shown up by that point. It doesn't make a lot of sense. But that's not even the weirdest part of it all."

Before I could offer an explanation, Mei waddled out from the kitchen carrying two steaming plates of her signature chicken stir fry. She beamed with pride as she placed the saucy, spicy Szechuan meal in front of us.

"Chī hǎo," she bowed. "Enjoy!"

"Thank you, Mei," Nick answered, grabbing for his chopsticks. I followed suit, savoring a few bites of the fragrant dish, the Szechuan peppers sending a tingling sensation throughout my tongue, clearing sinuses that I hadn't known were clogged. After a few mouthfuls, I had to take a break, gulping down the remainder of my water glass to put out the fire stinging my tastebuds.

"Wowza!" I yelped. "That's good, but holy shit. You could've warned me it was that spicy."

Nick laughed, taking another bite of his own dish, not a single bead of sweat swimming up to the surface of his brow.

"Sorry," he snickered. "I don't even notice the heat anymore, to be honest with you. I'm so used to it by now. It's all Amber likes to eat."

My ribs splintered in my chest at the mention of who I was sure was Nick's new girlfriend. Before I could stop myself from asking the clarifying question that I didn't want an answer to, the words tumbled out of my mouth.

"Is that your girlfriend?"

He paused midway through taking another bite of chicken before stuffing it into his mouth, giving him the perfect excuse to avoid providing a verbal response, nodding his affirmative answer instead. I sipped my water, the heat burning in the back of my throat no longer having anything to do with the food I had just consumed. A heavy quiet hovered between us, the only sound piercing the air that of Nick's chewing as he continued to shovel the stir fry into his mouth. After what felt like a lifetime of awkward silence, Nick took a long swig from his water glass and cleared his throat.

"So, you were saying there was something strange about the fire?" he reminded me of what I had been about to tell him before Mei interrupted our conversation. I nodded.

"When I asked Matt what happened to his brother, he told me that he died in the fire that night," I said.

"You're kidding," Nick's eyes went wide. "Did they recover a body?"

I shook my head.

"Not really," I answered. "Matt said all that was left of his father and Michael were bone fragments. Said it took all night for the department to put out the fire."

"Did he say what caused it?" Nick pressed.

"He was only ten, so he didn't remember much," I reminded him. "But from the sounds of it, I'd say it was arson. There would have to have been some kind of accelerant used for it to burn that long."

"And for the bodies to have been that damaged," Nick nodded his head in agreement. "So, what do you think?"

I bunched my eyebrows together, trying to pinpoint an answer.

"I don't really know what to think," I confessed. "I mean, I saw Michael with my own eyes. I know that the man I saw at Burg Interiors was the same person I saw in Mia's yearbook. But I don't know how he would've been able to leave his bones behind in a fire like that."

"Maybe he didn't," Nick suggested. "Maybe the bones weren't his, but everyone assumed that they were."

My mouth fell open, aghast at the statement.

"You think there could be another victim?" Nick shrugged in response.

"I'm just spit-balling," he said. "But if he was trying to fake his own death, then that'd be the way to do it."

I contemplated that for a moment, my mind drifting back to Evan's fake ID. Fragments of the truth danced before my eyes, fighting to fit together to create a cohesive whole. But no matter how I tried to force them into shape, the pieces just wouldn't connect.

"I'm gonna go back to Matt's house," I decided. "There's gotta be something else he knows about Michael. A reason why he would've—"

"No," Nick interjected.

"No?" I repeated, raising my brows in disbelief.

"No," he said again. "Look, you did great work with the DNA, I'll give you that. But this is too dangerous, Rachel. You're not thinking about this clearly. You're not a cop right now. You can't just—"

"Can't just what?" I snapped, the truth of his words igniting a fire somewhere deep in my gut. "Can't just finish what I started? What no one else aside from you even believes?"

"Listen," he put up his hands, attempting to ease the tension, "we have the DNA now. There's a clear link between the Hamlin and the Dunlap case. Once that comes back positive, and it will—"

"It still won't tell us where Michael is!" I half-shouted, the sound of my anger causing Mei to cast a look of concern over at our table.

I lowered my voice and continued, "If I'm going to find where he is, then I need to talk to the brother. That's all there is to it."

"Rachel," Nick's voice was strained, exasperated. "It's not up to you, okay? If the results come back positive, we'll send a team over to Matt's house right away to get more answers. You have to play by the rules. We can't have you risking your life for this. You have to be rational here. You think Mia would want you putting yourself in harm's way like that?"

"Fuck the rules," I seethed. "And fuck you."

"C'mon, kiddo, don't be like—"

"I'm not your 'kiddo!'" I screamed, tears blurring my vision as I shot up from the table.

"Rachel, please," Nick's eyes darted from me to Mei, who had given a small cry of fear at my outburst. "Please, just... sit back down. Let's talk about this."

I crossed my arms and shook my head in dismay.

"Thanks for dinner," I said bitterly, dashing for the exit.

"Rachel, don't—"

But I didn't stay to listen. Whatever words Nick had wanted to say were muted behind the thick pane of glass to the restaurant door as it swung shut behind me and I marched back to my hotel room alone.

CHAPTER 17

Date Unknown

I wake up to the smell of smoke. I'm in a room that I don't recognize, an orange glow radiating off the wooden walls that surround me. My wrists are bound together behind my back, chafing against the coarse, thick rope that I can't see but can feel digging into my skin the harder I try to wriggle free. I attempt a scream, the sound deafened by the cloth that's wedged inside my mouth. I press my tongue against the fabric, work my jaw with frantic grinding motions, desperate to call for help. But the cloth is tied around my head so tightly, nothing I do loosens it.

Smoke burns in my nostrils, the acrid odor scorching the back of my throat, rattling through my lungs until I can't breathe. That's when I start to hear it. This low rumble like the sound of a locomotive thundering down a set of distant train tracks. But there's something else, too. A crackling undercurrent, popping and snapping, each tiny explosion reverberating in my chest the closer it draws near.

I see it now. Giant flames licking up the sides of the walls, engulfing everything they touch. The curtains on the windows are made of fire, the floor is lava, the ceiling is a supernova, white-hot and dying to burst. And I'm going to be next.

I twist in place until I find a stone hearth behind me, its masonry chipped at the base, the edges sharp and jagged. Placing my wrists on the lip of the stonework, I begin to move the rope back and forth, back and forth, back and forth, sawing over the serrated corners until I finally feel the tension release. I shake loose the ropes from my wrists and bring my hands to my mouth, following the cloth around to the back of my head, fingers fumbling with the knot until at long last, it comes free.

I scramble to my feet, searching through the inferno to find an exit that hasn't been consumed by fire, black plumes of smoke stinging my eyes, making it impossible to see. To my right, everything is red. Red windows, red doorframe, red walls. Red, red, red. I stumble back from the flames, raising my arm to my mouth like a vampire disguising their identity beneath a velvet cloak. My lungs are burning, eyes watering, heart thumping against my ribs as desperate for an escape from my body as I am to leave... wherever I am.

As I back away from the carnage, I bump into a table and see my gun and badge are resting on its surface. I snatch them up and continue to snake away from the smoke and sparks that are inching closer to the center of the room. Shrinking away to my left, my back collides against the wall and I realize I've hit a door. I feel the handle with the back of my hand, ensuring that it's cool to the touch before pressing through to the other side.

I'm standing in a hallway now, the bloom of fire radiating out from the right, casting amber shadows across the walls, promising more destruction. I turn to the darkness on my left, finding nothing but a dead end at the end of the hall. With no other choice, I creep towards the haunting glow of embers, clouds of smoke billowing out from the end of the hallway like black tentacles reaching out from the depths of a murky seabed.

As I approach the end of the hall, I see the figure of a man, his frame backlit by the blaze devouring the world around us. He's facing me, but I can't see him, his features all but erased by the humming heat waves, the blinding light of combustion. But I can feel him looking at me, a prickle of unease erupting somewhere inside my stomach the longer we hold each other's gaze. He moves his hand, the silhouette of his arm punctuated by the unmistakable outline of a firearm.

BANG!

The gunshot echoes through the roar of fire, the vibration from the discharge causing my hands to tingle as I keep my weapon raised, ensuring my target has been taken down. I step forward cautiously, the barrel of my gun still locked on the man who is now writhing on the ground in the place where he once stood. As I draw closer to him, my heart fills with ice despite the sweltering heat, knees sinking to the fiery floorboards as recognition and realization dance together with the flames.

"NO!" I clamber to his side, the copper light in Nick's eyes fading fast, dulling to a muted russet. His expression is both empty and serene, peaceful and full of terror as blood trickles out from the sides of his mouth. I'm sobbing and sputtering, craning my neck around as though a savior might leap out from the embers. "SOMEBODY HELP! NICK! Oh God, Nick... please. Please, don't die. NICK! WAKE UP! WAKE UP! *WAKE UP!*"

I'm holding his head in my lap, begging the life to return to his irises. But he's slipping away. We both know it. A thin smile begins to stretch across his face, his lips moving imperceptibly, as though he's trying to speak but I can't hear a sound.

"*What?!*" I yell. "I can't hear you!"

I bend down closer until my ear is millimeters from his mouth, so close that I can almost feel his lips kissing the skin of my earlobe.

"Talk to me," I beg him. "Say something—*anything!*"

"Rachel," the sweet tenor of a young woman's voice caresses my eardrum, causing the hair on the back of my neck to stand on end.

This isn't happening, I tell myself. *This isn't real.*

"Rachel," Mia says again, louder this time. "Very soon, it will all be over, honey."

I jerk back at the familiar words, mouth falling open in horror as I see Michael Davies' face staring back at me from the floor. His mouth twists into a horrible smile, teeth stained scarlet with his own blood. He moves his lips and Mia's voice rings out once more.

"Rachel, wake up," she says. "Wake up, Rachel. Wake up. WAKE UP!"

***

May 31, 2023

My eyes snapped open with a start, the taste of ash hot on my tongue as I attempted to detangle myself from the bedsheets. I blinked the bleariness away, allowing myself to adjust to my surroundings as the burning building from my nightmare faded from view and the Holiday Inn hotel room took its place.

Just then, the boom of a fist smashing against the door thrummed into the room, startling me into full consciousness. I leaped from the bed and made my way to the door, stealing a glance through the peephole before flinging it open.

"Rachel, look, I—"

"Nick!" I threw myself into his arms before either of us knew what was happening. "Oh my God, I'm so glad it's really you. I had such a bad dream. There was this fire and I was trapped inside and I couldn't see, and then I saw somebody in the flames and I thought they were trying to hurt me, so I shot them but—"

"Shhh," Nick stroked my hair as I muttered the details of my nightmare into his chest. "Slow down. It's okay. It was just a nightmare."

"It felt so real," I whispered. "I thought you were dead. I thought I lost you."

"I'm right here," he assured me. I breathed out a sigh of relief, savoring the scent of baby powder that clung to his clothes as I kept my face buried in his shirt. Slowly but surely, the panic began to subside, a steady calm washing over me in its place.

You're safe, I assured myself. *It was just a dream.*

For a moment, I wondered what could have caused such a vivid hallucination to haunt my slumber. But the longer I stayed in Nick's embrace, the sharper my thoughts came into focus as memories of the previous night flooded my mind. Getting dinner at the Chinese restaurant. Telling Nick about the house fire. Storming out on him after our fight.

I pried myself free of his grasp, pushing away from him as I recoiled back through the door into my hotel room, the anger I had felt at the restaurant simmering its way to the surface. Nick detected the change in my demeanor, the muscles in his face slackening as he appeared to deflate like a forgotten balloon at an abandoned carnival. I folded my arms across my chest in defiance, ignoring the magnetic pull of his body as I denied myself the comfort of his arms.

"What're you doing here?" I grumbled. "I'm pissed at you, remember?"

"I know," he said sullenly. "That's why I'm here. I don't like the way we left things last night. Can we... can we talk? Please?"

"There's nothing to talk about," I insisted. "You made yourself perfectly clear."

"Rachel, please don't be like this," he begged. "Can I just come in for a second? I just have one thing I need to say to you and I promise if you still hate me afterward, I will leave you alone. Fair?"

Pride and forgiveness battled for my attention as my eyes narrowed, debating whether or not I should let him in. Maybe it was the earnest glimmer of genuine apology flickering in his eyes, or maybe it was the haunting image of his lifeless body resting in my lap as the world burned around us. Whatever the reason my walls came tumbling down, I didn't dwell on it. I simply stepped aside, widened the door, and allowed him to enter the room.

There was a computer desk at the far side of the room across from the bed with an uncomfortable wooden chair tucked beneath it. Nick pulled it out and proceeded to take a seat while I perched on the edge of the bed across from him, waiting for him to speak first.

"I know that solving this case is important to you," he started.

"*That's* an understatement," I huffed. He held up his palm, gesturing for me to stop.

"Please, just let me finish," he said. I pursed my lips, waved my hand as if to say, *Get on with it then*. He continued, "I know you feel like you made a promise, and you have to be the one to keep it. That there's no one out there who's more invested in this than you. And now the one person you thought was on your side is telling you to let it go, and it doesn't seem fair. But I need you to understand that I'm not asking you to let it go. I'm not trying to take this away from you. I made a promise, too, okay? To protect and to—"

"I don't need your protection," I bit. "I'm not a child. I know what the risks are. I know what—"

"Damnit, Rachel!" Nick slammed his fist on the desk beside him, the noise causing me to jump in my seat. "This is your problem, you know that? You spend all your time thinking you know better, thinking you can do everything on your own, but you can't and you don't. Look at what it's cost you already. Your badge, your career... us."

His words crashed into my chest like an anvil tumbling from the sky, sucking the air out of my lungs. I looked away before the tears came, ashamed of my own stubbornness.

"Do you even know how hard it was to move here without you?" he whispered. "How many times I'd wake up at night wondering if you were okay? And I'd keep telling myself, you know, she's fine. She's a good cop, she's got the department behind her. She's gonna be okay. But then Williamsburg happened, and you were out there on your own, and I was trying my best to be supportive because I know how much this means to you, but goddamn it, I was dying inside. Don't you understand that? I can't..."

He trailed off suddenly, forcing me to look in his direction.

"You can't what?" I ventured.

"I can't lose you," his eyes were glistening as he spoke. "I don't know what I would do with myself if anything ever happened to you."

"Don't talk like that," I chastised him. "You'd be fine. You'd still have Amber."

Nick turned his gaze to the floor, his shoulders sagging as he hung his head.

"No, I wouldn't," he muttered. A squeezing sensation pinched inside my chest.

"What do you mean?" I said. "Did something happen?"

Nick tilted his head back, an ironic bark of laughter piercing the air despite the tears that were evident in his eyes. He shook his head bitterly.

"We broke up last night," he told me.

"Wh-what? Why? I don't—"

"Because of you!" he yelled. "Jesus Christ, Rachel, I'm in love with you! I am always going to be in love with *you*. I am always going to be watching out for *you*. Even if that means that I have to be the one to stand in your way. I won't let you kill yourself over this. Please... don't make this harder than it has to be."

A flood of warmth melted away the icy walls that I had built around my heart as the reality of Nick's words settled over me. *He was in love with me.* Despite every hour I had spent obsessing over the case rather than passing the time in his company when we had been together, despite rejecting his proposal and forcing him to move to Charlotte on his own, despite finding a new woman to spend his life with, he still loved me. And yet there I was again, making it impossible for him, forcing him away when I could have been at peace in his presence. Why did I do these things? Why did I have to be so headstrong?

I extended my hand in his direction, an olive branch sprouting out from my fingertips, hoping to root itself in his palm. He slipped his fingers in between my own, sending sparks of longing soaring through my veins.

"I'm sorry," my voice trembled around the lump bobbing around in my throat. "I'm so sorry for everything. I was a terrible girlfriend, and I know that. I wish I could take it back. I wish I wasn't so obsessed with solving this. I wish I…"

I bit my lip, attempting to stifle the sob that wanted to rip through my body. But it was no use. In an instant, my chest was heaving, years of regret and loneliness bubbling to the surface, too painful and powerful to suppress. Nick kept my hand in his as he lifted himself from the computer chair and sat next to me on the bed. With his free hand, he tilted my head in his direction, wiping away my tears with his thumb.

"Don't cry, kiddo," he soothed. "I can't stand to see you cry."

"I can't help it," I whimpered. "I've missed you so much. All this time I've wasted without you when I should have married you when I had the chance."

"There's no such thing as wasted time," Nick tucked a strand of hair behind my ear. "There is only here and now. All that matters is what you decide to do with it."

My eyes drowned inside the copper pools before me as my gaze lifted to meet his, Nick's face mere inches from mine as we sat side by side on the bed. I lifted my free hand to cup his face in my palm, my heart catching in my throat as his lips grazed my wrist. He moved closer, the tip of his nose caressing mine, my lids fluttering shut as he slowly swam in for a kiss. As his tongue gently prodded my own, his hands slid down my back, fingers working their way beneath my shirt, timid at first, increasing in urgency as desire mounted between us. Before long, we were naked, our bodies finding a familiar rhythm, as though they had never known what it meant to live without the other.

When we were spent, we remained wrapped in each other's embrace for a long time, my palm resting firmly over Nick's chest, relishing the feel of his heartbeat. In that moment, everything from the past fifteen years seemed to fade into the background. There was no Mia Davis. No Michael Davies. No police department. No wasted time. There was only the here and now, just as Nick had said.

A loud, obnoxious ringing blared out from the pile of clothing that Nick had abandoned on the floor as an incoming phone call disrupted the daze of our lovemaking. He placed a kiss on my forehead before sliding off the bed to find his cellphone.

"It's the lab," he announced when he saw the caller ID. He slid his finger across the screen to accept the call, "Detective Gildan. Yeah... Okay... Mhmm... You're positive? ... Okay, I'm on my way."

He pressed the "End" button on his phone and set it on the computer desk before turning back to face me.

"They got the results," he said. I shot up to a seated position, eyes wide with anticipation.

"And?" I prompted, allowing impatience to get the better of me.

"It's a partial match," he informed me. "They said according to their findings, the sample belongs to a close relative of our suspect—a sibling, to be exact."

The fog of romance evaporated from my mind in an instant, heart rate accelerating as I pondered what this meant for the case that had dominated every fiber of my being for the better half of two decades.

"So, what now?" I demanded. Nick searched the floor for his clothes, hopping into his pants and dragging his shirt over his head.

"I have to head to the station," he answered. "We've got to get the judge's approval for the arrest warrant and send out an APB. After that, we'll assemble a team so we can try to find this fucker and get him behind bars where he belongs."

I nodded carefully, a strange sense of disappointment and defeat melding together in the pit of my stomach. Nick sensed the disquiet in my stare, stepping over to my side of the bed and taking a seat next to me before cupping my face in his hands.

"Don't worry," he assured me. "We're going to find him. And when this is all over, you're going to get your job back. I promise. Kane will never live this down."

He pressed his lips to mine first, then placed another kiss on my forehead.

"I love you, kiddo," he murmured.

"I love you, too," I told him. "Let me know how it goes?"

"Of course," he promised. "I know you only booked the room until today, but if you wanted to stay a bit longer, I don't mind. Or you could... stay with me? At my place?"

I blushed, the thought of being alone with Nick again making my insides ache with yearning. Every part of me wanted to say yes, but then I thought about the Davises, about how much they deserved to know what was happening, about the anger that Leah still harbored towards me and whether this new development might help give her some peace.

"I'd love to," I started, "but I think I need to go back to the Davis's. They need to know what's happening, and if I can't be the one to find Michael, I should at least be the one to tell them about all this."

Nick looked crestfallen at my response, his eyes straining as worry cast clouds of concern across his irises. For a moment, I feared that he might try to stop me, tell me it was too dangerous, convince me to stay put. But instead, he kissed my cheek and placed a gentle hand on my bare thigh.

"Text me as soon as you get there," he said. "And be careful. Don't do anything stupid, okay? We're in the home stretch now. There's no need to be a hero."

I gave him a smile that I hoped looked as reassuring as I wanted it to be.

"Okay," I told him. "You be careful, too."

"Always am," he winked. And with that, he was gone.

By ten o' clock that morning, I had made my way down to the hotel lobby and proceeded to check out, the funds that Nick had transferred making me feel confident that my bank account would not be overdrawn. As I made my way to my car, the drive to Sudbury on my horizon, I knew that I should have felt relief. I should have felt comfort or vindication or elation. But instead, all I felt was hollow. It was as though a deep cavern had carved itself out in my stomach, the emptiness pressing up against my organs, cold and unyielding in its grasp. Despite everything that Nick had said, the reassurance that he was leading the charge on the case, I couldn't shake the nagging feeling that I alone held the answers. That I alone had to be the one to end this.

As I closed the distance to Sudbury along the interstate, I saw the sign indicating that the exit to Red Rock lay just ahead. Echoes of my conversation with Cat clawed out from the corners of my mind, embedding themselves in my eardrum, deafening the rush of highway traffic.

He was forced to live at his grandfather's ranch in Red Rock when he was young.

His grandfather abused him.

All in Red Rock.

Red Rock.

Red Rock.

I swerved into the shoulder with a quarter mile to spare until the exit to Red Rock, Cat's words playing on repeat in my mind like a broken record. When I had gone to Matt's house, I had been so focused on the house fire connection that I hadn't thought to ask him anything about his grandfather or any of the abuse that may or may not have transpired there. If I had, would it have made a difference? There was only one way to find the answer.

Before pulling back onto the highway, I reached for my iPhone and navigated to my text conversation with Nick, selecting the "Share My Location" option before sending him a message:

Wednesday, May 31, 10:48 a.m.: I promise I'll be careful, but just in case, you know where to find me. I love you.

CHAPTER 18

May 31, 2023

Though I was parked outside of Matt's trailer no later than eleven-thirty that morning, I remained in my car for a good five hours waiting for his pickup truck to make an appearance, leaving only to grab a bite to eat at the nearby Waffle House.

Between the influx of cases he had been assigned after Memorial Day and the tedious processes involved with securing the arrest warrant, Nick must have been too inundated at the station to have noticed my text message. But I didn't mind. I didn't need him to worry about me. Soon enough, I would have the answers we both needed and he'd thank me in the end—even if at first my recklessness had made him angry. One day we would look back on this and laugh, our hearts made lighter with the knowledge that Michael Davies was rotting away in a prison cell thanks to my adamance.

It was nearly five o' clock by the time Matt's Chevy showed up, its tires following the familiar path of lawn that it had carved out as a driveway between the cigarette butts strewn across the grass. I didn't wait for him to make his way to the front door, choosing instead to flag him down before his feet ever hit the bottom step of his sorry excuse for a porch.

"Matt—excuse me, Matt?" I called to him, the sound of my voice jolting him to the point of dropping his keys.

"Good God," he grumbled. "You scared the heck out of me!"

"I'm sorry," I said, bending down to retrieve the house keys that had fallen from his fingertips. "I didn't mean to frighten you."

"It's... it's fine," he decided, accepting the keys from my outstretched hand. He ran a nervous hand through his stringy, blonde hair. "What're you doing here? I thought I answered all your questions last time."

"Yeah... about that—do you mind if I come in?" I gestured towards the front door. "There's been some new developments, and I'd really like to talk with you about it all. In private."

He raised a skeptical eyebrow over those haunting, icy eyes of his, a flicker of defiance threatening to send me away. As quickly as the thought passed through his mind, it evaporated with a heavy sigh.

"Fine," he decided. "But it's still a mess in there. I wasn't expecting company."

I fought the urge to ask him if anticipating my arrival would have made the slightest difference as to the state of his living environment, choosing instead to follow behind him in silence, the only sound coming from the creaking staircase as it struggled beneath the weight of two full-grown adults. The smell of stale beer and nicotine assaulted my senses as we entered the home, a familiar pile of pizza boxes and discarded cans leading me toward the ugly, pinstriped sofa like a trail of moldy breadcrumbs. I took a seat amidst the chaos, Matt choosing once again to sit across from me in the metal folding chair.

"So...?" he ventured, rubbing a pair of sweaty palms across his jeans. "What's this about now?"

"It's about your brother," I answered. "Michael Davies. Last time we spoke, you led me to believe that he was dead."

"Well, yeah, because he *is* dead," Matt insisted. "I went to his funeral and everything. There's a death certificate somewhere..."

He looked around the mess of garbage in his home as though the document might materialize from between the rubble of neglect. I waited for him to face me once more, eager to gauge his reaction to the words I was about to say.

"What if I told you that he wasn't dead?" I offered. "What if I told you that your brother has been alive all this time?"

Matt's eyebrows knit together, the color draining from his acne-scarred cheeks as his lip began to quiver. His nostrils flared as his breathing became labored, heavy with emotion. Genuine shock appeared to chip away at what little composure he had, leaving him shivering as he struggled to shoulder the weight of what I had just revealed.

"That... that can't be true," he stammered. "I told you, I went to the funeral. They found his bones. We buried him. He's dead."

"No," I eyed him carefully, "he's not, Matt. Your brother is alive. And I need you to help me find him."

His eyes widened, the action forcing tears to spill forth down his face. He smeared the saltwater into his skin with the base of his palm, the icicle of his iris darkening like an overcast sky threatening snow.

"I don't believe you," he whispered. "You have no proof."

My heart sank, his flat denial causing my confidence to dwindle. After all, he was right—I didn't have the same folders full of evidence at my disposal as I had when I went to speak with Cat at the county jail. If I was going to get him to open up, I needed to prove to him that what I said was the truth. But how?

A burst of excitement surged through my body as I reached for my cellphone, visions of the Burg Interiors website burning in my mind. My fingers danced over the device as I entered the address into my browser and pulled up the About Us page, scrolling until I located the headshot for Tim Clark, that glacial stare piercing through the screen, identical to his brother's sitting across from me. I leaned forward and passed the phone to Matt.

"Do you believe me now?" I nodded at the photo in his hands. Matt did a double-take, his face a wrinkle of disbelief as he pinched the glass, zooming in until his brother's face consumed the entire screen. The longer he peered into the portrait, the more difficult it became for him to deny what he was seeing.

"How is this possible?" his voice was ragged, breathless as the words escaped. I removed the phone from his lap and watched him begin to rock in place, his hands gripping at his hair as though he were trying to pluck the information that I had given him out of his head. His anguish and confusion seemed sincere—enough to convince me that he hadn't been harboring his brother after all. The emotion was too visceral, too all-consuming to have pointed to him as a possible accomplice.

"I know this is a shock," I said. "And I know it might not seem real. But I promise you, it's the truth. Your brother is out there somewhere, and I need to know where."

"How do you know this?" he demanded. "How do you know this isn't just someone who looks like him?"

I held his stare as I delivered my response.

"Because we found his DNA at the scene of two homicides," an audible gasp pierced the air as I spoke. "Your brother isn't just alive, Matt. He's a killer. And if we don't find him soon, he's going to kill again."

Matt gaped at me, his mouth opening and closing with involuntary indecision, as though the words were burgeoning in his vocal cords but he couldn't find the voice to speak. What little color was left in his face began to morph into a sickly green, his eyes bulging and watery. I recognized that look—it was the same expression that Cat wore moments before the vomit came.

As his stomach began to lurch, I leaped from the couch and reached for a nearby pizza box, opening the lid and placing it in Matt's lap just in time to catch the bile that had erupted from his stomach. I stood by his side, patting him awkwardly on the back as he continued to retch into the box, the acidic liquid seeping into the cardboard, leaving nauseating splotch marks in its wake.

"Sorry," Matt groaned, wiping his mouth with the back of his hand before setting the box on the ground. I tried not to think about how long it would sit there or whether it would ever find its way to the dumpster where it belonged.

"Don't apologize," I told him. "I know this can't be easy to hear."

"I just don't understand," he said, shaking his head. "It doesn't make any sense to me."

I stepped over the pizza box and sat back down on the couch across from him.

"Talk to me about that," I prodded. "What exactly doesn't make sense?"

He shot me a dark look as though I were the most hopelessly stupid person that he had ever laid eyes upon. I held up my hands in defense, understanding the source of his disgust.

"I meant aside from the fact that you thought your brother was dead," I clarified. "What about him being a killer is so difficult for you to believe? Can you tell me a bit about what he was like when you were growing up?"

Matt sank his head into his hands, dragging his fingers down his face until he inevitably let them collapse to his knees. He leaned back in his chair, folded his arms across his chest, and shook his head.

"I didn't know him very well at all," he muttered. "My mom, she was... it was hard for her, you know? She got knocked up by some guy who she barely knew, and her dad—my grandpa—he was real angry about it. I don't know the whole story; I wasn't even born yet when it all happened. But she told me that he disowned her, and she was forced to raise Michael all by herself.

"Eventually, she and Grandpa patched things up, I guess. Then she found my dad, and she got pregnant again," he straightened in his seat, his fingers gripping at his arms, a guilty expression on his face as he appeared to brace himself for the next part of his story. "My dad wasn't a loser or anything, okay? He was a good guy. Worked hard. But he didn't have any money, and neither did Mom. She could barely afford to keep Michael as it was. When she found out I was coming along, she didn't have a choice. She didn't do it to hurt him, you know? She had to make a decision. She thought she was doing the right thing."

"What did she do?" I pushed. "Tell me what happened."

Matt ran a trembling hand through his greasy hair, pushing the blonde locks from his face. He looked towards the ceiling, as though seeking forgiveness in anticipation of what he was about to say. When he dropped his gaze back down to meet mine, his eyes were bloodshot, shiny with fresh tears.

"She did what she had to do," he finally said. "A few months before I was born, she sent Michael away to live with her dad on his cattle ranch. It was just supposed to be temporary, you know? Until she could get on her feet. But... it ended up being a lot longer than she thought."

I nodded, doing my best to keep a blank expression despite the images clouding my mind. A confused and frightened child, begging to stay with his mother. A young, pregnant woman struggling to make ends meet. A broken family fighting to survive. I had to admit that in that moment, I began to feel sorry for Michael. For some reason, it made me think about the movie *The Crow*. How Brandon Lee's character tells Darla Mohr that mother is the name for God on every child's lips as he drains the heroin from her veins into the bathroom sink, forcing her to see the damage she has caused. I wondered how many times poor Michael called out for his own God, hoping to feel the loving embrace of his mother, receiving nothing but cold silence in return.

"How long did he live with your grandpa on the ranch?" I continued, shaking the visions from my mind. Matt closed his eyes and sighed.

"Eight years," he whispered. "He was sixteen when he came back to live with us in Sudbury."

I paused, thinking over the yearbooks that I had scanned through in Mia's bedroom. If Michael was sixteen when he returned to Sudbury, why hadn't his photo been in any of the yearbooks prior to his senior year? As if I had posed the question aloud, Matt began to answer.

"Really the only reason he came back was so that he could help my mom pay the bills," he said. "They got him set up with a fake ID and all that, tried to make it look like he was older than he was so he could get a job at the gas station. Eventually, they found out, though. Threatened to call child services on my mom if she didn't get him enrolled in school. But Michael was real smart, you know? He went to summer school, took a placement test, and was able to get in for his senior year of high school by the time he turned seventeen. Mom was real proud of him for that."

I froze. *A fake ID?* And at such a young age. Was it possible that this experience was what sparked Michael's fascination with false documentation? I didn't think that Matt would know the answer, but still I felt compelled to ask.

"Do you know where he got the fake ID?" As expected, Matt fixed me with an exasperated expression.

"I was eight," he said bluntly. "I have no idea about any of that."

"Right," I said, disappointed with the response despite the fact that I knew it was coming. I frowned, sinking back into the sofa as I wondered if there was any useful information that Matt might be able to offer. While I appreciated the insight into Michael's past, I was starting to feel as though our conversation had been a waste of time.

There's no such thing as wasted time, I could hear Nick's voice reminding me. I pondered that for a moment and whether or not

Michael or his mother would have agreed with the sentiment. If either of them had felt like the years they spent apart from one another had been squandered somehow. My mind turned back to the cattle ranch, all the time that Michael had spent there without a mother to guide him, Cat's words circling around my eardrum.

His grandfather abused him.

I sat back up in my seat with a start.

"Did Michael ever talk about your grandpa?" I pressed. "About what happened to him while he was at the ranch?"

Matt pulled his brows together, a deep crease forming along his forehead.

"What do you mean?" he tilted his head, daring me to voice my concerns.

"I mean, did he ever mention anything... bad happening there?" I chose my words carefully. "Anything that your grandpa might have done to upset him?"

"You mean like if he hit him or something?" Matt guessed. I nodded as he drew in a breath and continued, "Look, my brother and I were too far apart in age to be talking about anything like that. Like I said, I was only eight when he came back to live with us, and he was sixteen. It's not like we were having any heart-to-hearts. But if you're asking me whether my grandpa was abusive, I don't really have an answer to that. He's a rancher, you know? And he's tough—real old-school with his beliefs and all that. One time he clapped me over the mouth for talking back at the dinner table when I was a kid, but nothing more serious than that. At least not to me. As for Michael, I don't really know."

I absorbed the information, passing as little judgment as my heart would permit. Though my mother and I hadn't seen each other in years, my mind too focused on the investigation to justify a trip back to Arizona where she still lived, I knew that she would never abandon me. She would never have raised a hand to me—not even a "clap over the mouth" as Matt had so casually dismissed. If she had abused me in any way, would I have had the same nonchalance about it? Would I have forgiven her, blamed her pattern of behavior on generational differences? Or would the seeds of hatred have been planted too deep inside, rooting themselves within, thriving in the darkest parts of my soul until I couldn't stop the poison from overtaking me?

My thoughts drifted back to Michael, whether his insides were struggling to fend off the inky black growth of loathing. Whether the torment of his childhood had made it possible for something else to fester. Like rage. Or wrath.

Or revenge.

"Is your grandpa still alive now?" I gripped my kneecaps rather than the edge of the couch cushions as I posed the question, waiting on bated breath for his response.

"Yeah, he's still around," Matt answered. "I go to see him about once a week, but..."

He trailed off, the muscles in his face gone rigid, as though he had just remembered something terrible. His jaw clamped together, eyelids stretching wide around the icy wasteland in his sockets.

"But what?" I pressed him. He shook his head, clearing away whatever concern had caused him to become so tense.

"I'm sure it's nothing," he insisted. "Like I said, I go to see him about once a week. That's why I moved to Red Rock after Mom died—to be closer to him. Give him a hand when he needs it. He usually calls me to invite me over, but it's been longer than that this time. Probably just busy, I guess. He's old, but he still works that ranch like he's thirty."

The air became still, heavy—and it wasn't just the humidity hanging like a thick cloud between us. Whether he wanted to admit it or not, we were both thinking the same thing.

"Why don't we go pay him a visit?" I suggested.

"Now?" Matt balked.

"Yeah, why not?" I said. "His ranch is right here in Red Rock, right? I've got some questions for him anyway, and if he's as old-school as you say, he probably won't take too kindly to some lady cop showing up on his doorstep unannounced. If you're there, it could help him open up. He might even be able to help me find your brother."

"I don't know," Matt hesitated, searching around the room as though he might find a valid excuse for denying the spur-of-the-moment trip. Finding nothing but an assortment of abandoned garbage, his shoulders sagged, head bowed as he let out a sigh of defeat. "I guess... I guess it's fine."

"Great," I got up from the couch, careful not to bump into the vomit-filled pizza box as I crossed the room to head for the door. "We'll ride in my car. You can show me the way."

***

The sky was thick with purple clouds devouring the last remnants of orange sunset that lingered through the trees as I made the final turn into the cattle ranch. It was a large expanse of property, not a single indication that the land belonged to anything other than the cows that grazed in the fields—at least not from the dirt road beside which the farm was situated. As the car puttered along the gravel driveway, the occasional loose rock kicking up into the wheel bed, I could see the silhouette of a house blackened against the indigo horizon.

"There it is," Matt pointed to the inky outline in the distance.

We made our way deeper into the property, the speck of a structure gradually increasing in size the closer we drew near, though not by much. It was a modest home, more like a log cabin than a farmhouse with its faded wooden siding and A-frame construction. Despite the dusky light, I could see that there really was nothing special about it, not even a porch to create a clear delineation between the outside world and whatever was housed within. Just a front door seemingly attached to the earth beneath. Though I had never been there before, looking at it gave me a strange sense of déjà vu, a sinking feeling building in my gut, urging me to turn around and get the hell out of there as fast as I could.

"What the heck?" Matt mumbled more to himself than to me. I turned to face him, following his gaze to the vehicle that was parked in front of us. "Whose car is that?"

My heart skipped several beats as my eyes fell on the familiar Jeep Wrangler, its paint job muted in the twilight, though still unmistakably red. Unmistakably Evan's.

I swallowed hard around the panic in my chest. Something wasn't right, little goosebumps of anxiety sticking needles in my arms until every hair on my body seemed to stand at attention. As I stared through the windshield, I realized that the Jeep's taillights were on, a soft plume of exhaust emanating from beneath the back bumper, telling me the engine was still running. I wondered how long it had been there idling. Why it was even there in the first place.

"Stay here," I instructed, feeling at my hip for the gun handle in my holster as I made to exit my own car.

"Like heck," Matt argued. "I'm coming with you."

"Matt, get back in the—"

"No," he insisted. "I'm going in there. I've got to make sure my grandpa is okay."

I rolled my eyes, annoyed with his heroics.

"Fine, but you stay close and you do exactly as I say—understand?" he nodded fervently in the growing darkness. "Wait by the car while I go check out the Jeep."

Matt hovered by the passenger's side of my sedan as I made my way to Evan's Wrangler, my weapon drawn as I inched closer to the vehicle. Aside from the taillights burning red behind it, the SUV was black, devoid of all life. I crept up to the driver's side door, peering into the window to make sure there was no one inside. When I was satisfied that no one was near the car, I motioned for Matt to come to my side.

"You stay right next to me, okay?" I made him promise. "Be quiet, and if there's any sign of trouble, you call for help immediately."

"Alright, alright," Matt assured me that he'd be cautious and the two of us proceeded to make our way to the house. As we stepped closer to the front door, I could see that it was slightly ajar, sending a shiver rattling down my spine. Shadows swam out from the darkened interior through the inch-wide crack, a sinister energy rushing out to greet me as I placed a cautious hand on the wooden door and pushed. A long, loud creak squealed out from the hinges like a horror movie, the sound making me nauseous with unbridled fear.

Don't be afraid, I reprimanded myself. *This is your job. Get a fucking grip over yourself.*

I sucked in a deep breath and held it in my lungs, summoning the courage to cross the threshold. Matt clung close to my side as we stepped into the home, the total blackness that surrounded us like an impenetrable veil, oppressive and tactile. We hesitated in the foyer for a moment, giving our eyes time to adjust to the darkness. Before long, the home came into view, the sight of it sucking the breath that was still trapped in my lungs right out of my body.

In front of me was a small living area with an archway on the left that led into a bigger room, the stone fireplace contained within visible even from where we stood at the front door. To the right was a narrow hallway, its opening as black and ominous as the mouth of a forgotten bat cave. I didn't need to venture into its depths to know that a dead end would be waiting for me at the end of it. My insides twisted with agony as my gaze fell to the center of the room in which we stood, the image of Nick's body lying limp on the floor still fresh in my mind.

This isn't a dream, I reminded myself. *Nick is in Charlotte. You're fine.*

"Jesus," Matt groaned suddenly. I whipped around in his direction, pressing an agitated index finger to my mouth, urging him to be quiet.

"Shh!" I hissed.

"Sorry," he whispered. "It's just... it smells in here, don't you think?"

My brows bunched together, confused at first by the statement. I drew in a deep breath through my nose, attempting to detect the odor to which he was referring. As my nostrils filled with the indoor air, my blood froze. I had been so focused on the parallels between this place and the burning building from my nightmare that I hadn't noticed the most glaring similarity of all until Matt forced me to contend with it.

I smelled gas. A lot of it.

But there was something else, too. A sweet, sickly scent thick with the promise of decay. I knew that smell all too well. Had felt it clog my senses at every Holiday Inn hotel room where another suicide victim was waiting to be found. My stomach flipped.

"Stay here," I commanded quietly. Matt shook his head with vigor.

"I'm coming with you," he said in a hushed voice. I bit my tongue, stifled the urge to shout at him, scare him back to the car. Together we stepped deeper into the home, my handgun at the ready as I walked across the floorboards where Nick had laid dying in my dream. I shook the image from my mind, tried to focus on the reality unfurling before me rather than the tingling sensation tugging at my soul, telling me that this wasn't just a strange coincidence.

We skulked into the grand room through the archway on the left, the massive fireplace looming like a phantom on the opposite side of the wall. Aside from a sofa and a coffee table to the right, the room appeared empty. Quiet. Disconcerting. I turned around to face Matt.

"I don't think there's anyone in here," I whispered to him. But he wasn't listening to me. His eyes were transfixed, face contorted in an expression that I could only describe as sheer terror.

I watched his mouth fall open, the skin on his pockmarked cheeks almost bubbling with horror as he peered past me into the shadows. The skin on the back of my neck began to crawl as I heard the creak of floorboards moaning out behind me, the shift of weight as a body traveled across them, inching closer to where we stood. Gripping my gun tight in my hands, I prepared myself for a fight, using all my nervous energy to propel me in the opposite direction and meet my unseen attacker. But I never got the chance.

As I steeled myself to spin around, I felt a pair of hands reach out from the shadows, wrapping themselves around my mouth and nose, pulling me closer to a man's body. I sucked in a sharp breath, a powerful chemical aroma overtaking my senses, dizzying my vision the harder I struggled to break free from his grasp. Beneath the industrial odor, I could detect an earthy sweetness. Like spiced pine. Or worn leather. Or both.

Before I knew what was happening, the world began to wither away. My extremities weakened. And just as my knees were about to crash to the floor, everything faded to black.

Acknowledgements

To my husband, AJ, I'll never be able to adequately express how much it means to me to have your unwavering support—not just in writing but in every aspect of my life. Just being in your presence makes me a better person, and I'm so glad we get to take this journey together. I can't wait to see what comes next.

To my sister, Sara, you are the most incredible human and I am so grateful to have you in my life. Your constant enthusiasm and belief in me are what keep me going. Thank you for always making time to listen to my stories.

To my best friend and editor, Lauren, your keen insight and thoughtful critiques have made me a better writer than I ever thought imaginable. Thank you for investing so much time and energy into my work. I couldn't do half the things I do in this life if it weren't for you.

To my mother, Donna, you are the best cheerleader anyone could ask for. It means the world that you are so willing to step out of your comfort zone so often for me. You are the sweetest, most loving individual of all time, and I'm so glad I get to be lucky enough to be on the receiving end of those gifts.

To my father, John, you made me the person I am. Not a day goes by that I don't think about you and wonder what you would say if you were here to see this happen. Thank you for believing in me all your life, for encouraging me to take risks, and for instilling in me the importance of creativity.

And finally to you, dear reader. Without you, none of this is possible. Thank you for selecting my book out of the countless options available to you. I hope you enjoyed it, and I look forward to the opportunity to share more stories with you in the future.

About the Author

K.T. Carlisle is the pseudonym for a writer located in rural Vermont. Since early childhood, Carlisle has dedicated her life to the written word. Earning her B.A. in Writing Arts with a concentration in Creative Writing in 2015 from Rowan University, Carlisle received the Excellence in Writing Arts award from the university—an honor reserved for students who exhibit exceptional skill as a writer and teacher of writing.

When she is not busy working on her next novel, Carlisle spends her days enjoying all the natural beauty that the Green Mountain State has to offer alongside her incredible husband, four crazy dogs, and flock of chickens. For more information, or to inquire about rights, permissions, speaking engagements, and more please visit www.ktcarlisle.com.